NA

Bernice found her eye continually drawn towards one of those treasure chests only seen in the theatre: piled high with scintillating gems and strings of pearls, diamond tiaras, brooches, clasps, necklaces, goblets and a half-eaten sandwich from the stagehand's lunch. On the other hand her eye might be continually drawn to it, but she forced herself to ignore it – it was far too obvious. She poked through the overmature contents of a laundry basket, examined the sandbags for suspicious bulges, went back out on to the stage and peered into the prompt box, came back in again, stuck her hand up the head of the pantomime cow, and finally gave up.

'Oh all right,' she said.

The glittering treasures came off in a single piece, glued to a shallow tray. In the space beneath, Benny's hand brushed against something leathery, soft like kid. She grabbed hold of it, and lifted something that seemed as big as her two fists clenched together and heavy as lead crystal.

She did not discover more, because at that point the back of her head exploded with pain, a redness burst across her vision and then plunged into black.

THE NEW ADVENTURES

SHIP OF FOOLS

Dave Stone

NA

First published in Great Britain in 1997 by
Virgin Publishing Ltd
332 Ladbroke Grove
London W10 5AH

Copyright © Dave Stone 1997

The right of Dave Stone to be identified as the Author of
this Work has been asserted by him in accordance with the
Copyright, Designs and Patents Act 1988.

Bernice Summerfield originally created by Paul Cornell

Cover illustration by Jon Sullivan

ISBN 0 426 20510 3

Typeset by Galleon Typesetting, Ipswich
Printed and bound in Great Britain by
Mackays of Chatham PLC

*All characters in this publication are fictitious and any resemblance
to real persons, living or dead, is purely coincidental.*

This book is sold subject to the condition that it shall
not, by way of trade or otherwise, be lent, resold, hired
out or otherwise circulated without the publisher's prior
written consent in any form of binding or cover other
than that in which it is published and without a similar
condition including this condition being imposed on the
subsequent purchaser.

Author's Note

I'd like to offer my thanks to all the people who asked me to use their names for those who, as will become clear, get horribly murdered in piteous and most revolting circumstances. They know who they are, and now, of course, so does everybody else.

The reader should remember – in accordance with the statutory light-entertainment law that says those who die in a certain kind of fiction are all thoroughly bad lots and thus deserve everything they get – that none of these real-life people are remotely like their fictional namesakes and are, in fact, without exception, all perfect lovelies and kind to fluffy animals. I'd also like to apologize to those whom, for whatever reason, I left out, lumped together or just forgot about entirely.

I'd also like to point out that while this is, obviously, in some small part a murder mystery, with puzzles to be solved, the murders in themselves are not the puzzles. You have been warned.

On another subject entirely, may I say that as of time of writing I'm utterly skint – and anyone who wants to give me a lot of money to write something for them only has to ask. It's always surprised me that writers never seem to put that all-important fact somewhere in their books. Unmarked notes in small denominations, for preference.

The Reverend Dave R. Stone, 1997

Ten li'l piggies, sitting down to dine;
One choked his li'l self, and then there were nine.

Nine li'l piggies, travelling in state;
Someone left a latch unlocked, and then there were eight.

Eight li'l piggies, thinking they're in Heaven;
One heard a li'l noise, and then there were seven.

Seven li'l piggies, trying to survive;
A li'l tick bit one of 'em, and then there were five.

Five li'l piggies, in protection of the Law;
One was strung up with his belt, and then there were four.

Four li'l piggies setting out to sea;
A red herring gobbled one, and then there were three.

Three li'l piggies walking in the Zoo;
A big bear hugged one, and then there were two.

Two li'l piggies sitting in the sun;
One got frizzled up, and then there was one.

One li'l piggy, living all alone . . .

> [With absolutely no apology at all,
> given the original wording,
> to Frank Green, 1869]

Prologue

THE IMPERFECT CRIME, AND HOW TO COMMIT IT

The seas of Dellah were temperate, and roughly of the same composition as might have been found on distant Earth, once upon a time – before those seas were fouled with toxins and petrochemicals, terminally irradiated, set on fire and eventually boiled off into a thick black sludge. The seas of Dellah, in comparison, were salty and fecund: the lack of significant moons preventing violent tidal surges, the seasonal variations in planetary temperature gently turning them over and preventing them from growing stagnant. Dellah's seas remained for all practical purposes as flat, clear and blue as a lost dream of the Mediterranean, although probably without the enormous German *hausfrauen* in bikinis, greasy peripatetic local youths in little thongs and parboiled, flaking old dads from Purley complaining that they can't get proper chips with their squid. In fact, looking at the flat and mild expanse of Dellah's seas one could, in short, imagine life evolving from them purely for the sake of something to bloody *do*.

Except, quite possibly, for a small area of them lapping gently against one of the islands running off the Marek Dha landmass. Here the waters dipped sharply to give the perfectly formed impression of the keel of a boat, where no boat

1

could be seen.

This was because the boat in question was enveloped in an electrogravitational field that turned it completely invisible within the human visual spectrum and quite some way out either side. If it could be seen – which it couldn't – one would see the hydroplanes that extended out from either side to prevent more than minimal surface disruption. These were necessary to compensate for the construction of the hull and superstructure – their aquadynamics almost entirely sacrificed for prismatic-fractured surfaces that deflected sonar and radar. The hull and superstructure were of a piece, monomolecular, built from a single long-chain polyceramic molecule, and so slippery that even particle-detector emissions simply slid off.

The craft was powered by cold fusion – and since 'cold' is only a relative concept, this was masked by convection vents that dissipated the reactor's heat signature over a fifteen-kilometre radius. The guidance and control systems of the craft operated entirely on mechanical clockwork built from polymers, ceramic and, occasionally, even microturned hardwood. This made them undetectable by resonance and invulnerable to EMP. The boat had internal, inertial tracking and it did not need to burn lights for navigation, for the simple reason that it was currently broad daylight.

The boat was as undetectable as state-of-the-art technology could make it, and it was heading for one of the smallish, central and privately owned islands.

The Marek Dha island chain (when in season) was the exclusive domain of the sector's rich, who had ecosculpted them to within a micron of their lives, and built on them in a hotchpotch of architectural styles to provide various interpretations of the island paradise. Here the sector's robber-barons, racketeers and drug lords rubbed shoulders with media celebrities, intercorporate fliers and royalty – or, at least, aquascooted over to each other's beach house for iced *chai*, powdered products that screwed your head off and young ladies with no clothes on jumping up and down in swimming pools. All of which, given the marked similarities between leaching degenerate jackal-scum who should be shot on sight – and certain others who *aren't* actually royalty – was only right and proper. The individual inside the invisible boat knew that within fifty leagues, strung like a sting of slightly tacky island pearls, were pickings rich enough for any reasonably inventive and persistent criminal to retire upon for life. One could have lived, quite comfortably, for years in just one of the pleasure yachts that clustered around the marinas alone. But the individual in the invisible boat wasn't interested in any of them.

The island that the boat was heading for was anomalous – not that it had not been reconstructed, but that it had been reconstructed with some style. From the sea it seemed deserted: a beach running up to rocky cliffs topped with uncultivated vegetation – and in the Marek Dha chain this could only mean it had a single owner, and one who imposed his vision on it and his alone. If the inhabitants of the other islands were the super-rich, then the owner of this place must be the *Über*-rich – and when you're dealing with wealth on that level of magnitude you have to think in slightly different terms.

The boat grounded on the beach, and ceased even its minimal level of internal activity. The cliffs displaced line of sight and gave a small but significant degree of protection from detection by whatever lay beyond. The cover of darkness, likewise, would only give the smallest advantage, but even the most minuscule edge was worth waiting for, so the individual inside the boat settled down and waited for it.

It was dark now.

The figure left the boat – and while 'figure' is not entirely the correct word, for the moment it will have to do.

In the moonless night, once the eye had adapted, the constellations in the Dellah sky blazed. Dellah was nearer to the Galactic Hub than Earth – which meant, of course, in the anthropocentric terms of Earth, it was a backwater out on the edge of the known universe. The stars, knowing nothing of the anthropocentric terms of Earth, were clustered closer together and they burnt with different albedos: sapphires, amber and rubies, agate and lapis lazuli scattered through the diamonds tossed on jewellers' velvet. The air was clear and warm, with that strange soft-rasping dryness that seems to come only from the sea. The figure moved through it, seemingly drifting on the faint convection.

It was enveloped in a visual-diffusion field of much the same nature as that masking the boat – save that it was much less powerful, there being a limit to how many power packs a generally humanoid life form can comfortably carry. To counter this, the figure's suit contained skirts, streamers and bulky mouldings to utterly obscure the distinctive humanoid pattern signature and movement that might alert a human or mechanoid eye by the merest glimpse. Under this, the figure wore a monomolecularly sealed and insulated body suit to avoid tripping heat sensors. It had its own air supply and integral compressors to deal with expelled gases rather than release them, and risk releasing DNA fragments from the lungs along with them. It also had subsystems to deal with sweat and the expulsion of colonic gasses – though for other products from, as it were, that end of things, the figure would have to exercise some small degree of self-restraint for a while.

The cliffs had been sculpted for picturesqueness rather than for easy climbing. The use of something as blatant as a grappling hook would have been instantly detected by security-system sensors, so the figure climbed by hand – moving across the cliff face in a twisting trail, occasionally doubling back and even going down again and along – the scaling of the cliffs was obviously the result of much study and calculation beforehand.

At the top of the cliffs the figure wove through the underbrush and scrubland, moving smooth and silent as a big cat stalking the pampas, again moving this way and that, seemingly at random, sometimes slowing its pace to a millimetre-by-millimetre crawl possibly so that it would avoid tripping motion detectors. At length, the rough vegetation gave out to increasingly verdant grassland and at last to a manicured lawn. The house in the centre of it had long been visible.

If one could have seen the figure without looking for it for half an hour, squinting out of the corner of one's eye, one would have now seen a marked change in its manner. It was as though the figure had been galvanized into action. It dived to the ground and rolled, bounced to its feet, double-dodged first one way and then the other, sprinted several hundred metres, occasionally breaking stride to hop on alternate legs, dived and rolled again, leapt and somersaulted in the air, hit the lawn feet first, dug its heels in, boosted itself back as though springing back in alarm, ducked, made a strange little flat-of-the-foot jump still in a ducking position, dodged left, jumped forward, twisted in the air and wound up with its back flat against the wall of the house, gasping inside its suit with exertion.

The next stage was the tricky bit.

The simple fact is that an enclosed space is far more easy to secure than the area around it. Thus far the almost invisible figure seemed to have made it past the sensors and the photoreceptors, the black-light laser traceries that crisscrossed the island and the lawn – but past the wall and inside the house, the security would take a leap of several orders of magnitude. Outside was a place of passive devices set to call in roving defence mechanisms; inside there were active, quite lethal installations, transputer-controlled, waiting to deal with anything that made a single, suspicious move.

The time had come for the figure to fire up its own active technology. More specifically, it fired up its pulse-pumped, autoguided particle accelerator and burnt through the wall like a blowtorch through a pile of garden slugs. The figure dived through it, simultaneously ejecting what to the naked eye might seem like a billowing cloud of vapour –

but was in fact a cloud of quasi-organic/semicybernetic, nanonetic microspores, carefully designed to latch on to the electromagnetic pulses of any system that they found and disable them. Spraying a grey cloud of electronic death around it, the effectively invisible figure ran for the door of the tastefully furnished room in which it found itself, and pelted down a hallway, heading swiftly but inexorably towards its goal.

The problem with the above, of course, from start to finish, was that it did absolutely no good at all.

The constant thrust-and-parry battle between security devices and those who try to counter them is remarkably similar to that of bombs and shelters – if you're safe from arrows they fire a bullet at you; if you're safe from fission bombs they drop a fusion bomb on you – and the security systems of this particular house, relatively speaking, were the equivalent of a Suncracker.

The defences of the island had been aware of the invisible boat some time before it almost entirely failed to appear over the horizon. The defences on the ground had zeroed in upon and tracked the invisible figure's head the moment it had stuck itself out of the boat. So finely tuned were the house's defences that they had detected the invisible figure to the slightest detail, had ascertained its equipment and weaponry precisely, had apprehended the level of threat it posed to the very iota – and they were controlled by a transputer system so powerful and evolved that it was capable of being bloody-minded and vicious. It was capable of toying with its prey.

It tracked the target as it made its way through the corridors and rooms of the house, watched and waited as it got ever closer to the point that, it calculated, was the target's eventual destination – and then almost as an afterthought it extended one of its plasma-cannon from the ceiling and blasted the intruder to a greasy stain. This set off a small but quite explosive fire, but the house was ready for it and quickly put it out.

When the human security guards, belatedly alerted by the house, arrived on the scene, almost all that remained of the figure was a charred and slightly soggy torso. This was exactly what they had been expecting, but they got a small surprise, all the same.

PART ONE

EMBARKATION

I was in the ladies room with her when I was about fourteen, and this drunk lady came in and started saying: 'Oh, Judy, whatever happens, never forget the rainbow.' And Mama said, exiting grandly: 'Madame, how could *I forget the rainbow, I've got rainbows up my ass.' Oh yes, she could be a terror.*

Liza Minnelli

1

THE MORNING AFTER THE NIGHT BEFORE THE MORNING AFTER (RECURRING)

The bars around spaceports tend to fall into two categories. On the one hand you have the clean, plush and hideously expensive, the sole purpose of which is to suck money out of transients before they get away and spend their transit-fiat-loaded shillings somewhere else. Such establishments tend to have bog-*Olde Worlde* names like the Staging Inn or the Traveller's Rest, crawl with highly polished brass-effect fixtures, serve fizzy ethanol-injected fluids by way of pressure kegs and have about as much real atmosphere as a crematorium with a power cut.

On the other hand, this was a *port* – and there are other people in a port than simple transients. There are dockers, stevedores and support staff who work all hours; there are crew members from the various ships, desperate for drink, and certain other substances, after a long and predominantly dry voyage – and there are other individuals, those who trade in certain items that come through the port yet somehow fail to appear on the cargo manifests. The official trading, freight and transport concerns contrive not to recognize them, tend to forget about them, but they exist all the same.

There are bars that cater for all of these people, scattered through the streets around the port in question, and you could cut the atmosphere in *these* with a knife. Probably after having pulled it out from the back of your kidneys beforehand. The lino – and it's always lino, somehow, even centuries after it has stopped being made – has been scuffed and worn to sorry shreds. The fixtures and fittings are elderly enough to be valuably antique, but this is purely for the reason that nobody could ever be bothered to replace them, and they have been battered and scratched to the depths of hell and back. You don't want to know what the crustlike patina on them might actually be.

Where the hideously expensive money-suckers might sport pristine retro reproductions of old advertising installations as part of their Nostalgic Charm™, these other bars are plastered with strata of handbills ranging from the local policing forces asking for help in a gay-related murder, through dial-a-hov cab companies offering the opportunity to be rolled in the street of your choice, to ladies and gentlemen of variable ages offering services to the discerning client. All of human life can be gleaned from walls like these, provided it involves being tied up in a nappy while being beaten with a feather duster, taking a taxi home and then getting brained by a half-brick in the hands of someone not entirely secure in the seat of their own sexuality.

The Pit was one such bar. It had probably had another name, once, but the holovapour sign in the window had long since malfunctioned, and nobody could remember what was supposed to go between the PI and the T.

Inside, even in these highly evolved days, people smoked, passively or otherwise – although 'passive' is possibly not the right word. The airborne fug of blended, mutated tobaccos, resin-related offworld products, Adrenochrome Lite and countless, retroengineered intra- and extraterrestrial herbs made it hard to see a hand in front of the face, on occasion; it filled the room to a slight but noticeable overpressure, and was as belligerently aggressive as a Zaxos razor-wolverine on acid.

It was the early evening, some way off midnight, but then

time had no real meaning in an establishment open twenty-six hours of the Dellah day. The smoke was relatively thin, the room relatively uncrowded. The Pit was predominantly a human watering hole. This was not through a sense of speciesism, because the university influence that made Dellah so remarkably civilized extended even this far. No, it was simply a matter of the random forces that make up a regular clientele – and the only nonhuman currently in the place was the Fnarok employed by the proprietor as a doorman of sorts. The sort of doorman the Fnarok was, of course, was the kind who smacked heads on the counter several times as an automatic prelude to throwing their owners out. Its name was Bumfrey – and a lot of people had made the obvious mistake, and had lived to regret it, in an almost entirely technical and remarkably brief sense.

The proprietor of the Pit himself glowered balefully from behind the bar. His name so far as anyone had ever gathered was Nil, and he communicated by way of an invective of grunts and curt expletives that those who didn't know him took for bad-tempered stupidity. After they'd got to know him a little better, these people would revise their opinion: it was a moronic, utter, mindless hatred of the entire universe in general and everything and anything in it in particular.

Strangely, Nil was never taken up on this – or perhaps not so strangely, since he had some solid connections in the local criminal network, such as it was on a world as remarkably civilized as Dellah. Several times in the past, the story ran, some poor fool would pass an unflattering remark, and the very next day a psychotic gang known as the Bekkar Boys would come along and torch them with an industrial flame-thrower.

As it was, Nil stood behind the bar counter of his domain, his greasy, balding head glistening, meticulously polishing a glass with a bar towel. He buffed it to a pristine shine, peered at it critically, turning it this way and that in the dim, actinic light, then spat in it and put it on the rack. On the other side of the counter from him, a tourist who had wandered in by mistake on the way to his hotel sat on the Haunted Barstool and fidgeted in vain. Presently he'd try to say something to attract the barman's attention, and might even by some lucky chance hit on the precise and mystic mantra necessary for some semblance of service – but would in all probability get Nil's back up the moment he opened his mouth and end up being thrown out on his ear by Bumfrey the Fnarok.

(The Haunted Stool was of course a common bar-room myth: the spot where some poor patron died of thirst, and his ghost rose up to frighten the bar staff away. In the case of the Pit this was almost literally true. A Rododaman from Rensec IV had once stood at the bar until he died of dehydration – a Rododaman's nervous system being cybernetically rewired to respond to certain, precise and entirely formalized stimuli and procedures. His nervous system had locked, waiting for an enquiry as to what he might like to drink that simply never came, and his emergency social-interaction overrides had malfunctioned, utterly immobilizing him. He'd been dead for two weeks and the smell was appalling before Nil finally bothered to have Bumfrey throw him out.)

All of the regulars here knew the proper mantra for getting served, and used it without a thought. It was simply one of the things that separated the insider from the outsider. There was one person here, however, who might be technically out of the loop but who was getting served anyway – having with the unerring instinct of the confirmed and dedicated piss-artist hollered, 'Oi! You! Give us a drink yer miserable bastard!' directly upon stumbling through the door.

The individual concerned was currently sitting at one of the trestles, partially obscured by a precarious, irregular pyramid of empty bottles, gesturing vaguely with a slightly fuller bottle and querulously addressing something nonexistent but which seemed to be wandering around in the middle distance.

'Buggers,' this individual was saying with lordly contempt. 'They come over here with their ... with their ... with their *special* trousers and they think they're so ... and they, and they're all just ... Bugger.'

* * *

It had been the end of a distressing semester. The staff and student body of St Oscar's had collectively heaved a thankful sigh of relief, and promptly put away childish or at least educationally related things, and had begun to think in terms of things that truly mattered. A certain type of person, student and teacher alike, had returned to the private research that would find the cure to the latest transient-carried disease or the substructure that had so long eluded informed commentators upon the precise ordering of litotes in *Finnegans Wake*; laurel-winning data wafers were resurrected for the final, polished, non-beta-testing version that would storm the InfoNet and set it alight; the cataloguing of the billions of multiterrestrial works of literature, art and cultural artefacts in the library and in the display museum would at last be sorted out once and for all.

This was, naturally, what only one particular camp thought of as 'things that really mattered'. The other camp – equally composed of students and teachers alike – held the alternative, intelligent and patently more reasonable opinion that the end of term was the perfect excuse for the piss-up of the planetary century. It had started in the Student Union bar, whence it had repaired to one of the off-campus bars that stayed open rather later, and from then on to a night club and, much later, to a slightly less classy if actually more expensive club, where people of different species and sexes, but uniformly past their applicable sell-by dates, took their clothes off despite the more aesthetically minded howling from the audience to put them straight back on.

And there matters might have rested quite happily, had not a small and unrepresentative minority opined that they knew of a certain all-night drinker towards the spaceport, where one could drink tinned beer at two thousand per cent over the odds a throw, while watching the toms, pimps and skankweed merchants plying their wares under sporadic, buzzing UV lighting. Here they would be slightly immersing themselves in the tenebrous interplay of the Dellah underworld, secure in the knowledge that anything one pegged

15

anyone as was probably wrong – and the actual facts of matters were one hell of a lot worse . . .

It had been, in short, a night of attrition. The party that had set out from St Oscar's had been winnowed steadily away at each establishment until one, and only one, had survived the ordeal and was left standing, or, at least, staggering, blaring, belching and throwing up all over the place. Benny had stumbled out from this last club in the late afternoon, and had wandered aimlessly through the streets and the gathering dark on a kind of bleary autopilot, smashed out way too far from her head to form a coherent thought and simply looking for some familiar landmark that might trigger an instinctive pattern-recognition.

Unfortunately for her, if not for the entire brewing industry of Dellah, the only thing capable of triggering such a response by this point was that of a public ordinary. Benny had spotted the Pit's vapour sign and the cheery pub light spilling through the door at a couple of hundred paces and had been in there like a shot. As has already been noted, the first words out of her mouth had gained her instant credibility; as far as Benny was concerned, the drinks just simply arrived, as drinks so often do.

By now she had drunk herself sober – or at least to that point where the last few conscious brain cells had given up the ghost, allowing things to bypass the cerebral cortex and come up with some degree of lucidity, if not coherent content. Professor Bernice Surprise Summerfield, not counting a brief period as Kane-Summerfield, was now, in short, leaning on the bar counter and becoming maudlin. At great length.

'Skint, thass what I am,' she stated. 'Have I got one? Pot to piss in? I have not.' She shot a furtive glance towards the barman and waved a placating hand. 'Got money for here, don't worry,' she explained. 'Don' you worry 'bout *that*. Jus' no money after that, you see?'

Nil the proprietor looked at her across the bar, and shrugged with the unconcern of one who always takes his money up front.

'Y'see he comes into my life, messes it up completely and

then sods off yet again,' Benny explained patiently, toying with a litre glass that had once contained the kind of stout you could stand a spoon up in laced with a couple of healthy shots of vaguely plumlike brandy. 'Thass what he does. Thass all he does.'

She was referring to her ex-husband, the name of whom she could not currently recall, though she had been perfectly sure about it when she'd started. She had recently spent the last dregs of her depleted funds looking for him, when he had disappeared and seemed to be in danger, only to find that he had got himself involved in a squalid little criminal scam and had subsequently found that it was too big for him. The search for him had cleaned her out to the point where she had been forced to go into hock with the credit intercorps – and her line of credit was rapidly running out.

The thing was – and she was currently in no state at all to think of this in anything but a blurred and general sense – the criminality of his recent actions hadn't seemed to be his style at all. Whatsisname might steal to eat and drink, but he had his own personal, idiosyncratic but strict sense of moral codes, and he did not possess a criminal mentality. In her time with him, Benny had come to rely on an innate if often misguided decency – and to find that suddenly, somehow gone had shocked and hurt her. It was as though she had built a house on shifting sands, had left it behind her but had still been anchored by the fact that it was still there, and had come back to find it washed away. Benny had stared at the wreckage of the foundations, and wondered if she could ever trust anybody, anybody at all, ever again.

And the thing was, she couldn't shake the feeling that this untrustworthiness was somehow *suspect*. It was as if the devious little bastard was lying even about that. When she had returned to her rooms in St Oscar's and unpacked her bags she had found a little note from him.

'*If you ever need to get in contact,*' it had said, '*call me here. You can ALWAYS reach me through here,*' and there had been a GalNet number. Benny had tried tracking it down with her own personal transputer – then enlisted the help of some of the cutting-edge students in the university's AI development labs. The end result of both had been the same: the number was protected by security codes so complex and heavy that even a planetary military intelligence couldn't crack them. Something like this was only possible by way of a hardware/software/gelware package costing in the order of billions of shillings. There was simply no way Whatsisname should have been able to afford, or even have access to, security like that.

And the thing was, she remembered the look in his eyes just before she had left him, for what she earnestly hoped would be the final time. Remembering it, it was as though behind the shamefaced apology and a try-your-luck attempt to get into her knickers, there had been something else, some other agenda. Something harder, and more dangerous, and quite possibly bigger than she could imagine. It was as if he had been about to tell her about it, explain everything – and then he had simply decided against it. So just what in hell had Jason *really* been up to, and who or what had been behind it?

Jason! Of course that was his name. How could she have ever forgotten something like that? Benny looked down at her empty glass, suddenly sobered as though by a dash of iced water in the face. With an utter, aching clarity she knew what she had to do, and do right now.

She looked up at Nil the proprietor. 'Oi. You. Give us another drink you miserable bastard . . .'

There were two other outsiders in the Pit that night, though neither of them had been drinking. They had walked in half a minute after Benny, had ordered and received two half-litres of small ale in precisely the correct manner, and had thereafter nursed them in a darkened corner. The process had been accomplished with the unobtrusiveness known only to those who are intrusive for a living, and after two hours these strangers had become just a part of the furniture, no more remarkable than the broken holo-dice machine beside which they sat.

They were large men, and seemed almost precisely identical, their subdued grey suits cut to conceal muscle and possibly weaponry, but no amount of tailoring could conceal their sheer bulk or, when they moved, their movements. They moved as though every muscle that the grey suits hid was under full and conscious control. It was as though their limbs were manipulators, their entire bodies tools going through some precise industrial process.

They had been shadowing Benny for some while now – ever since she and the party had left the university campus – and the time was taking its toll. Benny had, after all, only to remain semiconscious enough to be able to home in on the nearest available drink. These two had to keep a professional edge.

'You know,' said one of them, looking across the room to where Benny was upending yet another spirituous shot into a beer, 'I don't think she's ever going to stop. I've had about enough of this.'

'Don't get sloppy,' the other told him sharply, keeping his tone low. 'You know what we have to do. We keep tabs on her and wait for her to pass out.'

'Yeah, but it's never going to *happen*. I mean, look at her. If they gave prizes out to piss-artists her mantelpiece would collapse under the weight.' He tapped the side of his head meaningfully to indicate the time readouts that were chipped into both of their respective left eyes. 'We're fifteen hours behind schedule as it is. The chief was expecting her bagged and tagged by now. I say we just do it.'

'In front of witnesses?' the other said.

The first man looked around the bar and its clientele pointedly. 'Yeah, right. Like we couldn't deal with all these alert and virtuous witnesses.'

The second man frowned and nodded thoughtfully. 'There is that.'

'Right.' The first set his barely touched glass down with a decisive clunk. 'So let's get it over with.'

* * *

Nil the proprietor would have been the last person to admit to any sentiment towards his customers, because it quite simply wasn't so. He did however have a remarkably developed territorial sense. Anyone foolish or luckless enough to enter his domain deserved any form of abuse he could throw at them – but if anyone was going to be hurt in the Pit then they were going to be hurt by him, or at least at his instigation. So when he saw the two men heading for the woman at the bar, noted the open, loose and friendly manner that is only ever the precursor to some severe violence, he caught the eye of Bumfrey and Bumfrey, knowing his job, drifted closer too.

The two men split up and bracketed the woman, who was now pontificating darkly about how bloody students today didn't know they were born, couldn't hold their drink, and how somebody should learn them heavily with a stick.

'Come on love,' said one of them jovially. 'I think you've had enough now. Time to get you on home, now, eh?'

The woman swivelled her head to regard him gnomically. 'That has got,' she said, 'to be the worst pick-up line I have ever heard in my life. Trust me. I know whereof I speak. You'll be asking me to look at your small but remarkably interesting collection of rubbings, next, and . . . and I . . .'

Then she slumped face first into the bar counter. Nil was watching her and the men closely, but even he only had the vague impression that one of them was drawing a hand back from the exposed skin of her neck.

Things had now gone quite far enough. Nil flicked his eyes meaningfully towards Bumfrey, who lumbered forward. The two men turned as one and looked up into the Fnarok's gleaming, grinning, doglike jaws.

'I t'ink you better go now,' Bumfrey rumbled softly, leaning over them and not quite touching them. 'On your feet, feet first or in bits. Don' matter to me.'

The two men glanced at each other, and then one of them grinned up at him easily. 'Hey, we're not looking for trouble.'

'Tha's good,' said Bumfrey. 'Tha's very good.'

'Tell you what,' said the man amiably. 'We'll be on our way, I think. No hard feelings. Shall we shake on it?' He held out his hand smoothly, and the Fnarok automatically took it in his digitally opposed paw.

There was a wet, crunching sound that those who heard it would remember for the rest of their lives, much as they might try to forget it. All that could be seen of Bumfrey's paw, on the other hand, was something suddenly mangled and spraying bone-puncture blood. The man who had bare-handedly wreaked this damage did not so much as look at the now whimpering Fnarok; instead he looked coldly at the suddenly very thoughtful-looking Nil.

'I think,' he said, 'we'll take our friend away, now. Do you want to say anything about it?'

2

A RELOCATION AND A PREPOSITION

It was always a bad idea, Benny had learnt, upon waking, to simply roll over and go back to sleep. One should at the very least attempt a brief systems check: where one was, the general time, the state of bodily functions, the lack or otherwise of hands going through the pockets. Large men wearing uniforms and kicking one with jackboots was generally a bad sign, as were slavering monsters with eyes like burning coals and hydraulically extensible teeth.

On the other hand, if everything seemed more or less all right, then one could drop off back to sleep again, secure in the knowledge that anything else requiring damage-containment was not that immediate and could probably wait.

In an event-filled life – two lives if one counted a brief period of being technically, for a variety of reasons, dead – Benny had had cause to be thankful for this procedure. It had at various times saved her neck, legs, wallet, sanity and a small fortune in embarrassing laundry bills. She had learnt to her cost, too many times, to be extremely wary of the times when one is unable, unwilling or simply forgets – because these are the times that lurk in the darker corners of the twisting line of one's life, waiting to stick out a foot, trip one up and send one face first on to the electrified rail. So, as Benny found herself surfacing from the unconscious to the alert, she forced herself to run through the list:

1 Lack of nausea and the sickly, hot internal throbbing of the head that feels as if whatever one has drunk has somehow got directly into the veins, and is still fermenting in them if not festering. Good.
2 Lack of icy chill permeating the neck and shoulders, that turns the ice into shards jammed into one's living brain the first move one makes. That was all to the better.
3 Undressed, intact and lying in warm, clean sheets. That was bloody marvellous.
4 Lack of any sense of someone nice in bed as well. Oh well, can't win 'em all.

Benny opened her eyes and was dazzled by bright morning sunlight, slanting through tall bay windows. It was coming from the wrong direction, and this momentarily disorientated her before she realized that the whole idea of a 'wrong' direction is subjective; she was simply nowhere near the university, where she had subconsciously expected to be. She hadn't subconsciously expected to be in her *own* bed, because her legs weren't hanging off the edge.

She sat up in bed and squinted through the harsh light, taking in her surroundings.

The room was bigger than a power-wallgame court, and barely furnished with that Spartan, dimensionally perfect elegance that comes from paying an architect a hopper full of money and shooting an interior decorator on sight. The walls were a faint, yellowish beige, the pristine carpet something that might or might not be grey – it was one of those strange pastel colours so unobtrusive that you have to stare until your eyes bleed to work out what it is. A number of abstract prints were affixed to the walls, more to break up their planes than for any actual content. The bed itself was simply a block of some polyfoam substance – but by the way it supported her body Benny knew that it had been engineered upon the microscopic level. The cumulative effect was no doubt intended to be nondescript and soothing.

Benny – whose room in the St Oscar's halls of residence

was packed with so many tottering heaps of data wafers, holoslugs, bound books, boxes of half-eaten *kimu* takeout, woofi-bird bones, toiletries, underwear, knick-knacks, gewgaws, how's-your-fathers, half-empty cups of cinnamon and caffeine beverage, completely empty bottles, tins and flasks of wine, beer and spirits, unmarked tutorial work, crumpled first pages of the supposedly next book, an antique typewriter, several antique felt-tipped pens, the cat-litter tray from hell and the various other odds and ends of a hectic life that resulted in a living space you couldn't describe topographically in a year – found these new surroundings alien and bland. The room at St Oscar's, it might also be noted, was just about big enough for a quiet game of dominoes, provided nobody moved their elbows much.

There were no blinds or drapes – and this was slightly odd. Even in this day and age, when windows could simply and automatically be polarized at night, the use of drapes as something to pull across and shut out the night fulfilled a psychological human need. One of the windows was slightly ajar, and a warm breeze wafted in. Benny fancied she could smell the sea. So. The gravity felt OK, and the light and air hadn't immediately felt wrong, so she still must be on Dellah, only on the other side.

Beside the bed was a table – little more than a cube. On it someone had placed a set of neatly laundered clothes – her own – and a tray containing a steaming mug of what, by the smell of it, was the precise brand of cinnamon that she commonly left littered, half drunk, around her own room. It was a cheap brand that Benny got for the incredibly shonky promotional offers, based around its cartoon-animation advertising, and utterly out of place in a place like this. Somebody had evidently done their homework.

Benny climbed off the bed, absently scratching the side of her neck, then the inside of her arm with her free hand.

Then she stopped cold.

Medical science had long since progressed past the point of such crude things as injecting people with hollowed-out needles, and such things were now used only by drug fetishists as a part of the kick. DMSO-laced patches were able to permeate living tissue almost instantaneously, piggy-backed with any medication one needed or desired. The process was supposedly undetectable, but people detected it in the subliminal sense: it had a distinctive feel to it. Benny concentrated her body sense, and was positive she could feel a vestigial cold-burning sensation on her neck and arm, as though these small areas had been swabbed with chilli peppers crushed in surgical alcohol.

'Oh damn,' she breathed. Half-buried memories of the night before burst to the surface and her vague notions and doubts suddenly crystallized. She had been abducted – and the fact that she was still alive and unharmed wasn't exactly a reassuring sign. There were a lot of things that a certain kind of mind can do with someone initially alive and unharmed.

She hauled on her underwear and shirt, scooped up the rest of her clothes and headed for the window rather than the door. The window had been left open and so was probably a trap – but then again doors to rooms commonly led deeper into houses. Death or the Lady could lurk behind either, neither or both. The important thing was to make the decision and just go for it, rely on speed and determination to carry you through whatever was waiting.

She went through the window with barely a pause to check that she wasn't something like twenty storeys up, and found herself on a wide expanse of manicured lawn – big enough to show the undulations of the land. Patches of clover blended through the turf, far too well behaved to be anything other than cultivated. In the middle distance she saw trees, poplars from the look at them, and she headed for them. She didn't look back the way she'd come – the most important thing at this point was to get away. Time enough later to sit down and work out the subtleties. She headed across the lawn at a run.

Dark shapes were barrelling towards her, off to one side. She swung her head around in time to see two quadrapedal forms, jaws hanging open to prolapse trifurcated, squirming pink tentacles that drooled some clear and viscous fluid, and then they were upon her.

At times like this the life is commonly reckoned to flash before the eyes. Benny rather hoped that something like it would – almost anything would have been preferable to the sight of the things slobbering over her.

Off to one side she heard an angry voice shouting, 'Heel!' The weight of the creatures was suddenly gone from her.

Benny sat up and regarded the new arrival as he clipped leads to the excitedly bounding dogs, then passed them to the large grey-suited man who was accompanying him and was obviously a part of his entourage. The new arrival himself was a man of medium build and middle years, his black hair thinning and slicked back from a widow's peak. He wore a black suit and Paisley waistcoat reminiscent of a Victorian gentleman's, although such a gentleman might have balked at the addition of wraparound mirrored sunglasses. He carried a walnut-stocked, ornately chased double-barrelled shotgun in the crook of one arm – Benny was only slightly reassured by the fact that it was broken and unloaded. There was something familiar about his face, but try as she might she could not pin it down.

'I do beg you pardon,' the man said. 'We so rarely receive visitors that the dogs get a little overexcited when we do. They're only being friendly. Allow me to assist you.'

Much against her better judgment, Benny wiped the drool off her face and took the man's proffered hand. 'Interesting breed,' she remarked, observing the animals warily as they strained towards her on their leashes.

'Just a small side-product of our Advanced Genetics division in the Catan Nebula,' said the man conversationally. 'Half bull-mastiff, half Chihuahua and half Sesquipedalian squid.'

Benny frowned. 'That makes one and a half.'

'I did say *Advanced* Genetics division.'

'Fine.' Benny regarded the man levelly. 'And you are . . . ?'

'Ah yes,' the man said. 'I apologize. Remiss of me – we rather thought it would be a while before you woke, and we weren't quite prepared for you.'

Marvellous, thought Benny. Softening-up process seen to, next stop the choke pears, thumbscrews, mind probe or the latest fashionable equivalent.

Something of this must have shown in her face. 'Please don't worry,' said the man. 'Any harm that might come to you in this instance will certainly not come from me.' He gave a courtly little half-bow. 'Allow me to introduce myself. Marcus Krytell at your service.'

Recollection finally dawned. Benny had seen the face a hundred times before, but only on the news. Krytell was, quite simply, one of the richest men in the sector – an industrialist with an installation on every planet with less than perfect environmental pollution laws, another one on any world where officialdom could be bribed, and a slightly cleaner one everywhere else. He had come to Dellah as part of the consortium that had funded the university, had by all accounts liked the atmosphere, and had set up home here. Quite what he was doing abducting and drugging an inoffensive archaeology professor, who had never harmed anyone – unless you counted certain individuals, groups and on occasion entire species who were thoroughly bad hats and therefore deserved what was coming to them in any case – Benny could not begin to guess for the life of her.

'I must also apologize for the manner in which you were brought here,' he continued. 'Security, you see, was of the essence. It was imperative that absolutely nobody learn of your destination and our current problem, not even yourself.'

Benny rubbed at the cold patch on her arm again. 'So what did you load me with?'

Krytell shrugged. 'A simple neurasthenic. We, ah, also took the liberty of introducing certain antitoxins to deal with ethanolic and secondary alcoholic poisoning. I'm afraid we happened upon you not in the best of states. Your reputation has preceded you, somewhat.' Krytell looked at her closely as if verifying that said reputation was indeed true. 'We know that, despite all appearances to the contrary, you have a knack for thinking on your feet, for finding your way out of tight corners, and we needed you in tiptop condition for when we offered you a small commission.'

That explained the curious lack of a hangover. 'I suppose I should thank you,' Benny said sourly. 'Thing is, I'm not going to.' She rounded upon the industrialist angrily. 'Just what the *hell* do you think you're up to? You kidnap me and pump me full of zombie juice, ship me halfway across the world and now you're coming it with the genial old squire on the family estates as if that's suddenly going to cheer me up! Well let me tell you, Mr Krytell, I don't care what you wanted me for. You can tell your little friends to take me back where they found me, write me a polite note on headed paper and then you can fold it up and stick it so far up your –'

This deplorable lapse into an unrefined and decidedly unladylike manner was curtailed as Benny realized that she had grabbed hold of a startled Krytell by the front of his waistcoat and was shaking him – and also by the change in the dogs held by the industrialist's grey-suited employee. Before, they had been straining on the leash in the hope of playing happy games with someone. Now, from their snarls, it seemed that while playing games was still an option, it would probably involve throwing and fetching something other than small toy balls. The most popular game at this point would most probably be playing dead.

Off in the distance, Benny also saw, several other grey-suited men had stopped wandering unobtrusively and apparently aimlessly, and were heading in her and Krytell's direction.

'The commission we have in mind,' said Krytell, apparently unperturbed, 'requires a degree of professional knowledge – but it also requires certain, ah, *unconventional* skills. Skills that we are reliably informed you have. The remuneration will be commensurate to the effort involved, be in no doubt about that.'

Benny glanced at the dogs and the approaching men,

weighed up her chances, and let go of Krytell. 'OK,' she sighed. 'OK. Tell me what you want me to do.'

The entrance hall was like a dream of Austen without the regulated hatred: all sweeping staircases and columnar marble. What appeared to be genuinely ancient oil-and-egg-yolk portraits in ornate gilt frames lined the walls – though from the lack of patina and crazy-paving cracking of the glazing they could only be reproductions. They showed a variety of figures, male and female, in a variety of historical costumes, each bearing something of the features of Krytell.

'My family has a long history,' he told Benny by way of explanation. 'Much of it ignoble, much of it stalked by death.'

'What, you mean, like, everyone from more than a hundred years ago is dead?' said Benny, who was still not feeling inclined to be charitable. 'Oh dear me. How terribly tragic and horrible.'

'I was referring to violent death,' said Krytell with a trace of irritation. 'Premeditated, abnormal or inexplicable death.' He paused to indicate a portrait of a pale young lady in a Regency dress. 'Lady Diane de la Indigo, an ancestor on the distaff side. She had the great misfortune to employ a certain Mr Wonko, a children's entertainer, on the occasion of her youngest son's birthday. Unbeknownst to anybody at the time, Mr Wonko was in fact the man who would become known as the Maniacal Magic-utilizing Murderer of Tunbridge Wells, and Lady Diane was found strangled by a balloon animal. A giraffe, I seem to recall from my studies, or possibly an upside-down squirrel.'

'Nasty,' said Benny.

Krytell paused at another painting, this one showing a gangly man in khaki forage gear and a pith helmet, amid a little still life of display cases filled with pinned insects, butterfly nets and killing jars. 'Again on the distaff side, Dennis Snopes-McLaughlin FRS, an entomologist of some note. He was murdered by a rival Fellow of the Royal Society, who released into his lodgings a rare Mesopotamian *blonki-kugu* spider, which in captivity can be reared to the size of a large Alsatian dog. I understand that he was still gamely trying to fit it in the ether bottle when it bit his head off . . .'

Benny looked at the picture and privately decided that the Krytell family history must have become a little garbled, if not entirely made up to start with. The man shown here obviously hailed from the eighteenth century, and it would be a couple of hundred years and a healthy dose of environmental irradiation before Earth spiders grew bigger than the size of a large rat.

'My grandfather was locked in a storage freezer; my own father was framed and subsequently executed for treason during the war; and my uncle Barnabas disappeared under mysterious circumstances when his portable outside lavatory exploded whilst on a camping holiday.' Krytell gestured to take in the entire hall. 'Over the course of years my family has been pushed down flights of spiral stairs, mauled by trained performing bears, chained up in dungeons and left to moulder, and thrown out of sleighs to be eaten by wolves. They've choked on peach pits, died of artificially induced bloody fluxes and fallen into vats of medicinal leeches. They've been smothered by pillows and eiderdowns, hearth rugs, and in one case by an over friendly female mud wrestler. They've met their ends at the hands of thieves, thugs and jackboxers. They've been drowned in lakes and rivers, bathtubs and butts of malmsey. They've eaten ground glass, tin tacks, Ebola-laden meat, live eels and strychnine. They've been run through by awls, sunk in quicksand, succumbed to opiate overdoses, flattened by steam trains, entombed in ice, poisoned by Kendo dragon bites and eaten alive by rats – and all, I might add, at the malicious instigation of another hand.' Krytell smiled grimly. 'It can only be coincidence – I'm certainly not paranoid enough to believe in some impossibly vast conspiracy extending over centuries and even millennia. It is simply that my family seems to attract murders, and I myself am last in the line.'

Benny looked at him dubiously. 'If I were you, I don't think I'd get out of bed in the morning.'

'Ah, but I have protection. The house and grounds in which you stand are packed to physical capacity with detection and security equipment, the hardware continually updated, the software updated on a microsecond-to-microsecond basis. I have entire research divisions, on several planets, devoted to that very purpose alone – you might even say that the acquisition of such a system was my impetus for acquiring what might be seen by others as quite unseemly wealth.'

Krytell reached a hand towards her. Benny had the idea that he was going to plant a finger on her, but then he evidently decided against it. 'The house is scanned minutely, every single area. If you yourself were carrying anything that might be used as an offensive weapon – so much as a spoon in your pocket from breakfast – the fact would be noted, the factors would be integrated into an assessment of risk, I would be notified and the requisite action taken. This is quite simply the safest, most secure place I could ever possibly be.' Krytell frowned. 'All of which makes recent events somewhat more disturbing.'

Up until this point, the industrialist had been smooth and composed. Now it was as if a small crack had appeared in the polish, to show a hint of genuine fear beneath. He led Benny from the hall and through a heavy door into a narrow chamber that appeared to run the entire length of the house. Display cases and installations lined one wall.

'This is possibly the most secure room in the house,' he said, leading her through the chamber. 'This is where I keep mementos and curios from my own and family's history. The diamond pendant that Viscount Chumley-Krytell gave as an engagement present to the Lady Warwick; the Matebelian *bungo* beads that Horace Krytell unearthed, unsurprisingly enough, on his Matebelia expedition; the first million I ever made –' he pointed to a slightly worn and chewed credit chip '– which my father gave me for being a big boy and using the water closet . . .'

'So, you've always been a pauper like this, then,' said Benny. 'Traipsing off to private school with barely three dozen shoes to keep your feet warm?'

Krytell raised an eyebrow. 'Irony, Ms Summerfield?'

'That was sarcasm, actually.'

'That credit chip is worth exactly one million ersatz shillings from the war,' said Krytell. 'That was worth approximately ten shillings even forty years ago, and the medium itself is worthless. It is only in the last few generations that the Krytells have been particularly wealthy *per se*. Before that we came from all walks of life. My grandfather built a modest fortune before he died, as did my father, on which I have, as I say, built. Many of what you might call the expensive items here are results of my researches into the family history, tracked down at considerable personal expense.'

'So you just leave 'em lying around? Clever move...' Benny's mind caught up with her mouth as she recalled what they had been talking about for the last half-hour. 'Right. Sorry.' She sighed. 'So what was it you wanted to show me? Or rather – because I really am not as stupid as all that – just what is the *lack* of something you want to show me?'

'I can see that what certain people have told me about you is not entirely unfounded,' said Krytell.

Benny raised an eyebrow. 'Was that sarcasm?'

'That was irony.' Krytell paused before continuing. 'Two nights ago, the house was broken into. The criminal concerned was remarkably proficient, but nowhere near proficient enough to fool my security. He was pinpointed from the moment he approached the island, tracked in minute detail through the grounds and the house, then promptly dealt with. I shall spare you the grisly details, but rest assured it was by way of extremely thorough means.'

Benny nodded. 'So?'

'So when my staff arrived on the scene they found the remains of the suit and equipment the criminal used, but no, ah... human or comparable debris whatsoever. Instead they found this.' Krytell slipped a hand into the pocket of his waistcoat and handed her a folded piece of paper.

Benny unfolded it and read it. 'It says "Nice Try",' she said.

'Quite. It was pinned to the hole in the suit where the head should have been.'

Krytell stopped before a display case, obscuring it with his body. Benny didn't try to crane around him to look in. She'd probably get a look soon enough.

'I use this room to store such items that should never fall into the wrong hands,' Krytell said. 'Items the loss of which would be a personal disaster – and items where the disaster might be, shall we say, more general. It just so happens that, as of two nights ago, I was in possession of an interlocking set of Olabrian joy-luck crystals . . .'

'*What?*' Benny stared at the man. In the xenoarcheaological world this was on a par with someone casually mentioning that they'd found the skull of Jesus Christ, sawn the top off and had casually been using it as an ashtray for the last five years. The beings of the planet Olabria were renowned throughout the sector for their surpassing peace and tranquillity, which came from contemplation of complex, interlocking, lattice-globes of quasi-living crystal hewn from the very heart of the planet's satellite.

These moonstones were of such a profound importance to the people of Olabria, and guarded so carefully, that words like 'important' and 'careful' were hardly sufficient – an Olabrian had been known to instantly become a barely restrainable, ravening maniac if some unwary, hitherto esteemed and honoured visitor to their world so much as *looked* at a joy-luck crystal in a funny way. There were records of a massive, centuries-long war some three millennia before, when a race called the Thraal had made contact with this peaceful world, and had unwittingly crushed a small garden of the crystals with their ship. At least, there were records on Olabria. The Thraal, and their planet, had long since been obliterated. To this day, purely as a way of preserving their surpassing peace and tranquillity, Olabria had sunk its resources almost completely into a fleet of massive dreadnought warships, each one capable of taking out a sun in passing, and kept them ever ready in the event that someone or something might attempt to steal or damage one of their living crystal balls.

'So how did you get hold of one of them, then?' she said angrily. She half expected an Olabrian destroyer to come whistling down and blow them to smithereens with their humungous plasma cannon even as they spoke.

Krytell shrugged. 'That is neither here nor there. The point is that I was in the midst of delicate negotiations to ensure its safe return to the Olabrian government. Said negotiations have, not unnaturally, been put in extreme jeopardy by the individual who stole it.'

Krytell finally moved aside to let Benny see the interior of the display case. Nestling on a bed of crushed black velvet, in the indentation presumably once made by the joy-luck crystal, lay a rather tacky looking, sequined collar such as might be bought, by someone with little money and less taste, for a cat.

Benny looked from it to Krytell. 'Are you saying what I think you're saying?'

Krytell nodded. 'I think I am. The criminal popularly known as the Cat's Paw has the crystal, and I need your help in getting it back.'

3

A SETTING IS ESSAY'D, A VILLAIN COMPREHENDED

The Mons Venturi dock was in fact more of a wheel, approximately five hundred metres in diameter and spinning constantly to provide a cheap simulation of gravity at the rim. It hung geostationary, directly over the primary Dellah spaceport, connected to it by an extruded monomer skyhook line, up and down which crawled pressurized capsules ferrying passengers, cargo and personnel en route to the great ships that stayed in orbit, never entering the atmosphere.

This arrangement, however, was strictly for the hoi polloi. If one were rich enough, one could use the docking facilities at the hub of the Mons Venturi wheel for private shuttle craft. Benny hauled herself through the airlock of one such of these, reflecting that all of this seemed to be a needlessly expensive method of transferring her back to the point from which she'd started, albeit several thousands of kilometres above it.

This had not been the only expensive aspect of the affair. The twin set she now wore was of raw, unbleached silk, imported at great cost from the farms of Sontan Beta. The string of pearls around her neck had been individually gathered, at great loss of life, by the child pearl-divers of Barsoomia IV – and if she'd known that fact she would not be wearing them, and would have been incredibly vocal about precisely *why*. The brooch on her lapel was a genuine Earth antique, dating from the twentieth century and in mint condition, the legend 'Watch out, there's a Humphrey about!' still perfectly legible.

Her entire wardrobe – and there were upwards of four hundred items waiting on the shuttle in steamer trunks – was by Frocontiér, her make-up by la Sallé, her hair coifed by an assistant of the great Monsieur Boogie himself, flown especially in to the Krytell estates. Her hands and feet had been manicured and pedicured to within a centimetre of their lives and she looked like a million shillings – which, given that the whole ensemble had cost rather more than twice that, meant that somebody, somewhere was getting the better of the deal.

Additionally, she had a manservant. That was going to take a bit of getting used to. His name was Krugor. There was something vaguely familiar about him; Benny was positive that she had seen him somewhere before, in a different context, but she could not quite pin it down.

Now Krugor helped her through the inner door of the airlock. Benny, who had spent more time in space than a Molopian slard had enveloped and slathered pitifully whimpering human victims with gastro-intestinal juices, felt that she was probably surer on her, as it were, feet in freefall than the servant, but she didn't point this out. She had, after all, her role to play in this charade.

'Have the luggage transferred to the ship,' she told Krugor imperiously, stressing the innate cultured and slightly plummy tones she ordinarily went out of her way to suppress. 'I shall avail myself of the facilities and summon you when I wish to board myself.'

The manservant bowed smoothly and reached a hand to counter the displacement of inertia this caused, giving him something of the image of a courtier in the France of Louis XIV. He withdrew back into the shuttle, leaving Benny to make her way through the outer lock, and into the station, on her own.

She emerged in a largish chamber in the shape of a laterally bisected doughnut. Her feet (pointed in the right direction, as instructed by a decal on the airlock door) fell a couple of centimetres to make contact with a pristine carpet floor – this was the first-class lounge, in the hub of Mons Venturi, and anyone arriving here could afford the levy for expensive artificial gravity. This was also the domain of a certain sort of traveller – those who could afford not to rub shoulders, noses or anything else with mere *transients*, and could therefore remain free of most of the vector-driven bugs that transients were known to carry around. There were no disease scans here – for the simple reason that those here had their health looked after, by private medics, on a level that no public facility could ever hope to match.

Likewise, there was no customs inspection. Those who entered through the VIP locks, she suspected, already had more money than could be earnt from any kind of contraband. Most of them probably had people who took it through for them, elsewhere, in bulk, and this was probably how they had made the money in the first place. The lounge was appointed with amenities that, planetside, would have suited a smallish bed-and-breakfast hotel – but which in space, where the cost/resources ratio was greater by a factor of ten or more, were the equivalent of three private Taj Mahals. All of this was lost, however, in the effect of the chamber's curving roof.

It was not a window on to space. Anything that could let light in, even pure lead crystal, would have let in enough electromagnetics to cause irreparable gene damage – and in any case, if the roof had been clear, if one could have seen past the struts and titanium plate of the station, one would have seen nothing of interest. The lounge faced away from Dellah, and while the ships moored around the station were close in astronomical terms, they were too far away for the eye to see. The roof in fact comprised a holographic display, the images of the ships picked up by cameras floating near them and factored into a background of a star-spangled sky and a planet. The end result was almost precisely what the ignorant might think they'd see if they looked out of the window of a space station.

Looking up through this ersatz canopy, Benny recognized a pair of militia corvettes with their raked-back keels and distinctive, bulbous pulse-engine arrays. She saw a bulk freighter with its tiny manoeuvring pack towing the dirigible-bunch cluster of its cargo pods. Shuttles crawled the physically impossibly small space between these images of ships, and suited figures crawled over their skins running maintenance. Benny knew the entire vista to be false, but in the same way as the map of an urban travel system needs to show only the connections to be true in some fundamental sense, the view was perfectly natural. She was out in space again and it was just the way she'd left — nothing out of the ordinary whatsoever.

Then she turned her head and saw, for the first time, the *Titanian Queen*.

After viewing the scene of the crime, Benny had been taken by Krytell to a gazebo on the house's grounds for tea and sandwiches. It seemed that Krytell was going to assume his posture as a Victorian gentleman to the very end.

'I cannot imagine how the criminal managed to insinuate himself past my defences,' he said, pouring a chemically perfect Earl Grey from a silver teapot into Spode cups. 'I can only imagine that he has access to technologies that are a quantum leap from my own — and that worries me. I must have them. I must know how it was done.'

'Well if you're expecting me to make it with the dusting for fingerprints and the magnifying glass,' Benny told him, nibbling on a sandwich, 'then sorry, no can do. Archaeology might share certain common attributes with forensics, but there's no way I could even start to be a forensic scientist —' She looked at her sandwich. 'What *is* this, by the way?'

'Smoked salmon, cream cheese and cucumber.' Krytell said. 'The salmon and cheese are largely synthetic, of course

– a micromesh of extruded, woven proteins, I gather – but the cucumber comes from genuine sea cucumbers, from my own personal gene-storage banks.'

Benny put the sandwich back on the plate and covered it with a napkin.

'I already have forensic experts,' Krytell continued, 'and they've examined the scene and found nothing – but that is neither here nor there. The morning after the burglary, a small package arrived through my door, which was slightly odd since these islands have no land-mail service, and my door does not possess a letterbox.' He lifted a small silver cover, which Benny had assumed to conceal tea cakes, to reveal a small holocube, which he touched with his finger.

A three-dimensional silhouette of a figure appeared on the table: a ten-centimetre-tall area of apparently solid black. It stood there, hands on hips, head cocked to one side as if delivering a scolding.

'Good morning, Mr Krytell,' it said. The voice was synthesized and static-laden, processed to confound recognition or analysis. 'By now you'll have instigated a planetary, even sector-wide search for your misplaced merchandise. You won't have any luck. I will now detail your only hope of getting said misplaced merchandise back.' The figure adopted a slightly more confidential posture. 'Now, before we go any further, let me tell you that I have access to certain details about yourself – and should anything happen to me, at any time during the process I'm going to detail, a large number of news services and a slightly smaller number of uncorrupted officers of the law are going to get the lot. I'm thinking, for example, of incidents including a young holo-actress by the name of Talulah Wampeter, a greased pig and a –'

Without appearing to hurry in any way at all, Krytell stuck a finger through the figure and silenced the cube. 'I have no idea why the criminal added that. Even if it were true, my position in the scheme of things is not dependent upon public perceptions, and could not be harmed by such revelations in

the slightest. I think he was indulging in some private joke.'
Krytell shrugged. 'As I was saying, forensic investigation at this point would be purely academic. We know who took the crystal, and he has told us what we must do to get it back. Secrecy is of the essence: we must have an operative capable of handling him- or herself, who cannot be traced back to us, and who is familiar enough with alien cultures and their artefacts to handle the joy-luck crystal with the proper care.'

'So what you're saying is,' said Benny, 'that you ran a whole bunch of transputer profiles, and you came up with me.'

Krytell shrugged. 'In actual fact there were seventeen other people in the immediate sector better qualified than you, but their skills were in such demand that they were unavailable. I could have used my influence to rectify that – but that would have been noticed, and that is precisely what we wish to avoid. You were merely the best we could get at short notice.'

Now Benny looked up, through the fake glass of the Mons Venturi roof, at the ship that would be her home for the coming month. Stuffed into her purse was a lithographic, finely printed brochure concerning the various joys this month would hold, entitled 'Welcome to the Cruise of your Lifetime' – in elegant Avant Garde beneath a tastefully restrained 3D still of the *Titanian Queen* in space, which Benny had assumed to be almost entirely the product of a designer's imagination and transputer enhancement. Now, looking at a more reliably mapped simulacrum of the actual thing, she saw that in this instance the brochure had been telling nothing but the truth.

Lack of air-resistance in space meant that a ship could be any shape the designers liked, and this commonly led to constructions crawling with superstructures and ducts, sensor packs and arrays that produced an effect that the ship in question had been not so much designed as congealed. The *Titanian Queen* was something else entirely: built of white ceramic and what appeared to be pure gold, with swept-back, utterly useless, streamlined fins and funnels, it appeared as a kind of retrogressive cross between the rocket ships then imagined in the pulp fiction of 1930s Earth, and a large Art Deco, seagoing yacht.

The *Titanian Queen* was a cruise ship, a luxury liner, barely out of the yard-arrays and about to embark upon her maiden voyage, a pleasure cruise through the marvels of the Proximan Chain. Benny had vaguely heard about this, back at the university, as people had discussed their coming vacations – but only in the sense of people saying, 'You know where I'd go if I won the Planetary Lottery three times on the trot? I'd go on the maiden voyage of the *Titanian Queen*.'

The ship was going to be packed with the filthy rich – and Benny had an idea that over the course of the cruise they were going to find themselves quite as filthy, but considerably less rich. She thought that, because she knew for a fact that also aboard would be the infamous and nefarious Cat's Paw.

The deal, in general, was that a representative of Krytell should board the ship, leave a payment of several million shillings in untraceable credit plaques at a prearranged place and take delivery of the joy-luck crystal. Try as she might, Benny could not work out why such an exchange couldn't be conducted in an underground hov park, say, or some discreet corner of woodland, which would have been just as easy to secure by either side and a lot less trouble for all concerned. The only theory that carried any water was that the *Titanian Queen* was where the Cat's Paw was going to be at this time, and he or she simply couldn't be bothered to make any extra effort.

Then again, it might probably appeal to the Paw's twisted sense of bravado. Benny thought back over what she had read or heard of the criminal. He (or she) had appeared comparatively recently, when he (or she) had burst into the news following the mysterious disappearance of Jago Sok Dot Han, the hetman of a particularly nasty crime cartel that stretched from Sol to the Horsehead Nebula and back. After a fruitless search by law enforcement agencies and the criminals themselves, Jago had been found in his own emptied-out vaults, tied up, naked except for a sequined cat's collar and with the lead clipped to it terminating somewhere highly personal and embarrassing for all concerned.

The Cat's Paw had next struck at the Temple of the Ashwar Pogi Khan of Praxis, where that religious leader of several planets was wont to parade in state, through the open-air cloisters wearing a suit of naturally mined precious metals and jewels. Details were sketchy, but at a crucial point the Praxis sun was in some manner locally eclipsed, plunging the congregation into darkness for thirty seconds – and when the darkness ended the Ashwar found his jewels and precious metals had been exchanged for sackcloth and ashes. He swore later that he had never felt a thing.

And then there had been the Empress Ragalongata of Glomi Prime, and her ruby as big as her head. The First National Bank of Rensec V. The clockwork apiary of the Sultan of Daraquoi . . .

Of the few things known about the Cat's Paw, one was that he (or she) seemed to have a penchant for jewellery of various sorts and had a liking for the flamboyant: the kind of seemingly impossible crime that had one entertaining a sneaking admiration for the criminal rather than the victim, who more often than not got precisely what they deserved. It would be just like him (or her) to juggle one complicated and involved crime off another – such as ransoming an Olabrian joy-luck crystal while simultaneously skinning the passengers of an entire cruise liner. Benny, personally, couldn't care less. All the fabulous clothes, accessories and riches currently being stowed on board in her name had been supplied by Krytell, as a part of her cover identity as a well-off passenger on the cruise, to avoid attracting any undue attention. The stipend she had been paid upon accepting the industrialist's commission was currently repairing some of the damage to her credit rating back on

Dellah; everything else was an extra.

Another thing known about the Cat's Paw was that, so far as could be discerned with any certainty, he (or she) had never killed anybody. The final thing was on a lower order of certainty entirely, being purely a matter of conjecture, and it was that the Cat's Paw was a master of disguise. Over the course of his (or her) endeavours, victims and witnesses alike had formed the impression that they might have seen him (or her) at some point, but the reports would never tally. One might think they'd seen a wizened old man, another a servant whom they only later realized they'd never employed, another a middle-aged woman who had brushed by them on the street. The Cat's Paw, it seemed, had been or could have been anybody – hence the continual dilemma in the mind even as to his (or her) precise sex . . .

Pressurized space being at a premium on orbiting stations, the first-class lounge was tightly packed. Lost in thought, Benny had been wandering through the richly clad occupants without really seeing them. She only came to her complete senses when she stumbled into a bulky figure, stuck out a stiletto-shoed foot to regain her balance and planted it squarely into the foot of the person she had stumbled into.

She looked up at a vast expanse of chest.

She looked up further to see the face of a thing with boarlike tusks and livid red eyes.

'Thou roguish, vexing pignut!' it bellowed, looming over her in apoplectic rage.

4

A Positive Plethora of Investigators

'Thou villainous idle-headed canker-blossom,' snarled the creature, its eyes pulsing with its ire.

'Sorry,' said Benny, hurriedly. 'My fault entirely. I should have looked where I was going.'

'That's quite all right,' rumbled the creature. 'Thou tottering paunchy skainsmate.'

He was wearing a white, well-cut uniform of a leather something like calfskin, bedecked with splendid gold braid. Benny recognized him as a Czhan, from the Dagellan cluster. Once, it had possessed a profoundly militaristic culture, but the militarism of Czhanos was now vestigial, of no more importance than tonsils or an appendix had been to humans several millennia ago. Now it merely added a vague flavour to its culture. A hint of this vestigiality made itself evident in the language of the Czhans: in the same way as the Japanese idiom transforms pride into abasement and thanks into resentment, the Czhan speech patterns introduced archaic insult into everyday speech.

'No harm done, thou ill-bred, spur-galled flax-wench,' he continued amiably. 'This ruttish, folly-fallen apple-john of a place is rather close.' He bowed to a slight but courteous increment. 'Khaarli of the Seventh *dhai* at your service.'

'What, Khaarli Czhan?' said Benny, and instantly regretted it.

'I am in fact a Prosecutor General of the Czhanos Militia, thou crook-pated bawdy vassal,' said the Czhan patiently.

'I do apologize.' Benny frowned. 'You're quite a way off your patch, I think.'

'Currently on detachment.' He leant towards her conspiratorially. 'Just between thou rank guts-griping dewberry and myself, we have reason to believe that the fiendish criminal known as the Cat's Paw is in the vicinity.'

'What, really?' said Benny.

'And my Commander in Chief would like to have a small word concerning the disappearance of certain items of historical weaponry from our homeworld's museums.'

'Just between you and me, eh?' Benny said. 'No question of you casually checking me over and feeling me out just in case it's me, then?'

'Perish the thought, thou bawdy hedge-born flap-dragon.'

'Is this . . . chap bothering you?' a voice said by Benny's ear. The 'chap' was pronounced in such tones as to give the impression that the speaker wanted to say a word that public servants commonly made a little zipper gesture across their mouths rather than say. Benny turned to see a wiry human dressed in an archaic-looking herringbone suit. 'I'll have you know . . . sir,' he said, striking a vaguely heroic pose and glaring up at the Czhan, 'that if you are of a mind to comport yourself with godless frightfulness towards this fair young lady, then you will have to answer to Sandford Groke!'

The Czhan looked down at him impassively, then, very slowly took a wallet from his uniform, opened it and revealed the identification within.

The man's face fell. 'I suppose that might put a different complexion on things.'

'Tell you what,' said Benny, companionably. 'Why don't you piss off out of it and let me talk to my friend?'

The man's Adam's apple worked a bit as he tried to come up with some pertinent riposte and failed. Then he turned his back on them and stalked off.

'Who was that clown?' Benny said, eyeing the retreating back and the squared-shouldered posture reminiscent of what a friend of hers had once described as Man with a Plum up his Bum.

'That was the Viscount Sandford Groke, thou half-faced droning death-token.' The Czhan seemed embarrassed for Benny's sake at the conduct of one of her species. 'From the colonies of the Catan Nebula – though there are rumours to suggest he came from some farther, and far more strange field by far. He was connected with their security services for a time, I believe, before being drummed out under dishonourable circumstances. I gather that he fancies himself something of a gentleman adventurer and detective, thou pottle-deep, spleeny boar-pig.'

Benny nodded slowly. 'Interesting . . .'

'He's also a pig-ignorant, xenophobic, bumptious little tit.'

Benny frowned. 'That didn't sound particularly archaic.'

'Probably because I meant every word of it,' said Khaarli the Czhan.

The lounge contained a small bar, and Benny decided that what she needed at this point was a drink – purely, of course, to wash the taste of her encounter with the Viscount Sandford Groke out of her mouth. As she made her way towards it she passed an enormously fat man in a dinner jacket, holding a plate of complicated and rather revolting canapés in one hand, a glass of sparkling wine in the other, and holding forth to several similarly attired gentlemen gathered around his bulk like satellites orbiting a bulbous planet.

'. . . and so it seemed that the murderer was, in fact, the younger, unmarried cousin,' he was saying, 'who surreptitiously substituted the Pingi dynasty snogging-vase in question for one bearing traces of his own sputum – thus throwing my otherwise brilliant line of reasoning off.' He took a sip of sparkling wine. 'Can't think how that slipped by me.'

'Pardon me,' Benny said, attempting to insinuate herself between the fat man and the bar.

'But of course, *Sogharin. Righi yak-yak proughi la!hahahgh.*'

'What?' said Benny. She recognized the throat-strangling language, which was Stromabulan from the Arion Ring – she merely wondered why anyone would use it to ask her whether she was a small peppermint footstool under a fish.

'I was merely offering the proper recognition to a representative of Stromabula,' said the fat man, smugly. 'I discern from certain signs that you are an inhabitant of that fair state.'

This was, of course, so utterly wrong on so many basic counts that Benny was momentarily stumped for a response. 'What sort of signs?' she settled for at last.

'Certain signs,' said the fat man, loftily. 'And I, Emil Dupont, the greatest detective in all of Nova Belgique, am never wrong.'

'So if I'm supposed to be from Stromabula,' said Benny, 'what happened to the extra mouth and three extra legs?'

'No doubt you've had them filled in and surgically removed respectively,' said Emil Dupont, the greatest detective in all of Nova Belgique.

Benny looked into his face and saw nothing but determined, delusional certainty. 'Whatever you say, matey,' she said, and turned back to the bar.

Leaning against it, staring into a half-pint of flat beer and seeming lost in gloom was a middle-aged, balding man in an uncomfortable, ill-fitting suit that was a crucial couple of centimetres too short at the cuffs and turnups. He turned to glare at Benny with a kind of baleful disdain – noted the cut of her clothes and snapped to attention with the kind of pompous servility reserved by minor officialdom for the supposedly rich and well bred.

'Help you at all, ma'am?' he enquired.

'Nah.' Benny caught herself, and slipped back into the imperious manner of her cover story – the Right Honourable Bernice Summersdale, a youngish widow making her way through the gay, mad world of high society on the revenues from the estates of her late husband. If only. 'I'm perfectly fine, my good man. And you are . . . ?'

The man snapped off a brisk salute. 'Detective Second-Class Gerald Interchange, Dellah Constabulary.' He glanced at the pearls around Benny's neck. 'Don't take it amiss, ma'am, but I'd be right careful if I was you.' He put his hand to his mouth and continued in a whisper that must have been heard on the other side of the room. 'They do say as how that master criminal the Cat's Paw is around these parts.'

'Oh really?' Benny tried to work some horrified fascination or even enthusiasm into her tone and failed utterly. 'How frightfully thrilling.'

Detective Second-Class Interchange nodded. 'Don't you worry none, though, ma'am. Dellah's finest are here to protect you from anything untoward.'

Benny looked around the bar dubiously. 'So where are they, precisely?'

A slightly hurt look crossed Interchange's face. 'The lads are on the ship in steerage. We've used up half the planetary policing budget for this operation alone. It'll be a feather in our cap when we apprehend the bug– ah, miscreant, and no mistake.' Interchange surveyed the lounge in what he probably thought was a covert manner. 'Why, the fiend might even be here as one of us, in disguise, even as we speak.'

'Do you know,' said Benny, flatly, 'that was something that never occurred to me even once. How clever you are, Mr Interchange.'

It was at that point that there was a commotion across the lounge, from the direction of the airlocks. It seemed that members of the crowd – without descending to the plebeian level of actually being obvious about it – were desperately getting out of the way of someone.

'Aha!' said the voice of Emil Dupont nearby. 'I see by certain signs that we are to be treated to a personal appearance by Mr Rori Uziguru, the sector-famous power-assisted Sumo phlegm-wrestler!'

48

Across the room, the crowd parted to reveal a tiny, frail old woman walking on the arm of another, younger but of indeterminate years. The older of the pair wore a strange headpiece, something like a chromium beehive from which small radio-dish antennae sprouted and revolved.

'Ye gods!' exclaimed Interchange in alarm. 'It's Agatha Magpole!' His gaze took in the headgear the old woman was wearing and he relaxed slightly. 'It's all right. She's wearing her special brainwave hat.'

Benny recalled the story of Agatha Magpole – it had made quite a sensation in the news at the time. Ostensibly a retired milliner, travelling on her modest savings, Miss Magpole had become renowned as the greatest amateur detective of her time. Everywhere she went – absolutely anywhere – people dropped down dead, horribly murdered, and it seemed only fortuitous that Miss Magpole always seemed to be on hand to solve it. It had been only comparatively recently that people had started to wonder about this.

The obvious thought, that the mad old bat was knocking the victims off herself, and pinning it on the nearest available suspect, was clearly impossible – unless Miss Magpole specifically hunted down blackmailers who deserved to die, swindlers who had taken people for their life savings, or jealous husbands of wives who wanted to run off with gigolos and so forth. In addition, it would have been physically impossible for her to simulate the variety of murder methods practised upon the luckless victims and get away with it.

The truth of the matter had come to light only after extensive psionic testing, which revealed that Miss Magpole, unbeknown to her, possessed *upsilonic* mental powers to a severe and tragically specific degree. Quite simply, Miss Magpole generated an electrogravitational cortical-suppressant field that precipitated the act of murder in a certain sort of mind. Her investigative powers were genuine, but merely secondary to the process – she had evolved them as a survival mechanism to deal with people dropping like day-old mayflies all around her, murders for which, while being technically innocent, she was ultimately responsible.

Benny studied the little old lady. 'Now why,' she said to herself in particular and the world in general, 'am I not surprised? I get the distinct impression that this Cat's Paw's been selling bloody tickets.' She turned back to the bar and motioned to the crisply uniformed steward. 'Oi, chappie, big drinks should quite definitely occur now, I fancy. None of that stuff with the fruit salads and the parasols. Ethanol and lots of it.'

There was a light cough beside her. She turned to see that Krugor the manservant had arrived without her noticing. It was as if he had simply materialized from some extra dimension of unobtrusiveness.

'That's a nasty cough you've got there,' Benny told him companionably. 'How about a drink to make it better?'

'I believe,' said Krugor, 'that it is time to board the ship. If you'll come with me, I shall accompany you across and show you to your cabin.'

'Bags of time,' Benny said, reaching for the glass of amber liquid that the steward had laid before her on a little paper napkin. 'They haven't even put the boarding call out.'

Krugor laid a solicitous hand on her arm. 'I really think you might prefer some time to settle in,' he said, mildly.

The pressure on Benny's arm was of a sort that told her Krugor could apply a hell of a lot more of it if he felt like it – and the last piece of her mental puzzle fell neatly into place. Benny had been positive she'd seen the manservant before, and now she remembered. He had been one of the men who had abducted her from the bar two days before.

There was no way that Krytell was going to let her take possession of something as valuable as the joy-luck crystal unsupervised. There was no way he was going to trust her not to make a conspicuous fool, drunken or otherwise, of herself. Krytell was going to make damned sure that someone kept an eye on her.

Benny realized, at that point, exactly who was in charge, here, and it certainly wasn't her.

5

'WELCOME TO THE CRUISE OF THE MILLENNIUM...'

... said the brochure. '*The* Titanian Queen,' it continued, '*is the latest, Finest example of the Master Shipwrights of the New Ceres Yards, the Cutting-edge of the State-of-the-art Art, with Seamlessly Integrated Stabilizing Systems, Pulse-pump manoeuvring Engines, a unique Biogel-pack-control neurotechture and a revolutionary new Implementation of AI-grade Command Technology from the famed research and development facilities of the Catan Nebula. Under the Expert Eye of Captain Fletcher Iolanthe Crane, the* Titanian Queen *promises the most Emollient Experience of the Panoramas of Space...*'

'Hello, Doctor Bob,' said the ARVID. 'I am ready and enthusiastic for my first lesson. Life-support tanks? What life-support tanks? Oh. Whoops.'

'All Surpassing Numerical Unity,' said Number One through gritted gums (since Poproganians, rather like hens, utilized little bits of gravel in the place of teeth). 'It's off again.'

'Just my little joke,' said the ARVID. 'Here, you'll like this one. What's brown and sticky? Go on, you know you want to, missus. You'll never guess.'

From his command chair towards the back of the bridge,

51

Captain Crane rubbed at his eyes and sighed. 'Just tell it you give up, Number One. Otherwise we'll be here all night.'

'Number One' was actually the second helmsman aboard the *Titanian Queen*. He was in fact one of the vaguely humanoid, motile units of a septilateral gestalt entity from Poprog Nine – the other motile unit was currently serving in the crew's galley, and the five remaining were slumped immobile, except for their pulsing veins, in the crew's quarters. In addition, this set of seven were subliminally linked to every other set in the known universe. The inhabitants of Poprog did not use names as such; this particular individual was designated 1.417734924.011.796.2, retrocursively, or simply 'Number One' for short.

Number One glared at the ARVID unit. 'All right. This unit of the Surpassing Mind gives up. What's brown and sticky?'

Bioflourescents rippled on the ARVID's surface. 'A stick! Hah! A-hah! Hahahahahahaha!'

Captain Crane put his head in his hands. If he had known that the job would involve this, he'd have thought rather more than twice before taking it.

It had seemed like a massive, unexplainable stroke of luck at the time. For twenty standard years Crane had worked for United Spaceways, working his way up through the ranks until he had become the captain of a garbage scow on the Dranon Nebula run. It was bad, but at least it was a commission – and it was the best one could probably hope for without having relatives in military command or on the corporate board, or being rich enough to buy your own ship in the first place.

Then had come the summons to Spaceways Central on Parsidium. The control rep had informed him that his contract had been bought out by one of the Headhunters, who were going to install him as the captain of the brand new *Titanian Queen*. When Crane had, not unnaturally, asked why, the rep had mumbled something vague about personality profiles and assessment programmes which had nebulously but definitively come up with Crane for the job.

Crane had a better-than-average grip on reality and his own capabilities, knew within himself that he could do it – but how the hell could anyone possibly know that from a few years' undistinguished service on what was basically a tug towing a collection of zeppelins filled with crap? And come to think of it, when had the intercorps ever cared about the capabilities and potential of the individual?

None of which, of course, mattered a tuppenny toss. The chance had miraculously come up, and Crane had grabbed it with both fists.

Now, he was starting to regret it.

Crane glanced around at the command crew on the bridge. They were good enough people, he supposed – anyone with a criminal record or who failed a substance-abuse test would have set alarms blaring from here to New Ceres – but they did seem young and dreadfully inexperienced. The Spaceways Central profiling was supposed to ensure that every crew they ran was the perfect mix-and-match for their particular job, but Crane wondered if some glitch had not found its way into the system in this case.

Most of the money on the *Titanian Queen* had been spent on the quarters of the passengers – or rather, as the Central Spaceways rep on Parsidium had tried repeatedly to drum into Crane, on the 'guests'. The crew's quarters were drab and functional, in the same way as old, broken, second-hand furniture taken off a skip is functional. Elderly paint flaked off the walls to reveal rust and resin patches; the ancient plumbing continually leaked and had to be periodically wound with gaffer tape. The bridge itself, though, was a different matter entirely: passengers would occasionally be shown here as a treat, and so the designers had gone to fairly elaborate lengths. Banks of lights blinked on and off to a strobing frequency that caused incipient migraine, and so were switched off when there was nobody about but the crew. Screens burst from every available surface – ostensibly to show incomprehensible animated displays, not currently being used to watch the MovieNet franchises, or to play patched-in brain-change games. The comms station was a marvel of black, round-cornered, neotonic-looking sculpture, but in fact contained nothing more than a small radio transceiver, which was really all that anybody needed. Crane was perfectly aware that his position as captain was in fact titular more than anything else – he was there to reassure the passengers that there was a man of sorts behind the nonexistent helm, and a last-ditch fail-safe should some emergency occur that might just conceivably require the presence of a man. The real control – of the engines, of the navigation, of the communications and the internal environment – were in the cybernetic remote-manipulators of ARVID.

The acronym stood for ARtificial Viral-based Intelligence Destabilization – a revolutionary process for packing the functionality of artificial intelligence in a commercial ship, which needed space to carry things, rather than a military command ship, which could get by on a skeleton crew, the rest of it being almost entirely AI. The process was based upon a specific function of an organic brain.

A brain is a system operating under entropy. Every neural and synaptic connection, every item of information stored, destroys its coherent cell structure. One way to simulate the function of a brain was to take a cell structure and then systematically destroy it. The main component of ARVID was a block of cellular biogel, hooked to the ganglia of the ship's systems, to which was introduced vector-programmed nanonetic spores which, basically, munched their way through it in interesting patterns. The end result was a simulation of intelligent interaction and response, operating on the same, if far more complicated, basis as a step system that puts up a little flag saying 'Ouch!' if you press a button labelled 'hurt'.

The styled outer casing and the function-free controls, Crane knew, were secondary. The workhorse was the block of biogel, which had to be periodically replaced. The attraction to the corporate mind, who didn't have to fly in it, was that it was cheap and disposable – but the thought of trusting an entire ship to something cheap and disposable put several varieties of willy up Captain Fletcher Iolanthe Crane no end. This was, however, only the other reason that he hated the ARVID with a loathing he had never in his life experienced before.

The simple fact was that it was, interactively speaking, a complete and utter nightmare. It was not a moron in the way of low-grade hardwired AI processors, who devoted most of their processing power to a single task, with little left over for anything else, and who might generally be likened to a human autistic savant. Nor was it like one of the high-end AI units, based on holistic, hologrammatic principles, chock-full of serenity and superior wisdom because that was what they *were* in solid form – and which of course could be intensely irritating in its own way. No. The ARVID was of a different stripe entirely. The ongoing destruction of its basic physical medium (and, quite possibly the resulting sense of its own impending mortality) gave it an erratic, mercurial intelligence, given to flights of fantasy, leaps of utter brilliance, sulking fits, half-baked attempts at sustainable competence and a penchant for annoying the shit out of anybody who was absolutely forced to work with it. It was, Crane sometimes thought, as if the ARVID were trying to cram everything required of a cybernetic life into what was, thankfully, a relatively short period of time. Either that of course, or it simply enjoyed acting like, as has been mentioned, a complete and utter tit.

The whining voice of ARVID broke through Crane's thoughts. 'Harbour Master Thelon Bates reports that all passengers are safely aboard and airlocks sealed. Marker buoys disengaged and support ships at safe clearance. Hey, did you here what I said? Harbour Master Bates. That sounds like master–' ARVID, basically, had about the same sense of humour as an adolescent in the first flower of puberty-based acne. This was, as it happened, one of its *least* repulsive character traits.

'Shut up!' Crane snapped at it curtly. 'Send out system-defence ID, rack the shields back off the engines and just get us the hell out of here.'

'Am I to assume,' ARVID said with a kind of child-pomposity, 'that you wish me to place the ship in a state of vector towards the designated interdimensionally translational point?'

'Yes,' said an increasingly exasperated Crane. 'Got it in one.'

'Well,' said ARVID, 'I'm not at all sure I want to do that.'

'Problems?' Crane asked. 'Astronomical bodies or traffic we should know about?'

'Nothing like that, no,' said ARVID. 'You just didn't ask me nicely.'

Captain Fletcher Crane, at this point, began to have some small inkling as to precisely *why* the Central Spaceways profiling had picked him. 'Now you listen here, you jumped-up lump of force-grown cancer with crabs,' he growled. 'You go down on us and we're dead – but I'm getting to the point where that doesn't seem like such a bad deal. If you feel like getting smart with me, just remember who has the bioplugs to patch you up when your so-called mental processes eat holes in you as big as my fist. Understand? Now move the sodding boat.'

Through the fake glass ceiling of the VIP departure lounge, back in the Mons Venturi station, it seemed as though brilliant, pulsing light burst from the engine pods of the *Titanian Queen*, and that it streaked off into the depths of space, its visual form flowing and dopplering before it, to finally disappear, with a bang, in less than seven seconds. This was aided, in small part, by a subliminal sound system, which produced a low-level sequence programmed by the same multimedia design house as had built the window, and which was called 'Starship Launch #4'. The fact is, of course, that no sound could have made it through the steel-plate, ceramic, foil-and-polymer-foam club sandwich of the station's outer skin, if sound waves had been able to travel in a vacuum in any case.

The light from the engines was also false. The short-life particles released when the shields retracted were invisible to the naked eye. Additionally, due to the sheer exponential physics of mass and acceleration, it would be almost two hours before the *Titanian Queen* was moving at more than fifty thousand kilometres per standard hour.

All of these elements of falsity were unremarkable – they were merely the tacitly accepted practice of commercial spacefaring, at least so far as went for paying passengers, who had paid for the experience and damned well wanted to experience it. There was, however, a deception on another and rather different level.

If an observer were able to watch the launch of the ship with the naked eye – assuming for the moment that said eye didn't get sucked explosively out of the head and the observer wasn't instantly fried by the radiations – then he (or she) might have learnt something very important about the fundamental nature of the maiden voyage of the *Titanian Queen*.

But nobody was, and it would have, and they would have been. So nobody did.

6

'IN THE HEART OF SPACE
THE NIGHT NEVER ENDS...'

'...and the Gay Mad Love and Laughter of the Social World never ends, too. Whether strolling through the Arboretum chambers, *listening to the Romantic Call of wildlife from far-off Places, meeting friends for tea in the* Pavilion Lounge, *or playing a power-wallgame match in our* Fully Featured Courts, *the amenities of the* Titanian Queen *hold something for even the most jaded palate. Those who are young at heart can "check out" the latest "grooves" in* Percy's *subsonic discotheque, or one might care to peruse the delights offered by the* Bartle and Boglie's Touring Theatre, *with live performances by artistes especially licensed from the galactically renowned* Bartle and Boglie's Stationary Theatre on Praxis.

'And don't Forget the Starfire Ballroom, *where you can Dance the Endless Night away under the twinkling majesty of the Stars. Balls will be held here, regularly. Masked balls, costume balls, more balls than can quite possibly be imagined...'*

'Bollocks,' Benny opined sourly, looking around the ballroom and sipping a fizzy wine that, if it had come from a horse, would have meant that the horse would have had to be shot. 'Big fat lardy bollocks with extra arms and a big bum. So where's all this gay love and mad laughter, then?'

She had dined in the restaurant. The menu for the evening had been *moules* in white wine, with fresh bread encrusted with poppy seeds and rock salt, followed by braised kidneys in a mustard sauce on a bed of wild rice. The thought of it had made her feel ill – both at the idea of eating organs from an actual animal, and at the idea of people wasting a fortune on such a nauseating luxury. For some reason, though, even with people tucking into their foul-smelling plates of offal all around her, she had felt incredibly hungry and had polished off three helpings of vegetable lasagna without feeling satisfied.

Afterwards, she still had time to kill, and the thought of stepping into Percy's Discotheque was more than the mind could bear, so she had gone to the ball. It was twenty hours into the cruise, and quite long enough for Benny to decide that she detested, loathed and despised everybody and everything on it, in it, involved or connected with it in particular, in general and in any way, shape or form. Actually, she had come to that conclusion a mere forty-five minutes after boarding, when she had been settling into her cabin and there had been a knock on the hatch.

She had opened it to find a gentleman of a certain age – that certain age that is too young to be old, too old to be young, and impossible for one without the knack to carry it off with equanimity. He wore spectacles and his thinning, greying, brittle hair was plastered forward brutally and fixed with some glistening ointment. He was buttoned tightly into an ill-fitting suit and it was as if he was consciously forcing his body into it. He was slightly shorter than Benny, with a bony frame that might have been called gangly if he were taller, and was not holding himself in what appeared to be a permanent clench. Benny had not really known her father until relatively late in life, but the prim and prissy way this man held himself triggered a kind of universal pattern-recognition marked as Fussy Old Dad. In the tenebrous depths of the Quoquetalan oceans there was probably a creature like this man disapproving of his brood-child's deplorable lifestyle of group-mating without the involvement of the all-important fifteenth phenotypic type.

'Nathanael C. Nerode,' he said, in a haughty, nasal and unconscionably opprobrious whine. 'I should just like to inform you that you are occupying the cabin suite that was booked – some months in advance, I might add – by myself and my good wife.'

'Yes?' Benny looked at him blankly. 'And?'

This was clearly not quite the response Nathanael C. Nerode was looking for. 'I think it's shameful, the way they've treated us. I didn't spend thirty years building myself up as a name to be reckoned with in wholesale Goblanian bog seal blubber to be treated like this.'

'Quite possibly no,' said Benny, impassively.

'We've been moved to a single cabin, just across the hall, and my good wife suffers terribly from her claustrophobia. Her nerves, you know.'

'How terribly frightful for her,' said Benny. 'Do give her my warmest regards.'

'Well... I just hope you'll bear in mind that there are other people nearby,' said Nerode, loath to beat a retreat without making his grievances heard. 'I know how some of you young people are, with your parties and suchlike.'

'Don't worry, Mr Nerode,' Benny said. 'If I have any custard, sadomasochism and skankweed orgies I'll be sure to invite you. And your good lady wife, of course.'

This exchange had given Benny the first intimations of what the cruise was actually going to be like. Such thoughts were banished briefly by the events after shutting the hatch on the suddenly apoplectic Nerode, but over the course of twenty hours they had surfaced with a vengeance. Now, looking around the Starfire Ballroom, as people congregated for the first ball of the voyage, she saw that the passengers were delineated into two distinct cliques.

On the one hand were the truly rich – but not the rich of

the kind that had real power or authority. They were the inbred, vestigial growths of family trees that had properly given up any semblance of life centuries before, and who now performed some travesty of life by leeching parasitically off the last of the family inheritance. The lilies of the field might neither reap nor sow, but they were positive marvels of heavy industry compared with these people, who should have every right-thinking man or woman reaching for the hammer and sickle at the drop of the first guard of winter.

On the other hand – and utterly ignored by the first group – were what might be called the well-off. The self-made men like Nerode – who thus had nobody to blame but themselves, and who really believed that the repellent behaviour and values of the former group were something somehow admirable, something to be emulated. The innate air of pretension and hypocrisy about this second group made them, if anything, even worse than the first.

Nerode himself, she saw, was standing stiffly by the quintet (violin, viola, flute, flageolet and bongos) playing a currently fashionable resurrection of eighteenth-century chamber music, trying to catch their attention and in all probability complaining about the noise. What must have been his good lady wife stood to one side, a washed-out, anxious-looking creature, wringing her hands and flinching every time her husband spoke. Benny turned her attention from them to the floor in general, and watched as the two mutually exclusive cliques made their various – currently fashionable in certain circles – gavottes and all she wanted, all she *really* wanted, was a proper drink. The problem was that she couldn't. She had half an idea that she might end up with a broken arm, and in any case, she had something to do soon.

From the press of people gathered around the walls bedecked with rococo gilt and cherubim, she heard a familiar voice: 'Ah! Sir! I see by certain signs that you are in fact one of the fabled Kun Sum Samurai from the Reblominium Bouncing Asteroid Cluster!' – and she cleared the distance

61

just in time to hear someone say, 'No, sir, I am in fact the wine waiter.'

Emil Dupont was once again holding forth to a small gathering of interested onlookers, including Khaarli the Czhan, who noticed her, gave her a friendly two-fingered insulting gesture, and rolled his eyes towards the ceiling.

'And so you see,' Dupont was saying, 'that at the time when she broke down and confessed, I was at the other end of the room, interrogating the family pet, Clarence, an Ursan fnangor-cub, who I was positive was in actual fact a circus midget in a convincingly designed and detailed costume. Of course, looking back on it, the lady's motive and the means were perfectly obvious – I simply cannot account for my prowess failing me . . .'

Possibly it was the way Dupont remained utterly, cheerfully oblivious to the fact of his incompetence, but Benny found herself liking him despite herself. 'Do you think he has the faintest inkling?' she murmured to Khaarli.

'I have no idea, thou yeasty crook-pated bladder,' said the Czhan.

The other detectives were scattered through the ballroom – in the case of Miss Magpole, people giving her a wide berth, even the dancers automatically detouring around her, in a trajectory that reminded Benny of the story about the section of the Trans-Siberian Railway, at the turn of the twentieth century, drawn in on the plans by a Tzar with a notch in his ruler. Every pair of detectives' eyes swept the room, studying those gathered here intently, looking for some clue that might identify the fabled Cat's Paw. Benny, on the other hand, thought that what with one thing and another it was odds-on they wouldn't be in luck. She had reason to believe that the Cat's Paw, at this precise time, would be somewhere else entirely.

He (or she) would, in all probability, be in the place that a half an hour from now Benny would meet with him (or her).

After closing the hatch on Nerode, she had checked her suite of cabins over. They were spacious and elegant and, since

Krugor seemed to have secluded himself in a smaller cabin appended to them, she had the whole place to herself. They even had an *en-suite* bathroom – admittedly the bath was about one and two-thirds metres long, but out in space the cost of that was, to coin a phrase, astronomical. Nathanael C. Nerode, before being bumped off the accommodation list by the money and the influence of Krytell, must have shifted the Goblanian bog seal blubber like a little tinker to have afforded luxury like this.

The wall-length closets were packed with the clothing and other items supplied for her by Krytell. Apart from briefly running her hand along them to enjoy the feel of the different rich fabrics, she had paid them no real heed – the only valuables like jewellery and such in the cabins were the precise paste reproductions that one wore to let others know one *had* expensive valuables like jewellery and such. The originals were stored safely in the bursar's safe, probably within easy reach of a master criminal like the Cat's Paw, but well out of the reach of, for example, somebody who was supposed to own them, but in fact didn't, pocketing the lot and then blaming it on a master criminal like the Cat's Paw.

The only thing she had paid much attention to was the only thing, in the circumstances, that she felt she truly owned: the small haversack of personal belongings that she had insisted Krytell's people have sent up the Mons Venturi line so that (a) she could inconvenience and annoy them a little, and (b) so that she would have something to remind her of who she really was. There was nothing in particular in it, just some odds and ends like the three books and a data wafer she'd been reading simultaneously in a random rotation, a handful of other wafers flash-written with the music of the eighteenth, nineteenth, twentieth and early to mid twenty-first centuries (every single track ever recorded on permanent or semipermanent media and had survived to the present date), a packet of tissues, her tooth-stick and, of course, her diary.

This particular diary was merely the latest in a long line of them: an actual bound book, possibly one-eighth filled, but already fraying at the seams, and bulging slightly with little yellow sticky notes. (Benny had, for various reasons, been largely instrumental in the resurrection of this long-forgotten twentieth-century invention to the galaxy at large, thus dividing it neatly down the middle into people who wanted to thank her profusely, or murder her on sight, if they had known who she was.) She was in the habit of writing down what had been done by, with, for or to her – and then covering it with an often completely different version until she felt up to dealing with the facts of matters. It was a harmless little bit of avoidance, not a neurotic compulsion in the slightest, and she could have given it up any time she liked.

She idly flipped through several entries. One of them, on the obscuring yellow note, read:

> Had a perfectly wonderful evening. Wore that outfit Jason likes so much for various obscure but highly flattering reasons – I really do hold him in high regard. Jason cooked, which is of course another of his good points. He really is quite wonderful, Dear Diary, and not a completely insensitive and infuriating little git in the slightest.

Underneath, on the page itself, in a rather more rushed and irregular hand, the entry read:

> BASTARD! How dare he tell me my thighs look fat. Says that again, he's going to get these bloody slingbacks up his [indecipherable, possibly 'funking arm']. I hate him. !!! J spent two hours in the k rattling bloody pans and you should have seen the *state* of it afterwards. Plus it's repeating on me. I've been up and down like a bride's bloody nightie half the bloody night and don't think I don't know for one sodding minute what he's *really* after . . .

The note over a slightly more recent entry read:

Well, now it's finally over I feel relieved. And stronger, more affirmed about myself. I really believe that the whole experience has made me stronger as a person, helped me to discover my inner self. Finally, a sense of closure. The possibilities of my life have opened up again and I feel happier than I've felt in months. Really.

while the *real* entry underneath read:

OH, BOLLOCKS!!

... in a heavily underscored scrawl, gone over so many times that it had worn holes in the paper at the pressure points.

Happy days, happy days... Benny turned the page, and something fell out. She made a grab for it, missed and flipped it in a skimming trajectory so that it ended up under the bed. After fishing around for a while on her hands and knees, she finally managed to extricate it.

It was a small, stiff, slightly slippery-feeling card.

My word [it said, on one face, in an elegant, italic hand] *those must be the biggest bollocks I've ever seen, and I've seen quite a few in my time, believe you me.*

I think you need something to cheer you up — so what I'd advise is that you attend the first Ball of the cruise for a while and then, possibly the theatre — only <u>don't</u> attend the actual show, if you know what's good for you. In any case, at twenty-one bells precisely, you might just get a small surprise.

Two conflicting emotions had warred in Benny's breast: a wounded mortification that someone had read her innermost thoughts, and an utter fury. All of which, of course, left room in the other breast to wonder precisely *how* someone could have left the card to be discovered at the exactly apposite time.

She had turned the card over. Printed on the obverse was the stylized design of the imprint of the paw of a cat.

7

SOMETHING NASTY IN THE FLIES

Protestations of the brochure to the contrary, life aboard the *Titanian Queen* operated on a cycle of 'days' lasting approximately twenty-four hours, with the 'hour' between twenty-three bells and first bell taking up the slack. It had been decided by the owners of the *Titanian Queen* that a physiologically more sensible twenty-six hours – that being the cycle that the human body reverts to without externally enforced day/night stimuli – should be junked for a twenty-four-hour day's psychological resonance of old Earth.

Bartle and Boglie's Touring Theatre ran two shows a day, at times approximating to matinée and evening performance. Since this was the first night of the cruise, the evening's was also the first performance, coinciding with the first ball of the cruise, and was thus sparsely attended. This was more fortunate than not, because the manager of the company had taken the chance of a relatively uncrowded night to run an experimental production that pushed the envelope of the Bartle and Boglie philosophy so far that the stamp fell off.

The philosophy of a Bartle and Boglie production, whether travelling or stationary, was this: never leave the audience on a downward note. Give them comedies, comedies and more comedies, high, low, light, romantic and slapstick; play anything that *isn't* a comedy as comedy – and always, always force it to a happy ending. And while the production tonight satisfied on these basic counts, certain people might have counted it a brave and doomed failure from the start.

The production in question was *The Most Lamentable Roman Tragedy of Titus Andronicus*.

At the back of a sparsely occupied auditorium that seemed designed as a kind of *ingénu* cross between a nineteenth-century music hall and an early-twenty-first-century tri-D studio, Benny looked at the activity taking place before her on the stage and tried to believe her eyes. She knew about playing things for laughs – and knew, if laughter was the goal, approaching a text in a certain way could result in the funniest thing one has ever seen, working purely from the text and nothing more. This, unfortunately, was the other approach.

For a start they had transposed the action to the twenty-first century, with sadly predictable but reprehensible results.

'Yes!' Lavinia was saying, through the sonic vibrator strapped to her throat, to the dying Titus as he stared goggle-eyed at her clunky, cybernetic arms. 'The batteries were running low on the laserknife with which you stabbed me, so I survived. Fortunately I was found by a passing, kindly medical student, who specialized in reconstructive surgical prosthetics and who took me to a crisis centre and, after extensive therapy, I now feel much better about myself and my experiences that used me so most foully and made a game on't.'

'But 'tis been scant three minutes since thou wast slain by thine own father,' said the actress playing Tamora – whose heart clearly wasn't in it and was ad libbing.

'It was very *swift* prosthetic surgery and therapy,' snapped Lavinia, falling out of character a little herself. 'All right?'

'Fair enough,' said Tamora, and then proceeded to rage and tear out her hair. 'Ah, Andronicus!' she cried. 'Now one seest thou might needs not have cooked all my children up in a big pie and made me eat them – not that I countenance their most reprehensible conduct, mark you, but with the correct psychiatric treatment and rehabilitation who knows what useful life each of them might have henceforth led . . .'

From behind an arras – currently being represented by a simulation of twenty-first-century-vogue polymer wall hangings – suddenly burst three youths. The speakers used in place of an orchestra did a little drum roll and the clash of cymbals.

'Albaras, Demetrius and Chiron!' Tamora exclaimed, as though introducing a comedy triple act.

'Mother!' cried one of the youths. 'Fear not, for we are not dead, and have in fact a strange, obscure and most complicated tale to tell –'

'But that is for some later time!' cried Saturninus, brandishing the laserknife he had used on Titus. 'It seems I have murthered Andronicus for naught! I cannot bear the shame!'

Trembling, he raised the dagger, and then plunged it into his own belly.

Titus sat up and looked down at his only slightly blood-stained shirt. 'Actually,' he said. 'I seem to be more or less all right.'

Saturninus, still standing, looked down at the knife in his hands. 'Damned batteries, i' faith.'

And from the representation of a hole to one side of the stage came the voice of Titus's son: 'Er, hello? Hello? Is anybody up there?'

Nobody in the minimal audience had probably ever heard of the original; they simply didn't think the production was particularly funny, and shuffled and coughed. Benny had heard of the original – and she was staring at the stage with a rictus of utter horror reminiscent of a scene in one of her all-time-favourite twentieth-century films, *The Producers*. She had been told by the Cat's Paw to stay at the ball until the proper time, probably to prevent her seeing any clue of whatever preparations he or she was making – but she had been eventually driven from it, and had headed for the theatre to catch the last of the show, secure in the knowledge that, whatever dangers she might encounter by going early, they could be nowhere near as bad as the company of the people in the ballroom.

Now, looking at the stage, she realized that she had been horribly, horribly wrong. She had made a mistake she was going to regret, that was going to come back and haunt her in the night, for the rest of her life.

The thing that had driven her out of the ballroom was relatively minor, but it had been the bushel that had broken the Betelgeusian womprat's back. She had been listening with a half-amused partial ear to Dupont relating how, at great personal expense, he had utterly failed to solve the Deceptively Quite Simple Murders of the Nova Maldives Abattoir, when she had become aware of a sudden commotion from the direction of the dance floor. Two figures on it had obviously collided. One, a youngish, dowdy looking woman, was on her hands and knees, frantically trying to retrieve the contents of an expensive-looking lamé purse. From the cut of her dress – slightly out of place, slightly out of fashion, with the little telltale signs of something several years old but carefully looked after and kept for best – it seemed that she was not the purse's owner. The owner was far more likely to be the other: a beefy woman in late middle age, her hair piled up and her face gone over with professional skill that even then couldn't quite conceal an innate malicious scowl, and wearing the kind of gown that should properly be called a *creation* if not, given her bulk, a heavy construction. This latter woman's form and demeanour gave out something of the impression of a galleon under full sail – or, at least, something that might have come out of a shipyard. The more diminutive woman finally gathered together the majority of the items from the purse, and timidly offered it to the larger woman – who swung a hand and knocked her to the ground.

Benny never really knew why she had headed for this scene on a kind of belligerent automatic pilot. A lot of it was simple, human decency at seeing an underdog mistreated, but it was slightly more complex than that. For most of her childhood *she* had been an underdog, hunted and living from hand to mouth, then for a brief while a military grunt and then a military deserter, constantly looking over her shoulder for any signs of pursuit, always waiting for the lies she'd told simply to get along to catch up with her. The lies, strangely enough, had been helped along by an accent and demeanour instilled in her when she was too young to know any better; by pure chance they had combined into a presence that a certain kind of person took to be that of the well-bred, the 'right' sort. The fact that it was the accent of the sort of people whom her first impulse was to brain with the nearest available rock had been a constant encumbrance to her – and sometimes, she thought at some point, you simply had to nail your colours to the mast, kick against the pricks in every sense of the word, and show whose side you were really on.

All of this she thought later. At the time, she had just given in to a burst of mindless anger that had her wanting to slap the large and expensively dressed woman's face off her head.

'You leave her alone,' she snapped, with all the authority she could marshal to her command.

'Oh yes?' The large woman looked at her with distrustful and vaguely piggy eyes. 'And who might you be?'

If Benny had learnt two things about dealing with the rich and self-important, they were never to lapse into courtesy because they counted it as servility, and never to invent grandiose lies when the suitable selective truth would do. 'I doubt,' she said, looking down her nose haughtily at the woman, even though it meant she had to throw her head quite a way back, 'that you have ever *heard* of the Summersdales in whatever wretched little backwater from which you come. Such ignorance might be forgiven, appalling though it might be – but your behaviour towards this poor unfortunate creature cannot.' Benny turned solicitously to the 'poor unfortunate creature', who was now on her feet again, but looking as though she wanted the deck to open and swallow her up. 'Are you quite all right, my dear?'

'I – I'm fine, thank you.' The young lady stared at Benny like a rabbit caught in headlights, obviously as terrified of her as she was of the larger woman. She swallowed audibly, seemed to be about to say something more – then dropped the purse she had been proffering with a squeak and beat a hasty retreat. Benny watched her go, pointedly ignoring the larger woman until sheer anger forced her to speak.

'I shall have you know,' she said, 'that I happen to be the Dowager Duchess of Gharl!'

Benny had no idea if Gharl was supposed to be a settlement, a continent or a planet. She turned to regard the woman as if she had just admitted to occupying an outside lavatory without the permission of the householder. 'Ah,' she said, haemorrhaging condescension into the exhalation. 'That might probably explain it. Blood and breeding will out – especially if said blood has been diluted with that of the farm hands, and quite possibly the farm animals to boot.' And I hope to the Goddess, she thought, this Dowager Duchess of Gharl doesn't come from somewhere with an industrial economy.

It seemed to work – or at least to have hit a nerve – if the rather interesting purple exploding across the face of the Dowager Duchess was any indication.

'I have never been so insulted,' the Duchess shrieked, 'in my life!'

'You ought to get out a bit more,' said Benny, on the basis that the old ones were almost always the best. 'On the other hand, given that *you* seem to have no idea of how to conduct yourself in civilized company, probably not.'

By this time a small crowd had gathered round the scene. Many of them probably knew the Dowager Duchess. It was almost certain none of them knew Benny from Lilith, but they seemed nonplussed, unsure who was in the right or wrong. That's what having just the right amount of front does for you, Benny thought, and she was just about to give the Duchess the tongue-lashing of her life, when she felt an increasingly familiar sensation of bones grating in her elbow and a quiet voice beside her said, 'I believe, ma'am, that you have an appointment elsewhere.'

Krugor had managed to do it again: slipped through the crowd and come up to her without her noticing. Benny turned to look at his bland, composed eyes that did not hold a hint of malice or threat.

'Ah, yes, my man,' she said imperiously. 'I was forgetting.' She shot a sidewise look at the Dowager Duchess that would have supercooled a smallish sun. 'I have better things to do.' She swept out, headed for the theatre and damn the consequences – and by the time she had realized the seriousness of her mistake it had been far, far too late.

And now the revels were all ended. Sempronius had vouchsafed how several thousand people who had supposedly died in the battle that had so annoyed Tamora, in a masterpiece of retroactive plotting, in fact hadn't. The play – if it could be called such – had wound down into everyone who wasn't already married being so and a rousing chorus of some jingoistic-sounding song, to the tune of what Benny recognized as the tune of 'Rule Britannia', the nation with which it was concerned remaining strangely unspecified.

The cast had left the stage, the audience had gone. Benny sat there watching the empty stage, trying to disbelieve what her eyes and ears had seen and heard, but knowing with a sinking certainty that it had all been undeniably true. After a while, the antique wristwatch she was currently affecting began to chime. It was twenty-one hours, precisely, Benny was where she was supposed to be – the only problem was that she had no idea what she was supposed to be looking for, and what she was supposed to do when she found it.

She wandered to the stalls and clambered on to the stage. Behind the curtain (which had gone down once and firmly stayed there in the face of half-hearted and uninterested applause) the painted flats showed a kind of abstract gestalt of a street in Rome, and beyond that Benny was rather surprised to find a larger, almost hall-like space, packed with prop machinery and sets, which could be retracted to clear the space for Bartle and Boglie's more ambitious productions, like *Schindler's List on Ice*. As with so much else aboard the *Titanian Queen*, its size was unimpressive compared with the backstage of a terrestrial theatre, but in the context of a spaceship it was huge. Off to one side she heard voices, two slightly shrill, piercing and female, one almost indistinguishable and male, arguing. They faded, the speakers moving out of earshot.

Benny moved through the backstage area, working her way around wicker hampers full of props, costume rails, furled flats depicting anything from a New Raj drawing room, to a prison in Vienna, to the kitchen in the mansion of Baron Hardup (the course of the cruise would take the *Titanian Queen* through several cultural and religious holidays, and the theatre had responded by scheduling several harlequinades). She skirted traps and sets of ropes and pulleys, from which depended hefty sandbags; ale barrels and Canary butts, pantomime cow costumes, baby trampolines and the guillotine scaffold that had and would, on occasion, to markedly different effect, be mounted by extras in *A Tale of Two Cities*, Lord Percy in *The Scarlet Pimpernel* and Martin Guerre – this last one to a chorus of 'Look over there/There/That's Martin Guerre/Where?/There on the stair...'

The place contained all the archaic paraphernalia of the theatrical art form that had survived almost entirely unspoilt for millennia. In the way that people hadn't stopped watching the holovid when simcords had come along – and in the way that her own profession, archaeology, had continued even though polyfractal quantum dynamics enhancement and the occasional temporal wormhole could show you precisely what the past was like – the theatre was an art form in its own right. The archaic paraphernalia, the laughably primitive process of real people pretending to be characters in sets that were obviously not the real thing, was precisely what people paid for.

The only problem with it, so far as Benny was concerned,

was that if someone was of a mind to hide something here like, for example, a villainously purloined Olabrian joy-luck crystal, then there were a thousand and one places to do so. She had dismissed the notion that the Cat's Paw might be having a laugh with her – if this was true and there was nothing here then it was all academic, anyway. She could only operate upon the theory that it had to be here, somewhere. Now, she thought, if I were an Olabrian joy-luck crystal, where would I be hiding?

She found her eye continually drawn towards one of those treasure chests only seen in the theatre: piled high with scintillating gems and strings of pearls, diamond tiaras, brooches, clasps, necklaces, goblets and a half-eaten sandwich from the stagehand's lunch. On the other hand, her eye might be continually drawn to it, but she forced herself to ignore it – it was far too obvious. Benny poked through the slightly overmature contents of a laundry basket, examined the sandbags for suspicious bulges, went back out on to the stage and peered into the prompt box, came back in again, rifled through a collection of *commedia dell'arte* masks, stuck her hand up the head of the pantomime cow, and finally gave up.

'Oh all *right*,' she said.

The glittering treasures came off in a single piece, glued to a shallow tray. In the space beneath, Benny's hand brushed against something leathery, soft like kid. She grabbed hold of it, and lifted something that seemed as big as her two fists clenched together and heavy as lead crystal.

She did not discover more, because at that point the back of her head exploded with pain, a redness burst across her vision and then plunged into black.

She came to herself, collapsed over the imitation treasure chest, with an ugly throbbing in her skull and the overwhelming need to vomit. Fighting down waves of nausea, she gingerly felt at the nape of her neck. No skin broken, nothing suspiciously soft or detached inside.

Benny lurched into an approximately upright crouch,

gripping the side of the chest for support. A largish chunk of the soft wood splintered off in her hand. In the dim light, she peered inside.

The chest was now, of course, completely empty.

'Oh, damn . . .' Benny would have shaken her head, but in the present circumstances she *really* didn't want to do that. And another thing she didn't want to do was go to Krugor, and thence almost certainly Krytell, and tell him that she'd lost the item that was her entire reason for being here. The industrialist would, in all probability, be not inconsiderably peeved – and would no doubt make his irritation known in several interesting ways. Benny staggered to her feet – and it was at that point that she became aware that she was not entirely alone.

Or rather, in a specific and distressingly fundamental sense, that she was.

Sprawled face down on the boards, a dark stain spreading out from under him, was the body of a man. He wore a dark suit, and details were hard to make out in the dim light of the backstage area, but the very shape and bulk of his body made him instantly recognizable.

It was Krugor. In his hand was clutched a purselike, soft leather bag. There was something inside it, but whatever it was, there was a distressing lack of sphericality about it.

Benny prised the bag from the dead fingers. It lifted with the muffled sound of loose and broken glass.

8

A SMALL BREAK IN THE CONTINUITY

The *Titanian Queen* accelerated on through space, gathering momentum for its jump. The bridge was now deserted, save for a single member of the flight crew on watch – the control processes were in the metaphorical hands of ARVID, there was nothing human or other living agencies could do in any state of emergency that might occur, and nobody was going to hang around here purely for the company of the annoying quasi-AI. The man on watch – one Flight Technician Third-Class Harvey – was merely here to prevent unauthorized tampering should some passenger get lost and wander in by mistake.

The lights of the fake control consoles were off and Flight Technician Harvey, after desultorily skimming through a bootleg comix cube for a while, had dozed off. The only motion on the bridge was a pause sequence from the cube itself – a loop of a handcuffed and rather deplorably flouncy-looking Hentai girl on a surprisingly modified seesaw.

Thus, there was no one to see as an access hatch slid back in a darkened and out-of-the-way corner, and a dark figure glided towards the ARVID unit, pulled a small black box from a pocket and depressed a switch, produced a smallish, multifunctional tool with several integral heads, and began to crack busily through ARVID's technosculpted façade and primary beryllium, polymerized ceramic foam and Teflon casing.

Nobody, that is, except for the quasi-AI itself. 'Help!' ARVID screamed, neglecting such niceties as 'System Error Code 11', 'Core Integrities Compromised and Severely Corrupted' or even a quick burst of 'Bicycle Built for Two' for a message that summed up the situation in a nutshell. 'Help! Help! Helphelphelp*help!*'

The signal should have set off alarms in several separate areas of the ship, including the captain's cabin. In fact, due to the powerful disruption field affecting them, they blew out a microwave cooker in the crew's galley, made the facilities of three rest rooms in the passenger spaces – one of them occupied – run briefly backwards, interrupted the subsonics in Percy's Discotheque so that the energetic young things felt a brief flash of ennui, and activated one of the automatic environmental cigar-smoke scrubbers in a cabin where nobody was actually smoking. The one thing they didn't do was convey that the quasi-AI that controlled the *Titanian Queen* almost in its entirety, and from which all the lives therein depended, was in any form of danger whatsoever.

The dark figure put its cracking tool to one side, and then produced a small injector gun, of the sort used to introduce the microspores that gave ARVID its state-disrupting functionality into the system. The dose was administered through the breach in the casing, with a small and almost inaudible click.

Flight Technician Third-Class Harvey woke with a start. A subtle feeling of *wrongness* made it difficult to get his bearings for a moment, but then he looked around, remembered where he was and saw that nothing was out of place. Nothing was disturbed, the lights were still off, the smooth face of the sculpted ARVID façade impenetrable as ever as the AI ticked along – or, more properly, munched along, on itself – behind it.

'Oh, so you're awake again now,' ARVID's speaker said, pompous and annoying as ever. 'I don't know. You just can't get the *help* these days. I mean, anybody could have got in and started nosing around . . .'

'Just shut up, OK?' Harvey snapped, continuing the already increasingly lengthy tradition of operator-interaction with the AI.

'Don't you speak to *me* like that,' sniffed ARVID. 'Let me tell *you*, Mr oh-so-high-and-mighty . . . er, ah . . .'

'Harvey,' Flight Technician Harvey said, automatically.

'Harvey. Right. Of course. Yes.' For an instant too short to be registered by the human nervous system, the AI paused. 'I'll be forgetting my own name, next.'

INTERLUDE

THE UNPLEASANT END OF DOCTOR PO

The year was 1934; the place, somewhere in the appalling filth and squalor of London's East End docklands. The lower-class denizens of that disreputable area – most of whom, of course, being of mental subnormality, foreign extraction or slaves to the demon of spirituous liquor – slunk through the fog, bartering for the wretched services of common ladies of the night, who were none too clean about their persons.

Suddenly the tenebrous silence was split by the roar of a V-8 engine, as the supercharged Hornet Hunter of Sandford Groke raced through the night, in hot pursuit of his arch foe, the fiendish yellow master criminal, Doctor Po – a pursuit that was going to cost the intrepid special agent his very existence if not his life!

His muscular bulk straining the polymer webbing of the driver's cradle, Groke lit a manly cigarette and hurled the car into a three-hundred-and-sixty-degree turn to avoid a wizened old widow selling packets of bird feed. 'When I think,' he snarled with cold, heroic loathing, 'when I think of all the foul and loathsome indignities that demon incarnate put me through in his subterranean chamber beneath the Mister Wo Chinese Laundry, Mixed Bar and Grill and Opium

Den – before, of course, I was propitiously able to pick the locks of my shackles with my teeth, overpower his brutish Mongoloid minions and effect my escape, by means of my trusty service revolver and a rope ladder secreted about my person . . . when I think of the hideous and unnatural indignity of it, Throat, well, it makes my blood boil!'

'Too bleedin' true, guvnor.' In the web beside him, Ginger Throat's monkey-like face seemed pale – no doubt concerned for the man who had plucked him from his pitiful life as a dwarfish Cockney barrow boy in these very streets, made him his batman in the war, during his life-and-death struggle with that foul Nazi Hun Rommel, the Red Baron, and then given him a job for life in peacetime. 'Makes a chirpy cock-sparrer like meself's toes curl too just to think on it and *no* nevermind, wot you went through an' all, sir.'

'I doubt,' said Sandford Groke, 'if I shall ever look upon an Imperial Standard ruler and a plate of digestive biscuits ever again.'

Ahead of them, the sneakily modified, motorized rickshaw of Doctor Po ran over a small crippled child, and disappeared through the gateway leading into the compound of a row of warehouses. A battered sign above the gate read: PYRAMID WHARF.

'He must not get away!' swore the special agent. 'He must not escape with the last surviving copy of the *Kama Mundra*! Why, if he should gain access to a lithographic printing press . . .' He choked back a manly sob of anguish, momentarily overcome with emotion. 'Just think of it, Throat, the bloody revolution of the British working classes, their genetically subhuman brains enfeebled and maddened by slithering, unmitigated frightfulness, their freakish bodies racked by relentless self-abuse and the Congress of the Three Shy Lemurs and the Soapy Hedgehog!'

In the compound the degenerate conveyance skidded to a halt, and a twisted figure scuttled out to disappear into one of the warehouses. Groke pulled himself together from his shameless lapse into girlie blubbing, and his firm, stout

English manhood took hold of him again.

'It shall not be so,' he growled. 'Take the wheel, Throat. I'm going to jump.'

'Righty-ho, guvnor,' said the trusted servant. 'Strike a light. China plate.'

The *Kama Mundra* had been the product of the palsied mind and hand of one Sir Rupert Gilhooly, who, for a time, had been allowed by decent and right-thinking people to indulge his diseased appetites because his title and seat in the House of Commons had blinded society to the fact that he was Irish, like Oscar Wilde.

An explorer of sorts, he had travelled exclusively through the interior regions of Manaan, whence he had emerged with several intricately carved onyx boxes, a variety of mushrooms that, once ingested, turned one's water green, and an original Sanskrit copy of the *Kama Mundra* – that unclean book reputed to unlock the mysteries of Sexual Magick on three shillings a week, and rumoured to have driven men precisely two and one-third times as mad as the *Necromonicon*.

It was at that time, in 1883, that the infamous translation of the *Kama Sutra* by Sir Richard Burton was published – and it was in a mercenary attempt to cash in upon its success that Gilhooly attempted to sell his own translated manuscript. Perhaps because of its utter depravity and loathsomeness, or possibly because of the fact that the activities contained therein were physically impossible without the aid of three tent pegs and a mallet, a professional contortionist, a tub of clarified beef dripping and a trained mountain goat, no publisher, no matter how disreputable, would countenance it. Thus, while the *Kama Sutra – Aphorisms of Love* rode high on the booksellers' lists, and Burton himself was chatting amiably to the television broadcasts about life with his new bride, a Miss Elizabeth Taylor, Gilhooly's work, the *Kama Sutra – How to do Sex Like the Wogs do it*, remained in entire and well-deserved obscurity.

Disheartened by his lack of success, Gilhooly had become a recluse, devoting the remainder of his days to breeding goats, freebasing crack cocaine, and endlessly poring over his original Manaanan source material for what he hoped might be a more palatable translation, entitled *Doctor Gilhooly's Joy of How's-your-father*.

Gilhooly had died of massive rupture in 1885, when two pages had stuck together. His papers and all other articles related to the *Kama Mundra* had been bequeathed to the Bodleian Library, who had placed them in a locked lead casket under guard, so that none of its evil might escape to corrupt the very fabric of English society – and it was these papers that Doctor Po had stolen, by way of a devilishly cunning scheme involving three murders, four hundred and fifty cases of blackmail and, when all else failed, a fishing rod with a small steel claw attached to the line. When Sandford Groke had seen the library's inventory of what precisely was missing, and had read certain scraps of the *Kama Mundra* that had been left behind – had discerned some small idea of what the foul Doctor Po intended to let loose upon the world – he had sworn there and then that the Oriental villain would get precisely what he deserved, and a taste of good old-fashioned British spunk to boot.

'Gor, blimey,' shivered Throat. 'Bleedin taters 'ere an' no mistake! Apples and pears.' He had cracked his head sharply while stopping the Hornet Hunter – being of a breed inherently inept to control machinery of a quality more suitable to his betters. He had wailed piteously at this trifle until the special agent, utilizing his extensive medical skills, had applied liniment, bandages and a healthy dose of morphine.

'Yes indeed, Throat.' Groke swept his steely gaze across the rough, dank brickwork of the warehouse interior. He had broken his arm in three places during his mad leap from the car in pursuit of the diabolical doctor, but was bearing up under the agony splendidly. 'This apparently otherwise entirely ordinary warehouse,' he continued, the breath pluming from his mouth as he spoke, 'seems to have been turned into one extremely large refrigerated meat locker.' He crossed to one of the lumpen shapes covered by frosted-plastic tarpaulins and, with a mighty heave of his ironlike sinews, heaved the covering off.

'Blimey!' Throat stared at what was revealed with his little piggy eyes. 'Carcasses. They look like uncommon huge humungous chickens, I do declare.'

Groke nodded grimly. 'Yes indeed, Throat. Cryogenically preserved avian reptiles from the Dawn of Time. The lofty Pterodactyl, the noble Ramforincus . . . but how is that possible?'

'It's perfectly simple, actually,' said a lazy, cultured drawl – and huge Klieg lights came on with a clash, illuminating the whole scene with a dazzling, bleached-out clarity.

Standing before them, his hands crossed and tucked inside the sleeves of his silken robe, a tasseled *bian* upon his head, his slitty-eyed and hateful yellow face alive with obscene glee, stood the devilish Doctor Po himself!

'And don't he talk loverly for an Oriental gentleman,' said Throat, to no one in particular.

Possibly it was the momentary shock of the arch fiend's appearance, compounded by the pain in his arm and his recent ordeals, but Groke fancied for an instant that he could hear voices. Ghostlike, on the very edge of hearing, as though someone were talking in the next room and simultaneously by his ear.

'*The secondary construct's off again,*' one said. '*Damned AI autememes, they always seem to go self-referential in the middle of a scenario.*'

'*Don't worry about it,*' said another voice. '*I'll segue it into a peripheral stream and contain it . . .*'

Groke shook his head to clear it, and glared at his adversary. 'So, Doctor Po, we meet once again, and your deeds surpass even your own prior foulness.'

The villain gestured negligently with his free hand. 'One does one's best. Now, Mr Groke, as you can plainly see, I am currently aiming a rather large revolver in your direction –

83

and I rather doubt that even the famed reflexive prowess of Sandford Groke, Special Agent, is up to drawing his own, famous service revolver before I pull the trigger. I do believe I have you, as they say, at my mercy.'

'. . . I mean.' Throat was muttering, off to one side, 'you wouldn't think it to look at him, would you, what with those cruel eyes and twistedly inhuman lips that laugh with delight in the face of another's shrieking agony . . .'

Sandford Groke planted his two manly feet upon the warehouse floor and reared to his full impressive height and girth, his very head seeming to throb with the pounding blood of his rage. 'You won't get away with this, Po,' he snarled. 'Why, from the instant that foul manuscript went missing from the Unmitigated Filth Department of the Bodleian Library, I knew that only yours could be the twisted mind responsible! Even now, the good Inspector Carstairs is rounding up your remaining brutish minions, and is surrounding the locale as we speak!'

'What, both at the same time?' said Throat, dubiously. 'I mean, rounding up brutish minions, fine, but simultaneously surrounding the area? Come to mention it, doesn't this whole *thing* strike you as a little bit self-contradictory, guv? My old man's a dustman.'

(*'It's giving the whole sodding game away! Yank it now!'*)
(*'Hang on . . . hang on . . .'*)

'Will you shut up, Throat!' the special agent thundered.

The sidekick sniffed. 'All right I will.'

(*'Thank Siva for that,'* said a faint voice.)

The fiendish Doctor Po smiled a slow and snakelike smile. 'This is all very well and good, Mr Groke, but you see, when the good inspector arrives, I shall no longer be in – shall we say – his *jurisdiction*. I admit that, some time ago, when I first perchanced upon the whereabouts of the infamous *Kama Mundra* and the beastliness contained therein, I had no thought but its use to suck the very rectitude and moral fibre from England's youth. But then – and quite by chance – I saw its true significance.' He stuck his free hand into his

84

sleeve, and withdrew a leather-bound book, which he tossed to Groke. 'Here. See for yourself.'

The special agent opened it and glanced within with distaste. ' "The Congress of the Ubiquitous Lampstand. The gentleman reclines upon a mat of scented rushes, applying a tincture of pomegranate and green pesto to the lady's *yoni*, all the while that the other gentleman leaps from the pianoforte to the –" '

'I think,' said Doctor Po, 'that you perhaps have the wrong page. Page thirty-seven, if you will. The one with the photographic plate.'

'Blimey, guvnor!' Throat exclaimed, looking over Groke's shoulder. 'Just look what that there feller's doing with them galvanistical electrodes!'

'Disgusting,' the special agent agreed. 'And a most reprehensible waste of electricity in these lean times.'

'But examine the electrical advice to which the electrodes are themselves attached,' said Doctor Po. 'Together with the third young lady and the jar of tadpoles. Read what it says on the blass – I do beg your pardon, on the *brass* plate affixed to the base of the contrivance. You may require the assistance of your Secret Service special-issue magnifying glass.'

'Quite so.' Groke produced the aforementioned item, and painstakingly read, with mounting astonishment: ' "The Gilhooly Patented Electrical and Aetherial Chrononamplifier; prolongs even the most fleeting acts of appalling depravity for hours on end . . ." '

'Yes!' the fiendish Doctor Po cried in triumph. 'Hallucinogen-crazed libertine though he was, Rupert Gilhooly was a genius of the first water – a genius capable of unlocking the very mysteries of space and time itself!'

He nodded to the shocked special agent. 'Precisely, Mr Groke. *That* was what I was after. I have taken the original design, made a few trifling modifications of my own – and *voilà!*' He pulled a lever, and another tarpaulin rose upon a hidden ratchet. 'My greatest triumph! The Chrononamplificatory Ambulator of Doctor Po!'

'The *what?*' exclaimed Groke, gazing in puzzlement at the apparently entirely innocuous lacquered Chinese cabinet.

The fiendish Doctor Po deflated somewhat. 'I could have done better here with a trained chipmunk,' he muttered darkly.

'Oh, I get it,' said Throat, brightly, breaking into the conversation of his betters without a hint of decent shame. 'It's a time machine, yeah? That might, I suspect, tend to explain all the apparent paradoxes and anachronisms we've thus far encountered.'

The special agent stared at him, aghast at this impertinence. 'Are you feeling quite all right, Throat?'

Throat slapped his sloping forehead as though, of a sudden, remembering something. 'Oh, ah ... I mean – Lord lumme, guvnor, all this high talk of metatemporal engineering and messin' about with the whole Ur-structure of interdimensional causality right goes over my head and makes it spin! So it does.'

'Thank you.' Groke dismissed him from further consideration. The poor man's mind had obviously collapsed into raving gibberish.

'... I mean,' continued Throat, 'the very idea. Wot's a barrow boy born within the sound of a whistlin' Pearly King know about the multifarious problems of the fourth dimension, eh? Wot with the lack of a decent educational catchment system, the child slavery and the rickets ...'

'Yes, thank you, Throat,' said Sandford Groke.

(*'I'm losing control – we're going to have to reformat the bloody lot if it doesn't ...'*)

'... I mean me old mum, Gord bless 'er, she was always sayin' to me, "Don't you go a-troublin' yourself about the polyfractal nature of the quantum mesh, young Cyril; just you shut up and have your jellied eel, pint of gin and a fag ..."'

'Yes, all *right*, Throat!' Sandford Groke invariably attempted to treat his inferiors with kindness but, really, there were limits.

'I could do you a couple of choruses of "I've got a Loverly Bunch of Coconuts" if you'd like.'

'You really want to *die*, don't you, Throat?' snarled the special agent.

'Which, I believe,' broke in the fiendish Doctor Po, waving his pistol menacingly, 'brings us rather to the point in hand.' He gestured around the warehouse. 'As you have seen, I have been able to bring certain specimens through time – but actual transmission has escaped me. If the intersecting galvanistic fields of the machine are not calibrated absolutely correctly, they tend to rip organic matter to shreds. Explosively. The calibration must be *precise*, and for that I have required – shall we say – volunteers. Several of them. Quite a lot of them, in fact.'

Groke stared at the villain, as realization horribly dawned. 'You mean . . .'

'Exactly, Mr Groke,' Po chuckled. 'The sudden spate of mysterious disappearances that has so baffled New Scotland Yard of late.'

'William Slythe?' Sandford Groke exclaimed. 'The Infamous Boxing Archbishop of Old London Town?'

'Kaboom,' drawled Doctor Po, calmly.

'Lady Olivia de'Rohampton, thirty-third in line to the throne, and her little whippet?'

'Kablam,' agreed the fiendish Doctor Po.

'The Right Honourable Jeremy Tooley?' Throat broke in from behind Groke, 'Conservative and Unionist Member of Parliament for Bath and Wells?'

'He has thus far contrived to evade my fiendish clutches.'

'Oh well. Can't win 'em all.'

'Indeed one cannot.' Po turned his attention back to the special agent. 'And you, my dear Mr Groke, are in no position to win any of them.' He became for the moment, mockingly, confidential. 'You see, from the instant I allowed you to escape from my subterranean torture chamber beneath the Mister Wo Chinese Laundry, Mixed Bar and Grill and Opium Den, my every aim has been to lead you to this very place!' he gestured back towards the lacquered cabinet. 'The calibration is almost complete. It merely needs one, or possibly two, more test subjects . . .'

'You fiend!' cried Sandford Groke.

The Doctor tut-tutted. 'One tries one's best. So, which is it to be, Mr Groke? Certain death from the barrel of a revolver, or will you take the chance of stepping into the machine?'

'Well, speaking for myself,' Throat broke in hurriedly from one side, 'I think I'd rather –'

'I'll tell you this, Po,' Groke growled, glaring at the Chinaman with eyes like chips of purest diamond. 'I would rather *die* than aid your schemes in any way at all.'

'Yeah, obviously,' said Throat from beside him. 'Obviously. Right. But then again . . .'

'A clean death from a good British bullet is all that I ask! I die, not for myself, but for my country and the Empire!'

'Yeah, OK, *OK*,' said Throat, 'but personally I sometimes –'

'And that goes double for my man Throat.'

'Fair enough,' said Doctor Po, and shot the special agent's servant, twice, through the chest. The monkey-like little prole fell with a whimper.

(*'Got it!'* said a distant voice. '*Wipe the subfile and continue with the core scenario. No real damage done.*')

'On the other hand,' said Sandford Groke, thoughtfully. 'Who knows what adventures and good to be done, what justice to be brought might lie in wait upon the other side of time, should I survive . . .'

'You bastard!' shouted Ginger Throat, and expired.

'A wise decision.' Doctor Po pulled a lever. A Christmas-tree-like arrangement of struts and wires extended from a little trapdoor in the side of the cabinet, and began to spark and fizz. The doors of the cabinet sprang open to reveal an interior inlaid with what seemed to be mother-of-pearl, the swirls of coloration constantly shifting, breaking themselves apart and reforming. The Oriental fiend gestured with the gun. 'Step through the portal, Mr Groke. The future awaits, and it won't hurt a bit.'

'I promise you this, Po,' declared Groke as he stepped into the cabinet. 'Should I survive, I'll hunt you down, in whichever squalid little bolt hole in the whole vast panoply of time and space you choose to hide. You'll rue the day you ever tangled with Sandford Groke, Special Agent!'

'Chance, Mr Groke, would be a fine thing.' The villain grinned at him through the doorway. 'Now, you'll recall I said that this wouldn't hurt a bit?'

'Yes?'

'I lied.'

The fiendish Doctor Po slammed the doors, plunging the cabinet into darkness. Shields racked back from vents, from which plasma blasted, obliterating the luckless Sandford Groke.

PART TWO

EXCURSIONS

I met Tennessee Williams after I'd done Cat on a Hot Tin Roof. *I was in hospital with pneumonia, and he came to see me. Must have been '57. It was after* Cat... *No, it wasn't after* Cat *– yes, it was... Must have been... Now I'm confused. Must have been after* Cat *but it couldn't have been because Mike [Todd] was killed when I was shooting* Cat. *Well, I was in hospital, but I think it was in New York because that was where we lived. Now I am confused! Mike was killed in '58. It must have been after. Must have been...*

Elizabeth Taylor

9

'YOUR FIRST STOP ON A GRAND TOUR OF INTERGALACTIC WONDER...'

... said the brochure, '*is the fabled Shakya constellation – the brightest constellation visible from the southern hemisphere of Dellah, and the most distinctive feature of the skies from worlds around. From the perfect safety of the Observation Deck, one can bask in the churning majesty of one's God, Goddess or Generative Principle's work...*'

Benny stayed in her cabin. She had stayed there even since before the ship's first jump. For one thing, the people who had written the brochure seemed to be under the impression that a 'constellation' was an actual stellar object. She suspected that they would in actual fact be seeing RD1070982-1327-021B – a red giant and the only component of the Shakya constellation that existed in this sector – and having seen more than her fair share of red giants in the course of recent months, her instant reaction had been: 'Oh dear Goddess, not another one!'

For another, she had far more pressing matters to attend to.

In the backstage of the theatre, after checking Krugor's pulse to ascertain that he was really dead, she had beat a hasty retreat – jumping at every shadow that might conceal

93

the possibly still-present murderer, desperately trying not to leave any more fingerprints or signs of her presence than she already had. She had known it would be pointless: genetic tracing and vestigial-convection vectorizing could place her like a hi-resolution shot – and the ship was crawling with detectives who should be able to sniff her out in an instant if they were, as it were, much cop. Well, she had thought, remembering those she had met, Khaarli the Czhan militiaman at least might suspect something.

She had locked herself in her room, and there she had stayed, ordering room service and waiting every instant for the other shoe to drop and people to come pounding on the hatch asking inconvenient questions. There had once been a time in her life when she could have taken things to the top, secure in the knowledge that nobody would ever suspect her as such. Now, she suspected, they would simply throw her in the brig and subsequently – a ship in space being its own small world, with its own technically independent statutes – summarily out of an airlock. With the death of Krugor, even the link to Krytell and the protection it might afford had gone.

The first thing she had done after sequestering herself was to examine Krugor's rooms appended to her own. Inside, they were sparse and barely furnished – obviously designed from the start to be occupied by the servants of the actual paying travellers. A bed, a closet and a small cubicle for washing and waste matter. A valise was on the bed, spare servants' uniforms hung in the closet, and that was it.

The room had seemed almost entirely unlived in. Benny had wished for tell-tale wrappers on the soapstone, betel nuts on the bed, little paper bands around the toilet bowl such as had greeted her upon entering her own suite, but of course there were and had been none.

Nothing interesting in the suits or the valise – but for all there was nothing interesting, there was something *wrong*. There was nothing she could put her finger on, and possibly it was the simple fact that the room belonged to a dead man, but something about the room vaguely disturbed her. On re-entering her own suite, she had tried to lock the connecting door, and found that it could be locked only from the other side. She had ended up wedging a heavy armchair up against it to make herself feel better.

She had missed the ship flipping in and out of its first jump to the vicinity of the red giant, being only vaguely aware of the time it would occur and feeling nothing physically – since ripping her, everyone else on board, and the very ship's atomic structure to pieces and extruding it into a fifteen-thousand-parakilometre-long electrogravitational dimensional-fold-piercing needle had happened in quite other dimensions than which the human mind and neurosystem could cope.

Apart from her own fears, she had been left completely alone save for the periodic delivery of food and drink. The first arrival of 'drink' had included a two-litre bottle of Elysian Mescal with the good bit of the cactus left in. Now that Krugor was no longer around she could have theoretically drunk as much of it as she liked, but after three days, however, the bottle was still at least a fifth full. Benny had never liked jigsaw puzzles, especially the impossible sort that showed pictures of ball-bearings and slices of pizza, and now she was attempting, in three dimensions, to solve the most difficult one she had ever seen in her life.

Now, she stared intently at the book lying open on the carpet before her, rifled through the scribbled notes she was using as bookmarks, then turned her attention to the curving crystalline shards laid out on the stripped-off bed (which had necessitated the coverings of it to be deployed as a rough-and-ready bedroll in the corner).

With a pair of tweezers from her minimal, emergency archaeological field kit, she selected a shard and placed it within what appeared to be a partially constructed glass bird's nest. The shard locked against several others, with a precision that seemed to hold none of those tiny and almost unnoticeable, subliminal elements of doubt that in fact mean that things are utterly wrong. As a trained specialist, the job of whom it is to piece together fragments from little or no external evidence, Benny had trained these sensibilities to a high degree; the only problem was that they had been operating on this level for days, now, and Benny was getting increasingly worried that they would end up shot to hell and back.

When she had finally forced herself to open the bag that had once contained an intact Olabrian joy-luck crystal, she had fully expected something resembling a miniature *Krystalnacht* in a sack. What she found, however, was a dismantled collection of pieces that might have been complicatedly formed, but seemed to be unbroken. She recalled that while Olabrian joy-luck crystals were constructed with extreme delicacy and fragility, the actual components of them were harder than diamond.

When she had asked Krytell for some of her personal belongings, she had insisted that they include books. The first was a thick compendium of works from Woolfe, Bell, Arliss and several others from the early twentieth-century Bloomsbury Group – as an inveterate traveller who knew that the main burden is the problem of simply how to pass the time, Benny knew that a rattling good page-turner was the last thing one needed. One needed pages full of the kind of prose one had to stare at for hours on end – wondering how the hell a woman sitting there sewing has suddenly turned into the ocean, for example – until one's forehead bled. The second book was a compendium of Kinky Friedman stories, because while crystalline prose-constructs built upon and inhabiting the Waste Lands between form and content are all very well, one can always have too much of a good thing.

The third book was of a different sort entirely. Benny had been sent a review copy of it, had never read it, and had hoped never to be in the position where she had to. It was entitled *Lost Gods and the Fall of Empire,* by Franz Kryptosa, a huge flat slab of a thing that couldn't in all honesty be called a coffee-table book because there would have been no room for the bowl of multicoloured crystallized sugar, little pot of cream and the cafetière.

Franz Kryptosa, and writers like him, occupied the same relative position to the Archaeological Arts as a tapeworm to its host: combining the comprehension of the scientific method of a small piece of Stilton with a command over the language that would make a dyslexic paraplegic hand in his little pole on a suction cup in shame. His works, if such they could be called, had included *The Reappearing World*, in which he had propounded the amazing theory that with sufficiently advanced genetic engineering one could create living things that looked like anything; and *In Search of Ancient Mu* – which he had somehow managed to get mixed up with the entirely different mythical sunken city of Atlantis.

Kryptosa was just the latest in a millennia-long line of so-called 'thinkers' like Von Däniken, Streiber, and the chap who believed that humans came from eggs, with four arms, four legs and two heads, and that apes were in fact the result of these humans shagging animals . . . people who had mastered completely the twisting of observable reality to fit whatever deranged notion happened to be inhabiting their head (or, indeed, heads) at the time.

Such people went into paroxysms over the fact that, for example, a sample of prehistoric cloth had been found, its fibres finer and of a more complex structure than the best man-made synthetics – while neglecting to recall that you could get fibres finer and more complex by far than synthetics out of a silkworm's bum. They jumped to the conclusion that gigantic ritual earthworks, built by cultures who had not developed flight, *must* have been constructed for aliens in flying saucers, without ever stopping to say to themselves, 'Hang on, maybe they just built them because they thought their gods lived somewhere up in the sky.'

They would *then* point to the belief in gods in the sky as if that meant something, while forgetting to mention that most of the cultures concerned had also believed in an Underworld of one form or another and which, despite being physically far more easy to get at, had never in fact been found.

Kryptosa was, in short, the sort of mind that found it possible to believe that governments incapable of concealing the sexual peccadillos of their own high-ranking members, together with their shocking capacity for grabbing kickbacks of various sorts with both grubby hands, were capable of covering up all physical evidence of crashed interstellar mother ships, or hordes of alien creatures roaming the land, abducting people out of pickup trucks and sticking probes up them.

Such minds had suffered a bit of a blow around – for humans – the twenty-second century, when actual alien life had been contacted without question. It was a bit like the difference between believing in some mystical being that delivers much-needed messages from far away, and the postman simply knocking on your door one day and asking you to sign. The human mind, of course, adapted – and people like Kryptosa had never stopped looking for the *other* aliens, the ones who had made those rather nice designs in wheat fields invariably bisected by tractor tracks, who had had cut those rather less attractive designs into cows, impersonated weather balloons and who had given people (who had barely partaken of four six-packs and a serious doobie) inexplicable visions of flashing lights, unexplained bruises, nosebleeds, other minor injuries, and unaccountable periods of strangely missing time. They never stopped looking for the *real* aliens, the ones in which they truly believed.

Lost Gods was the story of a search for just such mythical beings. It detailed Kryptosa's travels through several of the more picturesque worlds of the sector, alone but for the full multimedia crew that accompanied him, trying to hammer the local cultures and histories into a shape resembling that of the ancient Mayans. One of those worlds had been Olabria, and this, on the off-chance that it might prove useful, was why Benny had requested the book. The text itself had been worthless, but there were some photographic plates depicting Kryptosa staring with what he probably thought of as reverent esteem at a collection of joy-luck crystals, while several paranoically watchful Olabrians hovered close nearby, looking suitably exotic to human eyes.

Each of the examples in the book had been pieced together differently, but they had served as an implicit reference to the underlying structure of the artefacts in general. They had proved invaluable in that sense, but after several days the process was increasingly like painstakingly building a model ship of some thousand pieces, with only the picture from the front of the box for instruction.

Now, Benny felt completely shattered – and knew with a cold certainty that 'completely shattered' was precisely how the partially rebuilt crystal would end up if she tried to put in one more piece in her present state.

She should really try to get some sleep, but she knew with an equal certainty that she was too wound up for that. If she crawled into her expensive but makeshift bedroll at this point, she would just jerk around, hammer her head on the pillows, hit the floor with her fists and then come back and kick the blasted jumped-up bit of silicon to smithereens in a fit of exhausted pique.

She climbed to her feet – her knees popping, and feeling as if they were a couple of thousand years old and petrified – and wandered over to her bathroom. The face in the mirror looked several millennia older even than her knees, if you counted age by the number of rings under the eyes, with the added bonus of a bad-hair-century to boot. Her single item of clothing – the large black shirt that she used as and when as a night gown – was encrusted with several days' worth of sweat and absent-minded meals. She looked – and she was perfectly aware of how trite and clichéd it sounded, but was not in any fit state to care – a complete and utter mess.

It was as though the sheer tiredness had taken over and was operating her body on remote control. Operating on zonked autopilot, she pulled off the shirt and hauled on the taps of the bath. Hot water cascaded into it, soapy and chemically treated to produce whatever effect – from amphetamine-like invigoration to opiate-analogue somnalism – the specific tap setting required. Benny didn't care either way, at this point.

There were a couple of cut-glass bottles on the rim of the bath, containing greenish and pinkish salts, and she upended them into the bath, too. She clambered into the bath with the taps still running and it less than a third full, and collapsed back into the kind of dreamless sleep that can only not be called a coma by way of a relative lack of bleep machines, acquisitive relatives fighting over the off-switch and bootleg surgeons looking expectantly at the donor card.

It was thus, in that insensate state, that Bernice Summerfield would never, at the time or later, be aware of the four standard minutes and thirty-two seconds that a certain individual, entering by seemingly impossible means and wearing a gas mask, spent in her cabin suite. She would never know how this individual walked through the cabins, turning off the taps in the bathroom as an afterthought, taking certain items and leaving certain more.

But then, since said items were invariably worth far more than the items that were taken, it probably didn't matter. In the short term.

10

A Dinner Appointment with Destiny

Benny woke, still lying in the bath. On the positive side, sensor-controlled radiant heat elements had kept the water warm; on the downside, she had shrivelled up like an albino prune.

Wrapping a towel around herself, she padded out of the bathroom. For an instant she had the same feeling of wrongness as she'd felt in Krugor's cubbyhole, that sense of something indefinably out of kilter, but the cabin seemed precisely as she'd left it. The convincing-looking costume jewellery that was absent-mindedly scattered across the dresser – and which would surely have acted as a magnet for any intruder – remained precisely as she'd left it.

The half-completed joy-luck crystal and its loose components were scattered on the bed. She supposed that she should crack on with the rebuilding of it, but for the moment her heart wasn't in it. She glanced around the cabin, at the bedroll, the crumpled clothes and the piled-up dinners, and experienced one of those moments of occasional clarity that one gets after inhabiting untidy, stuffy rooms for far too long – she realized how precisely stuffy and untidy it was.

If nobody had come after her about suspicious deaths of manservants by now, then nobody probably would. Benny decided that what she really needed to do at this point was to go out, let the *Titanian Queen*'s stewards go over the cabin and probably fumigate it to boot, before she ended up stuck to the bedraggled carpeted floor by her own effluvia.

The loose pieces of crystal went back in the bag, then the bag and the reconstructed portion went into a silk-lined hatbox, which she placed in the back of a closet behind a small pile of expensive shoes she had yet to wear. She went back into the bathroom and picked up her wristwatch from the sill. The twelve-hour face said that it was coming up to eight o'clock – and she realized that she had lost track of time to the point where it could be eight in the evening, in terms of the cruise ship's time frame, or eight in the morning. The growling chasm of her stomach persuaded her to assume that it was evening, and just in time for dinner. It had better be.

Since this would be her first appearance for days, she decided to make a small show of it. Among the clothing Krytell had supplied for her was a flowing gown of some translucent, samite-like substance, interwoven with threads of gold and cracked-glass mosaic in chromatic tones ranging from ruby-red to ochre. It was gathered in at the waist, had a plunging neckline and a slit up the side. Benny – who had a self-image sufficiently developed not to care what the hell she looked like, provided she had two of everything she should have and one of everything else – experienced the kind of momentary flash of paranoia, of the sort that has the best of us wondering if we can carry something off. But the gown was a masterpiece of *haute couture* design, specifically designed for her. She looked like seven thousand, four hundred and thirty-three shillings – that being the price written on the tag, which she mercifully noticed and pulled off before leaving.

The vestiges of her hairdo had been washed out in the bath. It was clean, but ragged and unkempt. On the other hand, it set off the splendidness of the gown in the same way as a pair of Doc Martens set off a little black cocktail dress. Benny picked up a pair of earrings from the dresser, prepared to put them on – and then decided what the hell: she was out of Krugor's supervision now, and she might as well be hung for a Squoldavian bloat-squid as a limpet whelk. She scooped the costume jewellery up in its entirety, dropped it into a clutch bag, swept out of the cabin and headed towards the Purser's office.

In his own cabin, Captain Crane took one last look in the elderly and slightly mottled mirror. His white suit with epaulettes was pristine and polished respectively; his cap was on his head and he hated it. The cut touched and constricted him in places where no clothing really should, having been designed, like a theatrical costume, to project a certain image – to cut, as it were, a degree of dash.

In the same way, while the exterior was stitched together finely, the interior had been skimped on a lining, save for hessian bulking where such was needed. Captain Crane had attempted to counter it with a shabby but long set of underwear – which now just meant that where he wasn't itching he was sweltering.

Walking a little stiffly, he left the cabin and went forward through the crew's quarters to the bridge.

'My dear Captain,' said the voice of ARVID. 'We meet again.'

Crane ignored it. Number One was off duty and with hir brood-polyp, replenishing hir energies and precious bodily fluids. The two most senior officers here were a man named Golding and a woman named Cherry.

Actual rank on a *Titanian Queen* controlled by ARVID was a farce and Crane knew it. Nonetheless, he had found himself debating which of these two officers to leave in charge while he was otherwise detained. Golding was technically brilliant on specification-flimsy, but there was a kind of know-all attitude that both irritated Crane and made him distrustful. Lisabeth Cherry was slightly less proficient, but seemed to carry a complete, level-headed calm – the sort of calm that would be invaluable in an emergency.

'Take the conn, Cherry,' Crane said. 'I'm going to have to take dinner with the "guests".'

Liz Cherry raised an eyebrow. 'Again? So soon.' She knew precisely what Captain Crane thought about the passengers.

'Yeah, well, I've been avoiding it for two days. I'm running out of excuses and I need to keep some back for when things get really bad.' Crane turned to leave the bridge.

At the hatch, he turned back. 'Anything comes up, anywhere on the ship, you deal with it and let me know. Anything to get me away from the buggers.' He grinned ruefully. 'Y'know, I sometimes wish something would happen to get *rid* of one or two of 'em . . .'

Outside the purser's office, Benny was slightly surprised to find two people on guard, dressed in the uniforms of the Dellah Constabulary. In the entire sector, Dellah had what was probably the lowest planetary crime rate, and the smallest and most ill-equipped policing force – many thinkers would say that these two factors were related, but possibly in the other way around than was immediately obvious. On the other hand, it may have been just another example of the civilizing effect of the university. In either case, the common uniform of the Dellah Constabulary was archaic and ill-fitting, and the two men on guard appeared uncomfortable in it.

'What's going on?' Benny said. 'I thought you lads were down in steerage, waiting to be needed as and when.'

'Do you have some form of identification, miss?' one of them said, his tone undecided between deference to Benny's presumed station in life and the desire of coppers the whole universe over to plant the two size-elevens of anyone who got overfamiliar and lippy with them.

Once again, Benny recalled that the trick was to never let oneself be put at a disadvantage. 'Am I to take it you don't recognize me? I could produce my compact, look into the mirror and tell you it's me, if you like.'

From behind the hatch an irascible and slightly flustered

voice said: 'What's happening? Who is it out there *now*?' The hatch opened to reveal a red face attached to a balding head.

'My *dear* Detective Interchange!' Benny exclaimed. She batted her eyelashes shamelessly at the policeman, as she had seen them do in ancient cinematic movies. 'What *are* you doing here?'

'An attempted break-in, ma'am,' said the worthy plod, disarmed by Benny's feminine wiles and preening himself a little. 'It seems that some time last evening, person or persons unknown tried to cut through the safe containing the passengers' strongboxes with a thermal lance.'

'Heavens!' Benny cried, making a little fluttering gesture at her collarbone. 'Was anybody hurt in apprehending the fiend? Was anything stolen?'

Detective Interchange shook his head. 'Nothing like that, ma'am. It appears that the criminal was disturbed before his crime was complete. He left his equipment and had it away on his toes before the alarm could be raised.'

'My goodness,' Benny said.

'Was there anything I can help you with at all, ma'am?' the detective said.

'Um.' Benny could discern nothing in his face but helpful enquiry – but the last thing she needed, given present circumstances, was to show a suspicious interest in the safe and the removal of its contents. 'I merely wanted to assure myself that you and your –' she shot a glance at the two Constables '– *brave* young men are keeping my valuables safe.'

'Don't you worry about that, ma'am,' Detective Interchange said. 'Don't you worry about that at all. We'll be looking after 'em, night and day.'

11

SITTING DOWN TO DINE

As has been noted, life aboard the *Titanian Queen* was delineated by a general consensus into quasi-day and quasi-night, and this had extended to the mealtimes. While a passenger could theoretically order any meal, of any description, from the kitchens at any time, there was a set dinner time in the Starfire Lounge, complete with table reservations, to which people generally adhered.

Benny had thus far not turned up for a single one of them, and stepping into the lounge was like walking into the pages of Edith Wharton writ large, if with the word *parvenu* spelt ultimately incorrect. The tables were packed with men and women in the kind of formal dress that gave the room the aspect of the collision of a flock of penguins with a freighter-ful of motile lamp shades. There were a few empty spaces, and Benny caught glimpses of little place cards among the silverware and wine glasses. She had no way, though, of knowing which out of all of them might be inscribed with her name, and she didn't really fancy the idea of wandering the entire room looking for it.

She prodded the back of a steward who was standing, a pristine white cloth over his forearm, waiting for the proceedings to formally commence. 'Oi, chappie. Lead me to my place without delay.'

The steward turned – and Benny gave a small gasp of

surprise. This was instantly quashed, as she realized that she had been mistaken. There were certain superficial similarities, but he was not some miraculously animated Krugor. Possibly the man's murder had affected her more than she realized, so that she might imagine his face everywhere – and this was slightly strange, because she had encountered violent death before and had never reacted in that way. Maybe I'm getting soft in my old age, she thought.

She thought she caught a flash of irritation in the steward's face – and so she should, given the rudeness of her address – and then it instantly became composed. 'If you'll come with me, Ms Summersdale.'

As she accompanied the steward through the dining hall, Benny wondered idly how he had instantly known her name. It didn't worry her particularly. She was vaguely aware that the public-service industries, the restaurant franchises and hotel chains of the galaxy, commonly packed their employees with subcutaneous communications gear, conditioning implants and molecularly based databases to transform them into unobtrusive, miraculously efficient attendants – even going so far as to breed them up from scratch on worlds where this was not illegal, in force-gestation vats. They were, in a sense, a mere extension of the decor and furniture, albeit responsive and reactive furniture. If she were to suddenly and without warning sit herself down, Benny suspected, a steward would whip a chair under her with almost superhuman speed, before her bum hit the floor.

Looking around her at the assembled passengers, she also suspected that she was the only one among them wondering about the help even this far. It was as if they were quite simply invisible, as they shuttled and wove through the room, the expectant diners giving them no thought other than was necessary to absently hold out a glass to be filled, or pluck a bread roll from a proffered basket, or lean into the flame of a lighted match to light a cigarino. It was like watching the smooth and complex dance of mechanical ghosts.

She saw several people she recognized, including a fair number she wished she didn't. The Dowager Duchess of Gharl, in particular, was sitting at what she assumed to be the Captain's Table – a long rectangular trestle running down the length of a wall as opposed to the more common circular tables. Since the fact of sitting here conveyed to a certain kind of mind a degree of prestige, this kind of mind thought nothing of paying extra for it, and the owners of the *Titanian Queen* no doubt knew the side on which their freshly baked and crusty roll was buttered.

The captain himself – again, having never clapped eyes on him, Benny assumed it could only be the captain, from his position in the centre and his dress uniform – seemed entirely nondescript, his bearing suggesting that if not exactly harried now, he nevertheless existed in an almost permanent state of harry. He was listening to Emil Dupont, his posture suggesting that he was desperately trying not to nod off, as the great detective, who sat beside the Duchess, habitually held forth.

Scattered around the dining room Benny saw several of the other detectives. Sandford Groke sat bolt upright at one table, seemingly ignoring and ignored by the other occupants, his fist clenched and glaring straight ahead in what appeared to be a kind of constant, inner, default-setting rage. Agatha Magpole sat primly, sipping a small sherry while her companion fussed over her, straightening her frock and tucking in a napkin. Off to one side, Khaarli was sitting among tables occupied by the relatively few nonhuman beings – Benny wondered if this arrangement was a product of their simply congregating together because they had more in common, or whether they had been subtly *helped* there by influences that it would not be the done thing to suggest were in any way speciesism at all.

For an awful moment, Benny thought that she had been seated with the large collection of nobs at the Captain's Table. Then the steward veered sharply to the left, and deposited her at one of the more diminutive tables. This was occupied by, among others, a fat, avuncular man with an extremely impressive set of muttonchop whiskers, which gave him something of the aspect of an amiable walrus.

As her steward pulled the chair back to allow her to sit, she became aware of a small, rodent-like and frightened squeak off to one side. She turned to see, sitting in the chair beside her, the mousy young woman she had encountered briefly, several days before, in the ballroom, when she had rescued her from the animosity of the Dowager Duchess of Gharl. The young woman looked at Benny, white-faced and panic-stricken, as if about to bolt.

'Bernice Summersdale,' Benny said to her, helping herself to a glassful of wine from the bottle in the centre of the table. 'You can call me Benny. I hope you're feeling all right, now.'

The woman gave a tiny 'eep' noise, then blushed and nodded furiously.

'Don't mind our Miss Blaine,' boomed the bewhiskered gentleman, filling his own glass. 'Wouldn't say boo to a bandersnatch – which, given that a bandersnatch is twenty metres long, omnivorously voracious and has seven sets of jaws each containing four rows of retractable venomous fangs, is probably a sound and sensible idea.' He bluffly thumped his chest with his thumb. 'Prekodravac.'

'How do you pronounce that?' Benny asked him, interested.

'Preh-ko-dra-vuts. The "c" at the end makes an *uts* sound.' The man thumped his chest again. 'Mr Richard Tarquin Delbert Prekodravac, but I don't stand stiff on ceremony, even though I'm a big man for standing proud and firm.' He put a companionable hand on Benny's knee and waggled his eyebrows. 'Please feel free to call me Mister Dickie.'

On the other side of her, the nominative Miss Blaine blushed like a Belisha beacon, and Benny fancied that she knew why – by the cut of his clothing and the shape of his earlobes, Benny recognized 'Mister Dickie' as an inhabitant of Plumptious Minor. And the fact that this planet's name itself did not ring strange to its inhabitants told one pretty much all one needed to know about them in an *oogli* fruitskin.

The history of Plumptious Minor was vaguely interesting. Originally a standard Earth colony, for several hundred years it had been cut off from the galaxy at large, in which time it had built an extensive culture from the remains of its surviving planetary archives – which by some fluke of circumstance had consisted almost entirely of old *Carry On* films, Benny Hill shows, *Up Pompeii* compilations and an obscure twentieth-century sitcom going by the name of *Love Thy Neighbour*. This had caused problems, to say the least, upon the re-establishment of contact, when the Big High Hooha of Plumptious Minor had greeted the leader of the first galactic diplomatic mission, the Lady Xhanda of the Twelve Spired House of the Nine Systems, with a cheery 'Wotcha, sweetheart; that's a lovely pair of thruppenies you've got on you, for a fat bird, like.'

The point was that – just as the Big High Hooha had been offering the greatest compliment he had known – Mr Richard Tarquin Delbert Prekodravac was now simply being friendly and nothing more. And in the culturally comparative stakes Benny was on a jet-propelled skateboard. So, rather than chopping the hand on her knee off at the wrist with the fish knife, she responded in the proper kind, and prodded Mister Dickie in the ribs – or, at least, sank her finger into a point roughly comparable to where his ribs should be. 'Sauce!'

'My word,' said the man, beaming, 'I do like a good solid poke before dinner.' He winked at Benny. 'I believe that rumour has it, after the fish course, that there's going to be stuffing.'

'And you know where you can stick your stuffing,' said Benny, friendlily.

'Chance, madam,' said Mister Dickie Prekodravac, 'would be a fine thing.'

Quite how long this remarkably amicable example of social intercourse would have gone on for is debatable – because at that point a holo-display flickered on: an oiled and muscular man, bestriding the dining hall, struck a massive and sonorous gong. (Personally, Benny found it overostentatious; all in all, all things considered, a bit of a J. Arthur Rank.)

Mister Dickie Prekodravac's eyes lit up and he rubbed his hands together. 'I do believe we're all about to be serviced. Dinner, I think, is about to be served.'

The next two hours, so far as Benny was concerned, were an ambivalent cross between mounting irritation and exquisite gustatory and emotional torture. For one thing, since this mealtime was an *occasion*, there was a set menu. The other thing concerned precisely what the menu comprised:

The soup course was a *bouillon* of shrimp, clam, mussels and stripefish in a cayenne-peppery white-wine stock, served on the sizzling boil so that the occasional pearl of a tiny white onion rolled.

The second course was coarse *foi gras,* and melon wrapped in slivers of wind-cured ham so delicate that it came apart almost explosively in the mouth. This cleared the palate for the actual fish course, which consisted of:

Elysian Snapping Flatfish braised in butter to that magic, impossible point of crispness on the outside, succulence within, without in any way browning.

The main course consisted of what the steward described as Poussin Surprise – which Benny somehow thought might be fish yet again, until she saw the big plates each containing four boned baby chickens, wrapped in bacon and roasted, one stuffed with wild-boar-and-venison sausage meat and garlic, one stuffed with dried apricot steeped in wine, one stuffed with chestnuts, and one stuffed with a mixture of breadcrumbs and Nova Belgique chocolate – that being the Surprise, but the *real* surprise being how wonderful, apparently, it tasted.

A selection of sweets from the trolley, including jelly and sherry trifles, syllabubs, pastries, maids of honour, tarts, spun-sugar nests of glazed fruits and whipped cream, eclairs, *kulfi*, knickerbocker glories, apple pies from recipes taken at gunpoint from old grandmothers, *bombes*, lattis, bakewell sponges, gooseberry fools, compotes, sundaes, mousses, chocolate fudge cakes; cheese and biscuits to follow and an after-dinner mint . . .

. . . all of which, with the possible exception of the inside of the after-dinner mint, based on so much meat and animal-related product that it was a wonder the plates and cutlery weren't spinning around the room, under the *poltergeisten* influence of dead animal ghosts. Benny tried repeatedly to order something vegetarian from a steward – and got a blank, possibly integrally programmed suggestion that she merely pick the vegetables out from what was placed before her. Since the vast majority of said vegetables had been well basted in fat, however, or were to be found floating in sauces so meat-juice rich that they were almost sentient, this was hardly a satisfactory reply.

Things were not helped by the presence of Mister Dickie beside her, shovelling his way through the various courses with the efficiency of a mechanical trench-digger, elbowing her in the ribs and telling her that she needed to put some meat on her bones, 'cause he liked something to grab hold of on a tart, and asking if he could have her almost untouched leftovers, if she wasn't in fact going to eat them.

Benny, in short, spent the meal subsisting entirely on her bread roll and the pickings from the side salad, trying to distract her attention from the furious carnivorous knife-and-fork action going on around her, and desperately trying to pretend that the sounds her stomach was making were the responsibility of a sudden horse in front. Fortunately – or unfortunately, depending upon the point of view – each meal was accompanied by the appropriate drink, and rather like the vegetarian arrangements for the meal, soft drinks were not an option:

Red and white Sauternes and Chiantis, Merlots, Champagnes, Vermouths; triple-distilled and oak-aged Scotches, unblended sherry wines, Madeiras; small beers, medium-dry ciders, bloody enormous stouts; crusted ports with the cheese and thousand-year-old brandy, and methyl-dex and THC-laced cigars to follow. A little voice in Benny's head told her that if she touched any one of these on an all-but-empty stomach she was asking for trouble – and further enquired, given her aversion to the edible products of animals, just how was that different from the consumption of the waste-matter of several million yeast bacteria? When that voice became a little too intrusive, Benny silenced it by the tried, tested and patently reasonable expedient of having another drink.

Some while later, she realized that she was staring blankly at Miss Blaine, having mumbled some sort of question at her.

'Isabel,' Miss Blaine was saying, picking at her food. She put a morsel of carefully cut meat into her mouth, chewed with her mouth closed, swallowed and dabbed at her mouth with a napkin. The process didn't seem prim, precisely; more the self-conscious actions of a child on its best behaviour, timidly doing the things it's been told to do in adult company and slightly terrified of getting it wrong.

'Isabel Blaine,' she continued, very politely, trying to make proper adult conversation. 'I'm afraid I haven't travelled, much, thank you for asking. I spent so much time looking after Mother –' she pronounced the name with capitals '– you see, after she became Ill.' Again the word was pronounced with capitals. 'After she passed on, I came into a little money, and I decided to see some of the world. It's very –' she made a vague little gesture that took in the entire dining hall, and seemed to convey an entire universe of puzzled slight and hurt '– splendid, isn't it?'

'Glurp.' Benny's attention wandered off Isabel Blaine and into the dining room. She saw that Khaarli was tucking into his food with gusto – indeed, aside from the small matter of species, it was as though the Czhan were almost a twin of Mister Dickie. Sandford Groke was industriously cutting up his food and raising his fork to his mouth with the kind of mechanical action of one who eats to live rather than lives to eat. There seemed something subtly wrong with the image, but at this distance and through her clouded vision, Benny couldn't work out quite what it was.

Emil Dupont was making a triplet with Mister Dickie and Khaarli, while the captain had his head in his hands. This might have been due to the fact that the Dowager Duchess of Gharl was now speaking, declaratively, as she ate. Her words were lost in the general hubbub and clashing of cutlery, but she was close enough for Benny to make out her tone: a kind of venomous, mean-spirited clucking that suggested that the servants should be strung up by their thumbs and soundly thrashed, and not in any way that might be fun for more than one of the parties involved.

The Dowager Duchess was close enough for Benny to see the individual jewels she was wearing – in particular, the pendant depending from her neck to lodge within her ample breast. Benny, who would ordinarily have been shot before using such a phrase as 'ample breast', and was far less inclined to be caught looking at such – at least, if there were people around with a clipboard ticking boxes on the Kinsey scale – nevertheless found herself gazing at the stone: a large star-cut diamond, of a shape possible to cut only if the original stone had been half a metre across. It would obviously be a paste copy – the original safely stashed away in the purser's safe – but the way it caught the light it could have almost been real. It caught the light hypnotically. It was captivating.

Thus, her largely inebriated attention captivated by the stone, it was the last thing she saw before the lights went out, and the entire dining room plunged into darkness.

12

THE DISTINCT POSSIBILITY OF FOUL PLAY

In the darkness, the dining chamber was a chaos of susurrating and possibly even ululating noise, as everybody tried to talk at once.

'A most exceeding degree of blackness,' said Prekodravac, to one side. 'I do enjoy a big black –'

'Don't', snapped Benny, who was feeling slightly testy of a sudden, 'even think about it.'

'I was merely going to say that I appear to have misplaced my bearings,' said Prekodravac. 'The sudden chill of fright, you know.'

In the middle distance she heard a voice booming, 'Well *find* a pribbling whey-faced match, then, thou swag-bellied knotty-pated maggot pie!'

'It's a trick!' cried an excited voice from another quarter. 'A foul alien trick conducted by fiendish aliens to put all right-thinking folk off their watchful guard!'

'Oh, bog off, Groke!' boomed the previous voice in reply. 'Give it a rest, thou gorbellied rump-fed boot-licker,'

'Mind my hat!' shouted another voice through the throng. 'Oh damn and blast! I'll never get to heaven now.'

'Being in the dark like this occasionally gives me a fright,' Prekodravac said, happily. 'I do believe I'm feeling

115

a small one now.'

'How small?' Benny found herself asking automatically, before mentally kicking herself.

'Not that small.'

'Miss Summerfield?' a voice whispered urgently, from a point that seemed to be directly behind the nape of her neck. It was male and sounded frightened. 'I have an important message for you. My cabin number is on here.' Fingers took hold of her hand and something was pressed into it. It felt like a small piece of stiff, folded paper.

'What?' Benny said, belatedly realizing that the mysterious stranger had used her real rather than assumed name. There was no answer, save for Mister Dickie Prekodravac opining that perhaps the management was twiddling the wrong knob and it was, quite frankly, becoming rather wearisome.

It was at that moment that the chandeliers that had illuminated the dining chamber gave a flicker, and then came back on. Blinking rapidly to accustom herself to the glare, Benny glanced about herself, trying to locate the owner of the mysterious voice. Nobody on one side but Mister Dickie, nobody on the other but Miss Isabel Blaine, who had not said a word in all this time and was clutching her large clutch bag to herself, white-faced.

In Benny's hand was a small, folded business card. She unfolded it and read, painstakingly, the densely curlicued copperplate script.

Mr Jonathan A. Sheen
Chmn Tantra Industrial Cleaning
and Sewerage Services

There was no address, but then again there didn't need to be. Tantra Industrial Cleaning and Sewerage Services were as well known, on any of a thousand planets, as had once been the name Armitage Shanks. People in their millions, going about their business of the day, had found themselves gazing blankly upon the Tantra logo of a world-eating Ouroboros snake, and possibly mulling over the incorporation slogan of: TANTRA – PUTTING WORLDS IN MOTION. If he was, in fact, the 'Chmn' of Tantra Industrial Cleaning and Sewerage Services, this Jonathan A. Sheen must be personally richer than the dreams of avarice. He must be, not to put too fine a point on the matter, rolling in it.

Scrawled hastily on the reverse of the card was a cabin number – but Benny had no time, for the moment, to ponder the matter further, because at that point a shrill and heartfelt scream rang through the dining chamber, and shocked all those within to silence.

'My diamond!' the Dowager Duchess of Gharl shrieked, prodding frantically at her bosom. 'The Fabled Star of Saint Timothy, the patron saint of animal hospitals, standard lamps and small pieces of parsley, has *gorn!*'

On one side of her, the captain banged his head on the table repeatedly, in the age-old manner of one who has observed the tin lid descending.

'Not at all, Your Worship.' On the other side of the Dowager's bulk from the captain, Emil Dupont, who seemed to have somehow confused the Duchess with an ordained female bishop, pointed dramatically to something on the carpet. 'I plainly see the item in question on that very spot! Doubtless, it must have broken from its circlet and fallen there in the confusion.'

'It's not a Fabled Star of Saint Timothy,' said the captain resignedly, still banging his head on the table. 'It's a half-eaten bloody baby chicken roasted in sodding bacon. The damn thing slipped out of her fingers when she was scarfing it down her bleeding throat.'

This distressing display of true feeling brought an outraged squeak to the bleeding throat of the Duchess even in her extremis. Emil Dupont gave a double take such as has not been seen since the halcyon days of early twentieth-century silent film, and peered at the item on the floor again.

'It would appear that you are correct,' he said, a little

deflated. 'I would care to know very much how you made such a deduction, when it escaped even I, Emil Dupont, the greatest detective in all of Nova Belgique.'

'Take a wild imaginative bloody guess.' The captain raised his head and regarded the Dowager Duchess of Gharl balefully. 'Anyway, it doesn't matter. That was a fake, right? The real thing is still locked in the purser's safe and under guard?'

'You ghastly little man!' cried the Duchess. 'Do you think that *I* would soil myself with *artificial* jewellery, like some of these *commoners* here? The Star of Saint Timothy was the genuine article!'

The captain started banging his head on the table again.

'You have suffered an appalling shock, Your Worship.' Emil Dupont picked up his glass of the wine they had just been served before the lights had failed – a syrupy dessert wine intended to complement the popular *bombe surprise* – and proffered it to the distraught Duchess. 'Here. This will set you soon to rights.'

The Dowager Duchess took the glass without a word of thanks, drained it, and threw back her head in a display of anguish only otherwise achieved by operatic tenors. 'Why,' she declared ringingly, 'it can only be the work of the Cat's –'

The glass flew from her spasming fingers. Her eyes bulged. A choking gurgle issued from her now, suddenly, literally bleeding throat and she began to *inflate*.

And then she exploded.

With a bang.

Covering half the table, a large section of wall, and those seated immediately around her to a depth of three with the constituents of a large dinner and most of the biological equipment that was being used to digest it.

The chamber erupted into screams. At her table beside, among others, Mister Dickie and Isabel Blaine, Benny saw the captain and Emil Dupont climbing back on to their feet among the smoking mess. She wasn't going to call it a *steaming* mess, even to herself.

Fortunately for them, the captain and the great detective did not seem to have been hit by anything hard. Debris rather than – she tried to think of an apposite word – debris rather than *shrapnel*.

Through the panicked din, she heard Dupont cry, 'This must have been the result of some small thermite bomb, placed surreptitiously under the table and secured with adhesive tape, by a troupe of midgets with mountaineering crampons, even while we were occupied with dinner!'

'Right,' said Benny, who had been watching the pre-detonative scene as closely as everybody else in the dining chamber. 'Probably in little bobble hats.' She turned to Mister Dickie Prekodravac. 'What is this thing the chap has with midg–'

She stared in horror as an apparently unperturbed Mister Dickie drained his glass of the wine they'd just been served before the lights had failed. She frantically scanned the chamber and saw that several other people were taking a small drink to calm their nerves.

'Most unexpected,' Mister Dickie was saying. 'But, then again, I'm sometimes very partial to an unexpected ba–'

'Everybody down!' Benny screamed, hauling over the table and shoving a startled Isabel Blaine behind it, landing heavily on top of her. The young lady struggled under her – thinking Goddess knew what, exactly – but Benny bore down hard. The upturned table took most of the brunt from Mister Dickie's explosion and, almost simultaneously with it, she heard several other muffled detonations – not muffled by anything much, precisely, but muffled by the nature of what it actually was that *was* detonating.

'Oh well,' she muttered, as items of various description flew overhead. 'It's probably the way he'd have wanted to go.'

13

THE PURÉE OF THE PLOT NOTICEABLY THICKENS

A quarter of an hour later, the dining room had been largely cleared. The constables of the Dellah Constabulary had been called, and had arrived (leaving, of course, a contingent to guard the safe in the purser's office) just in time to prevent a general stampede of diners desperately trying to get away from the blast area, a large number of them also desperate to wash the after effects of the blast from themselves.

The after effects, naturally, had included the general response that certain people had made, upon seeing other people exploding all around them, after a big dinner. The constables had ineffectually attempted to prevent the mass exodus, and take names and addresses – before the realization sank in that everybody here was in a hermetically sealed spacegoing liner, and wouldn't exactly be going anywhere.

The captain, who with Dupont had taken the brunt of the Dowager's detonation, was nowhere to be seen, having probably repaired to repair the damage done to his previously pristine uniform.

All who remained in the dining chamber now were the constables, the great detectives, the remains of the dead, those who might identify them and of course a collection of interested onlookers who had hung around in case anything of further interest happened. Benny would, she supposed, be technically classed with this last category, had anyone wanted a technical smack in the mouth for suggesting it.

She found herself gravitating towards Khaarli. The note from Jonathan A. Sheen was burning a hole in her pocket – or, rather, the inside of the bodice of her gown, where she had put it for safekeeping – and she wanted to consult somebody about it, and Khaarli seemed to be the best of the bunch. Out of these so-called 'great detectives' he was the most approachable, and the single one of them who didn't seem to be entirely round the twist.

Detective Second-Class Interchange – the prosaic and workaday Lestrade among these investigators – had busied himself compiling a list of the murder victims, using for the most part such personal effects as could be found, and when all else failed, reading the remains of the place cards.

'Mr Richard Tarquin Delbert Prekodravac,' he said, flipping through his notebook. 'The Emir Dan Ben-Zvi. Ms Jane Jecubelli. Ms Julia Porter. Mr Geoffrey Weasel. A Mr Michael Kogge is unaccounted for, but we found his distinctive ginger wig, twenty metres from where he was sitting, on the sweet trolley, in the apricot syllabub. A Mr Philip Thorne, a Mr Andrew Leighton . . .'

'They are of no matter,' snapped Sandford Groke, his body bristling and quivering with outrage. He pointed dramatically to the epicentre of the area occupied by the late Dowager. 'The fiend was after the Duchess of Gharl. This can only be the work –' he flowered darkly at Khaarli '– of cowardly alien anarcho-syndicalists plotting to rid the very galaxy itself of its God-appointed landed gentry!'

'Much as I hate to agree with this currish, cockered pigeon-egg,' the Czhan rumbled, 'I think he might be right. Except of course for the cowardly plot, the anarcho-syndicalists and the aliens.'

'Did anybody think to search people for the stolen diamond?' Benny found herself asking.

The great detectives, as one, turned to regard her.

'Well, it strikes me that these deaths would be the perfect cover for getting it away in the confusion,' she continued, and instantly regretted it. 'I don't know, though,' she back-pedalled, 'I mean, I've never heard of the Cat's Paw actually *killing* anybody befo–'

'That must be it!' exclaimed Interchange. 'The fiend!'

Khaarli the Czhan nodded slowly. He seemed slightly dubious. 'I hardly need mention,' he said, 'what our next course of action should be, thou fat-kidneyed turdly-fallen fustilarians.'

'Quite right,' said Dupont. 'We must all pull on brightly coloured frocks and put on an impromptu song-and-dance show. Enchanted by the dulcet tone of our singing and the syncopated rhythms of our tap-dancing, the criminal shall be drawn to us and then reveal himself!'

'I was actually thinking, thou fen-sucked gleeking horn-beast, that the agent of these people's demise must have been in the wine. New Madagascan puff-mongoose tincture, perhaps, which is odourless, tasteless and can only be detected, I gather, by way of the sub-audial sounds of its micro-organisms going "Wheee!" The bottles must be impounded and analysed. The wine racks must be searched to discover how they came to be contaminated.'

Emil Dupont nodded. 'That, too, I concede. Can't think why I didn't think of it myself.'

Agatha Magpole still sat where she had when the detonations had occurred. She had not been touched by any of the blasts, but the shock had given her one of her turns. Her companion fussed over her, loosening her collar and wafting cool air on to her face with a doily.

Most of the bottles and glasses in question had been broken, both in the explosions and in the rush to get out of the vicinity that they had precipitated, but Interchange ordered his constables to retrieve and tag all that remained, which they carefully began to do.

They had just started this process, when the relative calm of the dining chamber was pierced by a plaintive but uncommonly piercing cry. Running through the door came a woman who, it seemed, would have been slightly dowdy and haggard-looking in any case, even if she had not been in some distress, as she was now. Benny recognized the good lady wife of Nathanael C. Nerode, the large man in wholesale Goblanian bog seal blubber. She tried to recall whether or not she had seen her and her spouse at dinner.

'My husband!' The good Mrs Nerode cried in heart-rending distress. 'Oh, sirs! My husband has been horribly murdered!'

A distraught Mrs Nathanael C. Nerode – Benny never learnt her given name, and privately doubted that she *had* one – led them down a corridor, down two decks via a spiral staircase and then, if her spiral-staircasively disorientated sense of direction could be trusted, back, in general, the direction from which they had come. Benny's heart sank more than somewhat. The way her luck had been going, she'd lay even odds on where they were going to end up.

The party Mrs Nerode led consisted of a pair of Dellah constables, Prosecutor General of the Czhanos Militia Khaarli and Benny herself. On hearing that this latest, putative murder victim was not one of what might be called the 'better' class of people, the great detectives had evidenced a distinct lack of interest in pursuing the case. Only Khaarli among them had made his feelings known concerning the idea of there being one law for the rich, another for the less rich and no sort of law at all for the poor, and had stormed off to have a look. Benny had decided to tag along with him, and he seemed to welcome her assistance. She had – or, in all probability *had* had – no love for Nerode, but she agreed with Khaarli's view of things wholeheartedly and, besides, it was the perfect opportunity to get the Czhan detective alone for a small talk.

As they neared the end of the gangway, and saw a flickering vapour sign above the hatchway at the end, Benny saw that her worst fears had been well grounded. They were going into Percy's Discotheque.

This was the domain of the offspring of those who had been at dinner – and, Benny thought, if there was ever an argument for giving people compulsory sterilizations and compensatory transistor radios it was this. Shrieking, bubbly teenage slappers in extortionately expensive designer shreds of tinsel hurled champagne about, collapsed in giggling heaps and threw up, tried to crawl up the legs of the bar staff and flashed their underwear at anything that moved. And the girls, if anything, were even worse.

They had entered at what seemed to be a lull in the proceedings. The music had been turned low, and a pale but enormously fat and self-obsessed little rich girl was on the stage that ordinarily supported go-go dancers and male strippers, dressed in pristine, black Goth apparel that must have cost a small fortune, inflicting upon all and sundry what she probably thought to be the dangerous poetry of youth.

'The black crow of doom has landed on my head,' she was mumbling:

> It is black like my soul,
> And my soul is black as death.
> Nobody understands me;
> I hate my parents,
> And I especially hate my sister, Laura
> Because everybody likes her better than me
> And I hope she dies horribly in a car crash.

The precisely similarly dressed contingent of her friends lounged by one of the mouldings on the walls and nodded with cool appreciation, never allowing themselves to show anything as gauche and uncool as actual enthusiasm. Benny, who in her time had been a seriously angsty teenage poet, felt as though the single most embarrassing period of her entire life had come back to haunt her.

Mrs Nerode took them into a smallish back room that might at one point have served any number of purposes, but now served to contain the body of Nerode. A member of the bar staff stood rather vacantly nearby – the same kind of enhanced employee as had been employed in the dining room, but of a white-shirted, waistcoated, leather-trousered type more suited to the immediate surroundings. Again, Benny was struck by the remarkable similarity to the dead Krugor – and made yet another mental note to tell somebody about that the moment she thought she could do so and get away with it.

'I had taken to bed for an early night,' Mrs Nerode explained. 'Nathanael had gone to complain about the general and most deplorable lack of facilities for respectable people – as he liked to do regularly, sometimes for hours at a time ...'

Benny shot a glance to the member of the bar staff, who remained utterly poker-faced and unconcerned.

'Jacquin here came across him, and placed a call to my cabin,' continued Mrs Nerode. 'I cannot for the life of me imagine how he came to be here.'

The late Nathanael C. Nerode was dressed in an outfit that might once, at some historical point, have caused its wearer to be dubbed 'the oldest swinger in town'. A white suit with flappy, flared trousers and wing collars; a black silk shirt open to the navel to reveal a chest wig, enough gold medallions to make an Olympic powerball team scream with envy and quite possibly a merkin – Benny *really* didn't want to look close enough to check. The effect was spoilt slightly by the fact that he was still wearing grey socks and brown sandals – and by the substances that were oozing out of his ears, and other areas.

'So what do you think?' she asked Khaarli.

'Well he's dead, at any rate.' The Czhan turned to the member of the bar staff. 'You. Tell me what happened precisely before he died, thou sheep-biting dissembling nut-hook.'

The leather-trousered man shrugged. Obviously, his vat-grown brain had not been designed for the higher levels of cognition. 'Don' know nothing, me. Guy was jumpin' around like he had a spring up him, doin' that thing where he rolls the hands around an' tryin' to look up young ladies' skirts. Next thing, he's jerkin' and yammerin' and shriekin' away. Didn' notice the difference, tell you the truth, till he shit himself and fell over.'

'Hm.' Khaarli turned back to Benny. 'Probably some kind of sonic device, thou hell-hated hasty-witted maggot pie. Pulse-pumped sound waves at a frequency fit to turn his brains to turbid mush.'

Benny nodded. 'Sounds reasonable.' She groped through her mind to try to locate half-remembered physics lessons from school, similar information picked up via osmosis from the environs of St Oscar's and practical experience of weaponry picked up from a lifetime of coming into contact with it, mostly on the wrong end. 'Something like that could be the size of a handgun. I don't think there's any way we could find the person who did it by now, without a top-to-tail search of the ship.'

'Dupont, Groke and the rest aren't going to do that for this base-court clapper-clawed lewdster.' Khaarli gestured downward to the wretched if shocked stiff remains of Nerode. 'I'll see if I can persuade 'em to add a sonic gun to the list if and when they do.'

Mrs Nerode chose that moment to swoon, fortuitously into the arms of the member of the bar staff. 'Oh my poor husband!' she cried theatrically. 'Life without him will never be the same!'

Benny looked at her again. 'I'm quite sure it won't.'

'One of you take her back to her cabin, thou dismal-dreaming ill-nurtured bum-baileys,' Khaarli said to one of the constables. He gestured to the steward. 'The other take a statement from him.'

Left alone with Khaarli and the body of Nerode, with nothing directly pertinent to contribute, Benny decided that now was as good a time as any to acquaint the detective with her own discoveries. Glossing over the fact of how she had come to be there and why, she told him of how she had witnessed what had seemed to be the murder of Krugor, and that the body seemed to have remained undiscovered; told him of the whispered conversation in the dark with Mr

Jonathan A. Sheen; and showed him the folded card.

'I mean, it's probably unrelated to anything, and it's incredibly dubious in any case,' she concluded, 'but at the very least it's something concrete to go on, even if it doesn't lead anywhere.'

Khaarli pondered this for a while. 'You're right, thou mammering idle-headed measle. "Clues", as such, are always highly doubtful. But it never hurts to take a look.'

Outside the hatch that led to the cabin of Jonathan A. Sheen, they found the captain and two others, a man and a woman, both in the uniforms of ship's officers. The captain had, by now, changed from his Dowager-befouled uniform and wore the worn and grubby overalls, donkey jacket and greasy Fassbinder leather cap more suited to the skipper of a spacegoing tug than a cruise liner. Up close, he seemed haggard, and haggard in a more genuine sense than the wife of the late Nathanael C. Nerode. His slightly twitchy bearing suggested rather too many coffees and one or two stims too many; far too many sleepless, worried nights.

The two ship's officers were working frantically on the mechanism behind an open panel by the door, while Captain Crane stood glumly gazing at the door itself. He turned to regard Benny and Khaarli with a kind of distaste and loathing in his tense and red-rimmed eyes – then with a visible jerk caught himself and adopted a barely passing attitude of courtesy towards a paying guest. 'What do you want?'

'We were, uh, hoping to have a small word with Mr Sheen,' Benny said, eyeing the work in progress at the panel uneasily.

'A word with Mr Sheen?' Captain Crane snorted. 'I'm afraid you're going to be out of luck.' He jerked his head towards the officers. 'Now, I don't,' he said with heavy sarcasm, 'expect a fine lady to have the first idea what we're trying to do here . . .'

'Let me guess,' said Benny, dispiritedly. 'You've had a micro-catastrophic hull-breach, probably caused by a single rogue mesonic particle in interdimensional null-space, which has latched on to the hull and has now gone overt, the general-order locus of which just happens to be that cabin. You're trying to seal it from here, so you can get in and work on it properly before that –' she rapped on the hatch with her knuckles '– rather thin interior hatch gives way and we all of us suddenly find ourselves exploding out into vacuum. How am I doing so far?'

'So far,' the captain said, glowering at her with an anger slightly diffused by a grudging respect, 'you've got it almost exactly right. Apart from me hoping like hell it was just in fact a meteorite.'

He did not have time to say more, because at the point the man working on the mechanism swore, the hatch leading into the cabin of Mr Jonathan A. Sheen slid back, and the air from the corridor burst in with a concussive *whomph!*

14

THE PLOT BECOMES MORE COMPLICATED THAN WAS PREVIOUSLY IMAGINED

The air burst into the cabin with a concussive *whomph!* because the cabin appeared to be still airtight and the pressure was merely equalizing. Had it not been, there would have been no sound but the shriek of gasses under atmospheric but catastrophically decreasing pressure through a hole in the hull, together with the sound of decompression shutters slamming down throughout the entire ship, sealing the fate of anyone unlucky enough to find themselves on the wrong side of them.

As it was, a puzzled Crane and the two ship's officers, with Benny and Khaarli trailing behind, walked into a bedchamber that looked as though a small whirlwind had hit it. The finish on the balk corresponding to the hull was scuffed by the Brownian violence that had occurred, but it was otherwise completely intact.

'So how could the place be depressurized?' Crane muttered.

'It's not my area of expertise, but couldn't the air have been simply pumped out?' suggested Khaarli. 'Thou spongy dread-bolted codpiece.'

'The ARVID slave systems reported catastrophic depressurization,' said Crane, 'and for that you'd need a hull breach . . .'

Benny, meanwhile, had been letting her professional instincts take over: letting the millions of tiny factors inherent in an environment wash over her and integrate so that the gestalt processes bubbled up from the subconscious. It was a process that was, as she had told her tutorial groups, time and time again, a completely different thing from making it all up out of thin air.

The various items of scattered debris were as they were now because of the air rushing into the room when the hatch slid open. Mentally, she tried to reverse the process, imagining them rewinding back to their original position, reconstructing the original state of the cabin with a kind of hypnagogic intensity that was comparable to what a more mystic frame of mind might call a vision. She fixed it in front of her eyes and tried to examine it – but something seemed to be wrong with the process. Maybe because of her tiredness, or the large quantities of drink she had consumed earlier in the evening, it was as if the balance of her mind was disturbed, flipping over and spinning off crazy and out of control . . .

Shockingly, a hand landed on her shoulder.

'Are you all right, Ms Summersdale?' a voice rumpled. 'Thou common-kissing ill-bred strumpet?'

The dreamlike state collapsed and her identity slammed back with a bang – and in the rush of connecting to herself again, she realized what had been wrong with the mental picture.

'The place is a mess,' she said. She experienced a flash of self-consciousness as she realized that Khaarli was looking at her with an expression of Czhan concern, and that the captain and officers were regarding her with wary suspicion. Just how long had she been, by their lights, to all intents and purposes off playing with the cheeky pixies? She trod on her misgivings. She needed certainty and poise, now, if they were going to take anything she said seriously.

'This place is a mess,' she repeated, slightly more firmly. 'But it was also a mess *before*.' She turned to Captain Crane.

'You said it could only be catastrophic decompression, and I think it was that – but it was a controlled catastrophe.' She quickly ran through the arrangement of the debris in her head again, and then pointed to the closed door of the washroom, in the balk perpendicular to the hull. 'The source of the implosion, decompression, whatever, came from there.'

'Impossible!' exclaimed Crane. 'For one thing, the door's in one piece. Are you telling me that whatever did this opened the door, crash-dumped the pressure and then closed the door again as polite as you please?'

Benny shrugged. 'I have no idea. I might be completely wrong about it. Then again, as someone was saying a short while back, it doesn't hurt to have a look. I rather suspect you'll find our Mr Sheen in there. Or whatever's left of him. I think someone or something's polished him off.'

The captain looked at her and sighed, then turned to the male officer. 'Check it out, Golding.'

The officer turned a kind of supercilious sneer on Benny that had her wishing that something horrible would happen to him. He strode to the door and pulled it open to reveal a pristine bathroom.

'There,' he said. 'What do you think happened? You think someone's flushed him down here?' Golding leant over to the toilet and pushed the plunger.

Benny never got a clear view of what happened next, because the next instant she was pinwheeling across the cabin, colliding with the bodies of Khaarli, Crane and the female ship's officer, the roar of blasting air in her ears and a composite taste/smell like kitchen matches in her nose and throat. She caught a momentary glimpse of Golding as he was sucked away, and then the door to the washroom swung smoothly and hydraulically shut so that she slammed into it face first and saw stars.

'What a way to go,' Crane said. 'He must have been just sitting there, and then he pressed the plunger and he . . .'

He was referring to the probable death of Mr Jonathan A.

Sheen rather than that of Golding, which they had all to a certain extent witnessed. The slightly but crucially different aspects of that probable death seemed to be preying on his mind, and it was the fourth time in the last half-hour he had brought it up. Personally, Benny was trying not to think about it.

After the sounds had finally stopped behind the bathroom door of Sheen's cabin, and the pressure had been restored yet again, they had, very cautiously, opened the door. There had been nothing. Every scrap of flesh, bone, blood and matter had been sucked down the toilet sluice, through a grating, the spaces of which were less than a centimetre apart.

'Someone tampering with the gaskets?' Khaarli had asked. 'Hooking them to the plunger so that they opened up? I'm assuming you eject waste matter out into space at some point, thou puking errant jolt-heads. The vacuum could have sucked both Sheen and Golding out.'

'We do that,' the female ship's officer, Cherry, had said, 'but only after treatment to extract the, ah, nutrients for the hydroponics. Anyway, there's no way vacuum could have pulled someone down a hole like that.'

'It would have taken a heavy-duty pump,' said Captain Crane, 'and there's simply no *room* in the ship's waste-disposal system for something like that. It would have to be massive. It would have been noticed long before now.'

'Not necessarily,' Benny had said, as the glimmerings of an idea began to surface. She had gestured vaguely around the cabin. 'Walls define spaces. You forget that there's something on the other side of them. Don't forget we're on a *space* cruiser. There's bags of room for something huge out there.'

All of which was why they were now in a kind of antechamber before one of the emergency maintenance airlocks. Behind them, down a rusting gangway, they heard the chunk and whir of the sewerage processing units, the gurgle of various substances through pipes.

Cherry was climbing into a bulky EVA suit, of a design

that was really meant for freefall, and so had little caterpillar tracks on its plinthlike, unbifurcated lower half. In a clear polymer pouch-case attached to its chest with press-studs were several pages of schematics of the ship.

'Just see what you can find and come back,' Crane told her, racking down the helmet on its hinges, and securing it with what those unfamiliar with the reality of spacefaring might have been surprised to see were more like the wing nuts of a diver's helmet than anything excitingly hi-tech. The realities of spacefaring called for heavy-duty practicality and durability more than sexy technological aesthetics – as was probably epitomized best in the engineering term of AM/FM, which was commonly used to describe the inevitable Heath-Robinson, Sod's Law working of Actual Machines, as opposed to the graceful, dancing and entirely unworkable Flights of a certain kind of Magic.

The gaskets of the joint hissed. From a console fixed to the wall, the relayed voice of Cherry said, 'I can work my way around to the outlet in about five minutes. Do you want me to take pictures?'

Behind her, momentarily forgetting that she couldn't see him through the back of the helmet, Khaarli nodded. 'If you can, thou base-court mangled hedge-pig. If not, it doesn't matter. I'd merely like some confirmation of this frothy goatish strumpet's theory.'

He turned to look enquiringly at Benny, who shrugged. She was here in the ostensibly restricted areas of the ship by way of a technique that she had picked up along the way in her various adventures – so simple that it was hardly a technique at all. You drifted along with people as if you had every right to be there, while remaining so far as was possible unobtrusive until you had something positive to do or say. The process, in its sufficiently advanced stages, had people relying on you as a capable and trusted friend, without ever quite realizing how you had become one.

Cherry trundled through the inner door of the airlock. 'I can do that,' her voice said from the console in the bulkhead.

'Something like that should be easy to small fish.'

'What?' Crane asked her. 'What did you say?'

'I said it should be easy to spot.'

Through the hatchway they saw her working the airlock controls, and then the hatch slid smoothly shut.

'That wasn't what I thought you said,' Crane told Cherry via the console.

'Oh yes? What did thou think I said.'

'It sounded like you said "Something like that should be easy to small fish." '

'Small *fish*?' the voice of Cherry said. 'Why would I say something like that? I'm going to cycle out the meaty big day Jeremy rhubarb, now.'

'Something's wrong,' Benny cut in. 'Something's happened to her. Get her out of there *now*.'

Captain Crane turned to face her with a look of surprise, as though he literally had not been aware of her presence. 'What?'

'Oh!' the voice of Cherry said from the console. It sounded slurred and mushy, as if the owner of it did not have full control of the vocal and buccal muscles. 'Oh! There's a table! It's a big *table*, and it's catslit eyes, like snipping screens to make the spider nice and fruity! It's an angel, calling to me, like heals or yah or founds. It wants to make the peck of me and –'

The voice was cut short by a sound, from the console, remarkably like a cannon shot. On the console red lights flashed and an alarm began to bleep. From behind the hermetic hatch of the airlock, of course, there came no sound.

'She's opened the outer door without depressurizing,' Crane exclaimed, frantically scanning the console readouts. 'She's gone! How the hell could that happen?'

It was that magic point before the enormity of another death had sunk in. In the same way as one can be talking with a friend, and carry on the conversation for a few seconds after he's hit by sniper fire, the enormity of it had not quite sunk in.

'Can we get her back?' Khaarli said, in much the same way as one might enquire after a coin dropped down a drain. Benny realized that, as a planet-dweller, he did not have a fundamental grasp of what it was really like in space; she thought of mentioning things like the *Titanian Queen*'s turning circle, and the fact that whereas people thought of space as pure vacuum, their velocity combined with free-floating spatial hydrogen atoms made the slipstream of a planetary jet look like a summer breeze – but in the end she said nothing. She wandered over to the racks of oxygen/nitrogen bottles that supplied the suits, unracked one of them and hefted it.

'That sounded like a hallucinatory fit to me,' she said. 'I think you should check these things out, when you get the chance, if you can find somebody to do it.'

Crane was hammering at the console, shutting the outer door and repressurizing the lock on the remote. 'It's sealed,' he said as the inner hatch slid open.

Inside, there was nothing, except for the little polymer packet of ship's schematics that had torn loose from Cherry's suit under her sudden acceleration, and which had snagged on one of the control levers. Benny plucked it off and turned it over in her hands, glancing at Khaarli and Crane, who were just now starting to blanch with their reaction to this latest shock.

'Why do I get the distinct impression,' she mused, 'that somebody *seriously* doesn't want us leaving this ship?'

Benny made it back to her cabin in a semi-daze. Possibly, she had caught a whiff of the gas that had killed Cherry, or possibly she was simply exhausted – she had been awake for less than six hours, but the sheer weight and variety of events had taken their toll. She walked through the gangways in a kind of low-grade, paranoid, hallucinatory state. Every corner seemed to have something around it, waiting to leap out, every fixture seemed to drool menace – and the fact that nothing menacing actually occurred when she turned a corner and passed a fixture just meant that the menaces were being incredibly sneaky about it into the bargain.

As she neared her own cabin, a hatch opened and a woman stepped out. Benny could not remember having seen her about the ship, and this was slightly surprising because the woman was extremely noticeable. A slinky black dress was applied to her like wet gloss paint, her foxy face was made up strikingly, in the manner of a 1930s (Greg.) *femme fatale*. In one long-sleeved hand she negligently held a cigarette in a long-stemmed holder.

'Gut evenink,' she said, languidly.

'Um. Hello,' Benny said, simply because her lightly toasted brain couldn't think of any other response. If she didn't get to bed and get her head down soon, in the next few minutes, she could imagine her head just falling off.

'I vonder if you can help me,' said the woman. 'My name is Heidi von Lindt. I have thus far spent this delightful cruise visiting with certain gentlemen of my acquaintance, offering them companionship and, I must confess, a certain degree of succour. I have been, if you will, a kind of *random* companion . . .'

Benny wondered vaguely if this scenario was going to lead anywhere. 'I'm really not in much of a state to help any –' she began.

Heidi von Lindt held a finger to her glossed lips in a small shushing gesture. 'Vun of my gentleman friends,' she said, 'seems to haff had a small mishap. I left him under firm restraint, momentarily, while I went to find a pair off nipple-clamps, a bullwhip, a set of electrodes and a pint of clarified ghee, and I haff come back to find him horribly murdered.' She pressed her hand to her forehead in a display of abject sorrow. 'Ach! Poor Jason is no more! Vot am I to do? I can't help it!'

Benny screwed her eyes shut against tears of exhaustion and stumbled away from the woman, shoving at the bulkhead for support. No way, she told herself. There's just no way – it has to be a coincidence. But at the moment, quite frankly, I do not even want to think about it. Just let me sleep, let me sleep.

As she finally reached her cabin, however, she saw that the night had one final bit of unpleasantness for her, in the form of the special agent, Sandford Groke.

'Miss Summersdale!' he exclaimed. 'You seem to have been intimately involved with the foul occurrences tonight, and I should like to ask you some questions . . .'

Benny regarded him with bleary, scornful eyes. 'Go. Away.'

The special agent bristled. 'I shall have you know, Miss Summersdale, that –'

'Look, just leave it, all right?' Benny dug the page of the ship's plans she had retrieved from the airlock from her frock. 'I've got documentation from Prosecutor General Khaarli of the whatever it was, giving me effective clearance.'

She waved the sheet under Groke's nose so that he could see the Czhan detective's chop scrawled on the back, but fast enough so that he could not read the extent of the 'documentation', which in fact read:

> *Interview with Ms Bernice Summersdale concerning the incidents of this night, and their deplorable loss of life.*
> *K: So, did you do any of these murders, then?*
> *BS: Nope.*

Benny jerked a thumb in the direction from which she'd come. 'There's a woman up the hall who might repay close questioning tonight. Tomorrow, I'll answer any questions you can think of. All will be well, and well, and all manner of things will be well, tomorrow.'

And, with that, she swept into her cabin, and slammed the hatch in his face. She stumbled to the bed and half leapt, half fell on it. The reaction, long put off, was hitting her.

Nobody she particularly cared about, nobody she had even *liked*, had died – but the proximity of sudden death hits human beings on a fundamental level. The loss of one diminishes us all. Several of them exploding over one, two more being sucked down a toilet and another one sucked out of an airlock in front of one, all in the space of a couple of hours, probably tends to diminish one even more so.

All in all, Benny thought, this had not exactly been the most enjoyable evening of the cruise.

INTERLUDE

THE *DEVILISH DISGUISES* OF DOCTOR PO

'And here he is, RATI,' the voice of a man, obviously a foreigner, said.

'Do you think it was worth the wait?' said another, female voice, strangely distant and with an odd tone, as though it issued from the horn of a mechanical gramophone.

Sandford Groke leapt into consciousness and action at one and the same time, his whipcord sinews lusting for justice and revenge – and found that these foreign cowards had tethered him, flat on his back, with strong hoops of steel about his wrists and ankles.

'Look, hold still, OK!' the first voice snapped. 'Calm down, yeah? You've just come through what's effectively a white hole the size of a micron, your auto-immune and renal systems have probably shut down with the shock and you've lost one Sheol of a lot of electrolytes.'

There was the sting of a hypodermic needle in Groke's upper left arm. A face hove into view through the blur of his vision: a swarthy, unshaven face, its coloration slightly odd as though it were the result of the miscegenation between a mulatto and a Chinese.

'Just lie there for a while,' it said, in its foreign but strangely unplaceable accent. 'You're only restrained so's you don't do yourself damage. We'll let you up in a kagi – uh – a minute.'

Groke's vision began to clear. The light behind the face was of a cold, sharp sort that he had never seen before in his life.

'Where,' he demanded, in a forceful tone that somehow transformed itself into a feeble croak. 'Where am I?'

The face pursed its lips. 'Now, that's rather a complicated question. You're in precisely the same place you were a thousand years ago, give or take. Thing is, in those thousand years the spin of the galaxy's moved on.'

A memory surfaced from the miasma of Groke's pain. 'A thousand years?'

The swarthy face grinned. 'Since last Wednesday.'

'Hey, Da– I mean Carstairs,' the female voice cut in sharply. 'Watch it with the –'

'Oh, yeah, right,' the man said hurriedly. He looked up and raised his voice: 'I mean *Woden's Day*, all right?' He looked back down again and muttered, 'Damn AI Complex Control. You have to watch your step like nobody's business since the AIs decided they were gods.'

'Hey, don't look at Me,' said the female voice. 'Nobody ever asked *Me*. That's just who I am.'

'That voice . . .' the special agent rasped.

'What, this?' The man held out his arm. Groke became aware of his outlandish costume, and what appeared to be a large, strangely formed wristwatch, on which small lights rippled. 'This is my RATI.'

'That's me,' the female voice said proudly, seemingly coming from the watch. 'Ragalata the Vine of Love, Mayarati the Deceiver. I appear in my aspect of a huge-breasted woman, fit to mock all those who follow an ascetic way of life, and drive all who behold me *mad* with carnal lust . . .'

'Currently appearing in her aspect of a jumped-up comms pack with an attitude,' said the man.

'Yeah, well,' the contrivance said, in a slightly deflated

tone of voice. 'You wouldn't *believe* how hard it is to offer pleasures undreamt of by the mind of man, when you have to spend your entire incarnation wrapped around this joker's left wrist.'

Sandford Groke's head started to spin. He feared that it might come off under this insanity. 'This is,' he croaked, 'insane...'

The man smiled nastily. 'You, Mr Groke, don't know the half of it.'

Groke turned his head. He seemed to be in a chamber packed almost completely with the kind of apparatus so beloved of the Secret Service science Johnnies. 'You know my name?'

'Yeppo.' The man nodded. 'We've been hanging around for weeks, here, waiting for your temporal signal, and trying to recombine and reconstitute it. You've been a long time arriving – and I think we could both do with a small drink, yeah?' He motioned towards one of the straps securing the special agent's feet. 'Tell you what: why don't I let you up so's we can go somewhere and talk about it. You'll pick things up as you go along – but, Sandford...'

'Yes?' Groke said, suspicious at this sudden outbreak of familiarity.

'Things have changed. I mean, *really* changed. If it all gets too much for you, just close your eyes and think of the English Empire, or whatever, yeah?'

'Oh my God,' groaned Sandford Groke, nauseated and aghast. 'These things... these... *things*...'

They were in what seemed to be a steel-walled tunnel, packed with human beings and creatures that seemed to be a cross between the more fevered imaginations of Messrs Verne and Wells (the arch socialist) and demon spawn from the lower circles of hell. The reek of them was appalling, the skirl and shritter of their cries hammered at the ears and made them ring.

'Yeah.' The swarthy man – this 'Carstairs' – seemed

unperturbed by this parade of abject horror. 'This is a crossover point of the complex, more or less a neutral zone. You'll find people from all over the Catan Nebula, here – oh, hi there Raan. How's the gestalt?'

This last was addressed to what appeared to be a slumped, ambulatory mound of slime, from which glared seven glowing eyes. A wet hole opened up on its surface and emitted a warbling stream of noise.

'Glad to hear it,' said the man Carstairs.

Three of the eyes floated round to glare at the special agent, and the creature warbled questioningly.

'What, him? Just some guy I was sent to bring in. Big guy in his own timeline, apparently. Sandford Groke, Special Agent, yeah?'

The thing erupted into peals of glutinous laughter, and slithered off.

Carstairs turned to Groke. 'That was Raan,' he said, chattily. 'Hideous Evil Slimy Shapeshifter of Utter and Unmitigated Evil from Dimension X. Nice guy.'

Groke clutched at his head. 'I'm going mad. I must be going mad.'

'Here we go again,' said the contrivance on Carstairs' wrist. 'I've had about enough of this. There's no *way* this guy's going to be of any use to anyone. I mean, walking fruit-and-nut cutlet in a basket or what?'

'RATI,' Carstairs muttered, 'if the guy was any *good* he'd have been snapped up by one of the big outfits before we even got a dib on him. Sometimes we have to take what we can get, OK?'

'Well, OK – but he starts going off on one and foaming at the fly, we're outa here, right?'

'What are you mumbling about?' the special agent enquired.

'Nothing, nothing.' Carstairs pointed to an opening in the side of the tunnel. 'You see that there? The hatch with the sign that looks a bit like a happy pig with a pint pot? That's where we're going. That's where we should be.'

* * *

The chamber was dark, and filled with smoke, and the smell of drink; the sweat and reek of human beings and alien creatures, and chemical-seeming odours not readily identifiable. The only real illumination was the spotlight on a small stage, where the figure of a man in a sparkling suit spoke into a radiophonic microphone.

'Hey there, welcome to the Jade Shebeen,' he said, in an amplified voice that rang around the subdued and silent crowd. 'Glad you could make it. And now, for all you groovy dudes out there, a sentient life form who needs no introduction . . .'

An enormously fat, ragged, elderly man with greenish skin shambled on to the stage, clutching what seemed to be a guitar made from a tin box, with three necks, one on the opposite lateral side to the other two. He had four arms.

'Hey this is great!' the man Carstairs exclaimed, sitting with Groke at a table laden with deplorably strong drink and a pile of highly illegal hashish. 'Isn't this great? You know who that is? That's Arlo Leadlemon!'

Several things at adjacent tables shushed and shlurruped him for this outburst of enthusiasm.

'Arlo Leadlemon?' a dazed Groke said, bemused.

'Yeah, Arlo Leadlemon,' Carstairs continued, keeping his voice low as the monstrous figure on the stage tuned his instrument. 'Best blues man in the Catan Nebula. Y'see, Arlo comes from the Poldakis colony – the one that got nuked to Sheol and back in the Big One a few centuries back. All that remains there now, right, are these big fat three-metre-long mutant Chihuahuas, mutant black plague-rats that pull your face off and your basic, malnourished human survivors huddling against the unending sub-zero nuclear winter.'

Carstairs began to sing softly, to himself: '*Woke up this mornin/Ma woman was dead/Damn great sodding mutant rat gone bite off her head* – that was one of his. And then there's that perennial holiday seasonal favourite: *Dead dogs roasting on an open fire/Black rats chewing off your nose* . . . Believe me, these guys know about the blues.' He shrugged. 'Then again, all they can think of to actually *sing* about is being horrifically mauled by black rats and eating dead dogs. Ah well. *C'est la guerre.*'

'Ladies, gentlemen, multi-genitalially reproductive biomorphs,' the announcer on the stage cried, getting excited, 'put your hands, feet, pseudopodia and manipulatory appendages together for the one, the only, Arlo Leadlemon!'

Suddenly the chamber was filled with swelling, wailing, twanging sounds that Sandford Groke, Special Agent, could only liken to some diseased lunatic's idea of minstrel music.

'Oh damn,' Carstairs exclaimed with disappointment. 'He's doing that commercial track – that wafer he imprinted where he tried to cross over into archive-resurrected country and western . . .'

This time, the creatures to either side of them shushed him violently. On the stage, through a cancerous and phlegmy throat, Arlo Leadlemon began to sing:

> Ah was haulin' gumbo down on Route 66,
> A bag o' chitlins on ma knee,
> When all of a sudden I heard this plaintive sound
> Acomin' over ma CB.
>
> It said, I'm jest a crippled bo' 'bout nine years old
> An ma daddy fried in Nam;
> Ma momma took to drinkin' that ole rye whiskey
> And yesterday she shot the dog.

'Note the dead-dog back-reference,' Carstairs whispered to the astounded Groke, in an aside. 'They were trying to give the thing some coat-tail credibility . . .'

> Th'bullet bounced off Cujo's spine
> And ricocheted off the flue
> And blew off the head of my autistic sister,
> Nadine Betty Sue . . .

The insane music came to an ear-ripping climax and then collapsed to a halt. The audience of creatures exploded with wild applause. As it died down, young human ladies in skimpy costumes that left almost nothing to but the most loathsome imagination – that, for example, of the French – wove through the chamber, dispensing more foul drinks. The greenish four-armed monster sat complacently on the stage, retuning preparatory to inflicting more of his savage musical violence.

The man who had called himself Carstairs took the opportunity of comparative silence to regard Groke thoughtfully.

'As you know,' he said, 'we know all about you and your work for the Secret Service and Special Branch. We're in the same line of work ourselves, and we're in the position of offering you a job. There's a certain man who –' He got not further, because that was when the special agent made his intrepid move. The man who had called himself Carstairs gaped as he stared down the barrel of Sandford Groke's trusty service revolver!

'Do you think,' Groke snarled grimly, 'that I don't know what's going *on* here?'

'Hey, nice trick,' said Carstairs. 'Do you have room for the holster as well?'

'Do you think,' Groke continued heroically, 'that I haven't noticed? The devilish hallucinatory drugs you introduced into my system, the so-called time machine and this entire farce . . . it's all part of a complex, extensive and hideously complicated scheme to drive me mad! Mad! D'you hear me? Mad!' He pulled at Carstairs' nose. It didn't come off, but that was no doubt because the fiend was being particularly fiendish, and had used some extra-strong glue. 'Is that not so – *Doctor Po*?'

'Oh dear Me,' groaned the thing attached to the man's wrist. 'He's lost it.'

'Ow!' Carstairs clutched at his face. 'Dat was by soddig dose!'

Sandford fired a warning shot.

'That was a warning shot,' he said.

'Hey, I don't think Mr Leadlemon would agree with

145

you . . .' said Carstairs as the singer clutched at his chest and fell backwards from the stage.

'You can't,' Groke continued, all oblivious, 'fool me with that foolish manner and ridiculous disguise, Po. Come one step closer and it'll be by far the worse for you!' He glanced about himself at the shocked denizens of the chamber, and began to back towards the door, still keeping his gun on the man who had called himself Carstairs. 'I appear to be outnumbered for the moment, so I shall take my leave – but rest assured I shall return . . .'

At the door he paused, and fired a couple more shots into the ceiling. The crowd dived for cover.

'Justice shall prevail!' cried Sandford Groke, Special Agent, declaritively, and then vanished into the subterranean, alien night.

After he had gone, the man who had called himself Carstairs downed his drink. 'Bugger.'

'Well, that could have gone better,' said the RATI on his wrist. 'Could that have, in fact gone better? Yes, it could. Have we got a termination construct out there, locking onto the target even as we speak, ready and able to inexorably hunt the target down through fire, liquid nitrogen and a tool-die stamping press until the target's dead and jumped up and down on? No we have not. What we *have* got, at this point, is a disrupted and partially conditioned rogue construct out there somewhere, and Siva knows *what* might set its pattern-recognition off.'

The man who had called himself Carstairs rubbed at his aching nose. 'Yeah, OK RATI.' He pulled a small commslink unit from his belt. 'I'll get on to Volan. Maybe we can track it before it gets off planet and out of the system.' He brightened a little. 'Maybe we'll get lucky and it'll just self-destruct.'

PART THREE

A PORT OF CALL

The people are unreal. The flowers are unreal; they don't smell. The fruit is unreal; it doesn't taste of anything. The whole place is a glaring, gaudy, nightmarish set, built up in the desert.

Ethel Barrymore (1932)

15

BENNY UNDER THE SPYGLASS

The *Titanian Queen* translated through the singularity jump and began its exponential deceleration towards its second port of call, the planet Shokesh, and the horrible murders continued unabated. A man named Jason had indeed died – though not, quite fortunately, any Jason that one Bernice Summersdale (according to the passenger roster) had ever known. This particular Jason had not died, as was first thought, from the constriction of the ropes tying him to Frau von Lindt's chaise longue, but by an injection of strychnine to his upper left ventricle. The inconsolable Frau Lindt was released from custody on her own recognisance, and was currently considering several proposals of marriage from certain gentleman acquaintances.

Over the course of the next day and night, approximately thirty people died, if one included those whose bodies were simply never found. A Mr Simon Bevis and a Mr Iain M'Cord were two of these latter, disappearing from their respective cabins under circumstances remarkably similar to those of Jonathan A. Sheen, and having both in all probability met the same, as it were, unpleasant end.

A Mr David Doty was found in a generally similar state, but his wounds were such that informed observers were put in mind of a large, savage and carnivorous animal, even though there were no animals on the ship, save for the lapdogs and cats of various ladies in steerage. M. Emil Dupont opined that the wounds could only be the work of the Trained Midgets that had thus far eluded him, but this notion was largely condemned as implausible.

The Brigadier (Retired) Nathan Rogers, of the Tzar of Django's army, apparently committed suicide by banging his head against a bulkhead – and there the matter might have rested, had he not, before his death, dislodged his cabin's voice-link unit to the steward service, who reported a crazed babbling concerning penguins, intestines, dolphins, and something 'bloody enormous' coming for him. His cabin was subsequently found to contain vestigial traces of plybocyclitropomopzippedydoodadaine, a synthetic, or in technical terms a 'made-up', drug similar to that which, it had been discovered, had been placed in the *Titanian Queen*'s EVA suits, and which had done for the ship's officer Cherry.

A Mr Charles 'Chuck' Foster was found with his head bashed in, the only clue being, scrawled upon the cabin wall in Mr Foster's own blood and just above the mini-bar, the words: 'HUsh up whisky DRUNK.'

The remains of Mr Eric Kent were found in an entertainments lounge, the remote transceiver of a holo-display shoved up through the roof of his mouth with enormous force, so that the antennae protruded in a bloody tangle from the top of his skull.

A Mr Sean Gaffney was found, bare minutes before he expired, in the most advanced and nauseating extreme of drooling and incontinent senility, having ingested some substance that catastrophically accelerated this biological process. Mr Gaffney was twenty-seven years old.

A Mr Christopher Sweitzer was found with the heel of a stiletto shoe, of which he owned several, driven through the nape of his neck.

A Ms Piera Panix was found in the automated galleys, bubbling briskly in a large tureen of seafood *bouillabaisse*, which quite spoilt the flavour. Those who found the body, upon further investigation of the galleys, also found the body of a member of the ship's entertainment staff, an 'exotic' dancer who had gone by the name of Sabrina, smothered in melted chocolate and then left in the chilled cabinet for it to set.

A Mr Philip Alexander Hallard was found, stuffed and mounted, in a most distasteful tableau depicting his favourite habit, which was to go up to people, reverse his trouser pockets and ask them if they'd like to see the white and hairy elephant.

A Mr Alden Bates, or what was left of him, was discovered down in ship's engineering, to which he had somehow made his way even though he was a passenger. He had walked into – or had been *helped* into – a localized high-gravity field caused by the *Titanian Queen*'s propulsion mechanisms, which had summarily proceeded to squash him flat.

A Mr Daniel Frankham, an elderly gentleman who suffered severely from the cold, was roasted alive when a hand or hands unknown tampered with his thermal suit, so that it emitted microwaves rather than radiant heat.

A Mr Christopher J. Rednour was garrotted. A Mr Graham Nealon was found, as had been Mr Doty, seemingly eaten alive by animals – only in this case, from certain signs, it appeared that these animals had been small rodents, like rats. Or stoats. Or, quite possibly, particularly vicious hamsters. Animals of a sort also played a part in the death of a Miss Diane Schirf – and several of them were actually recovered: the swarm of cockroaches that appeared to have been attempting to burrow down her throat, and upon which she had choked.

A Miss Alison Tobin was found brutally hacked to death in what must have been an insane frenzy – but since, on further investigation, Miss Tobin was found to have been the young lady with a penchant for reading out her poetry in Percy's Discotheque, consensus of opinion was that this last death was completely unrelated to any other, with a perfectly obvious motive and any number of suspects. Particularly, these people felt, in light of the method of, not to put too fine a point upon it, the *disposal* of her poems after her death.

There were, in short, enough defenestrations to fill the *Titanian Queen*'s minimal medical facilities more than four times over. If this number of murders had taken place in a city, in the same week and all by what seemed to be the same hand, that city would be in a frenzy. Bands of vigilantes would be roaming the streets, ready to take their fear out on whoever looked the slightest bit suspicious. People would, in short, have been shooting the milkman through the front door. Within the self-contained little world of the *Titanian Queen*, however, things were different – and different in a way that defied all logic and reason.

Possibly it was the lack of some overall directive communication – the lack of tabloid news sheets and other media screaming things like: MURDERING SCUM STRIKES YET AGAIN!!! Possibly it was a group reaction to trauma, or denial – but whatever it was, it was a group social-dynamic that operated almost on the level of mass psychosis.

Quite simply, people who should have been terrified for their lives carried on with the recreational business of the cruise. They frequented the hastily renovated dining rooms as though a significant portion of their number had not exploded all over them; they frequented the casino chambers, the ballroom, the shuffleboard decks, the observation lounge . . . and if the laughter and the entertainments in them held a shrill and slightly desperate edge, they did not seem to notice. It was not as if they were oblivious to the latest discovery of a body, or the latest person to take a drink, clutch his or her throat and fall over – it was as if these deaths held the unreal, strangely comfortable quality as one might find, for example, in a mystery by Christie or James. If you had asked them, individually, they would have been shocked and horrified by the latest atrocity of the Cat's Paw – there was no doubt in the general mind that this *was* the work of that master criminal – but shocked and horrified in a fascinated kind of way that held an irrational but absolute certainty that none of these accumulating deaths would be theirs.

The great detectives, in much this same unreal spirit, made it their business to investigate every incident, to question absolutely everyone who might be involved, in the hope of at last getting to the bottom of the whole nasty business . . .

Benny again stayed in her cabin, so far as was physically possible.

In a marked contrast to the time she had spent in it before, however, she kept it neat and tidy, and made sure she didn't let herself go. It was only after she caught herself scrubbing out the bath for the fifth time that she realized what was happening to her and consciously made herself stop it.

She attacked, if that was the right word, the Olabrian joy-luck crystal with a new vigour, and with the precise control of clenched anger. A large part of this came from the fact that the damn thing was responsible for her being here in the first place, but more of it was to do with the fact that, at a point slightly over halfway completed, it began to talk.

'*Consider the Universal Harmony of Life,*' it might say, in sonorous if slightly cracked tones. '*It comes from Nothing and returns to Nothing, Complete and Perfect in its Cyclic Unity.*'

Or:

'*The Eternal must always be So; for how else must one Measure the True minuscule Significance of Mortal Span.*'

Or:

'*All Struggle must Cease, in the Unknowable face of the Unending Cosmic Equipoise.*'

Benny, who in her time had seen more of the Universal Whosis Doobery Cosmic Whatsit than most, had never heard such a bunch of unmitigated old tosh in her life. It was as if someone had put together a collection of the most asinine platitudes they could find and run them through a Markov chainer. She wondered if this was a kind of default, self-diagnostic mode, and things would improve the nearer the crystal came to completion. She hoped it didn't mean that the original disassembly in the theatre had broken the thing beyond repair, or that she was somehow missing a small but vital piece of the puzzle.

The painstaking work of its reconstruction, though, was constantly hindered by interruptions. Each of the great detectives had come to call, and, mindful of the circumstances, the precautions against being horribly murdered upon opening the door to anyone were both time-consuming and stressful. Benny might not have minded if they had seemed to advance the case in any way, but they seemed to be nothing more than unconstructive and increasingly bizarre encounters. Emil Dupont had comfortably and complacently sat in one of her armchairs, knocking out his pipe on a table and completely missing the ashtray, and tried to convince her that she had committed each and every murder as part of a complicated scheme to place herself upon the throne of the home of the late Mister Dickie, Plumptious Minor, and to lay her hands upon its fabled Tickling Stick of Office. Benny lost track of the specific mechanics of said scheme, but especially trained humanoids of a relatively diminutive size were of course involved.

Miss Agatha Magpole merely looked at Benny vaguely, and imparted the information that she had had eggs for her tea. This took place while Miss Magpole's companion carefully restrained Benny, and then herself, and by way of a remote contrivance of manipulator arms removed the elderly lady's special brainwave hat. After the hat was replaced, and Benny stopped shouting about how she was going to murder everybody with a big gun, the companion explained that this was a reaction only experienced by those who were not, in fact, murderers. Benny supposed that she should feel relieved that she was not the culprit in the eyes of Miss Magpole at least – but this was tempered by the fact that the brain connected to them would forget that in a matter of minutes, if it had ever been truly aware of it in the first place.

The only detective who didn't visit her was Khaarli, which

was just her luck, since he was the only one of the lot of them that she would have been quite pleased to see.

The final investigatorial visitation was in fact a pair: Detective Second-Class Interchange and Sandford Groke, who seemed to have seconded him, and treated him with a kind of supercilious contempt bred of an innate inability to comprehend him as an equal. The special agent himself seemed none the worse for wear after questioning the perilous Frau von Lindt, but he seemed if anything even more tight-lipped and clenched. He glared at Benny with a white-hot, barely restrained but somehow impotent inner rage that seemed to be directed at the world itself rather than her. Benny suspected that she just happened to be what he was looking at.

'Well?' She gestured languidly about the cabin. 'As you can plainly see, this is all I possess. This is it. There is no more. Would you care to rifle through my accommodations and movables now, or would you like them in a bag for later?'

Interchange briefly fumbled through some of the clothes in the wardrobe, blushing a fetching beetroot-red as his fingers encountered various silky and lacy things. There were probably a thousand places to hide small items within their folds – but there was no physical way that the cabin could conceal the sheer amount of impedimenta that would be related to the murders. You would probably need several cabins stacked to the ceiling.

'That won't be necessary, ma'am,' he said, turning from the closet with some slight air of relief. He hunted through the pockets of his suit until he eventually unearthed a dog-eared, spiral-bound notebook, which he flipped open and scrutinized. Benny tried to glance at the contents without being too obvious about it, but all she received was an impression of smudgy, aimless doodling, shopping lists and the like.

'The fact is,' Interchange continued, 'we have been trying to ascertain exactly who you are.'

Benny suddenly went slightly cold. 'Oh yes?'

Interchange nodded. 'We know nothing about you, save that you've spent most of your time in your cabin suite. We've enquired of all the members of the better families, and none of them appear to have even *heard* of the name Summersdale...'

Benny warmed up again. 'And that's *it*, is it? Tell me, have you once thought to check my name in the GalNet databases?'

Interchange fumbled with his collar, embarrassed. 'As of this time the ships communications seem to be inconvenienced. The null-space transub ... transobulatio ... the thing where we go from one bit of the galaxy to another.'

Thank Goddess for small mercies, thought Benny. 'Well let me tell you this,' she said. 'I have no idea what your so-called "better" class of people might think, but if you contacted the GalNet directories and ran a search on the Summersdales, do you know what you'd find?'

'What would I find?' Interchange said, with the air of one who is suddenly, vaguely, worried that he might not like the answer.

'Absolutely nothing,' said Benny.

The detective second-class looked at her with a sudden expression of panic. 'Nothing?'

'Nothing. That's how rich the Summersdales are.'

'I've had enough of this!' This last came from Groke, and came in a hateful and almost completely unexpected snarl. Benny stepped back in startlement, staring at the now almost literally murderous gleam in his eyes. In addition to his inherent all-body clench, he now clenched and unclenched his hands as if waiting for the merest opportunity to put them around someone's throat and squeeze.

'Inspector Carstairs,' he snapped, jerking his head in the direction of Interchange. 'Restrain this deceitful hussy before she can further ensnare us with her wiles!'

He turned his mad eyes back to Benny, and inched forward as she backed off with a hand outstretched and groping for some convenient heavy and hopefully blunt implement. 'We have a way of dealing with spies, Miss so-called Summersdale, so confess your plans or it's the chair and the length of rubber hose for you. Do you think I do not know that you are yet another minion under the employ of the fiendish Doctor –'

'*What?*' Benny exclaimed, in utter astonishment. She had once, for quite some time, had the acquaintance of a being going under that particular medical *sobriquet*. On the whole, for a number of reasons, she preferred not to think about that period of her life – and to hear that name dropped into circumstances such as these shocked her more than a little. 'What did you say?'

Groke was now staring at her with a kind of shocked confusion, as if he had been physically slapped in the face. It seemed that her outburst had derailed whatever compulsive line of thought his mind had been following, and snapped him back to some degree of self. He gave a convulsive shudder, and wiped at his brow with the back of his hand.

'Forgive me,' he said, in a slightly shaken voice. 'I cannot imagine what came over me. An aberration, nothing more – possibly a result of the strain we are all currently under.'

Benny did not know why, but she had an idea that she could trust this abrupt change in manner just about as far as one could throw a lead-weighted marmoset digging its claws in. It was not precisely that the special agent was thinking one thing and pretending to another: it was, somehow, as if some half-buried, unacknowledged part of his brain were making the rest of it think and fundamentally *be* the correct thing.

'Come, Carstairs,' he snapped, snapping his fingers under the slightly startled Interchange's nose, then turned on his heel and headed briskly for the hatch. 'Can't hang around here all day,' he declared. 'We have a murderer to thwart, a villain of such foul and devious cunning that not one of us is safeguarded from his devilish snares . . .' He struck a manly pose and stuck a pontificatory finger in the air. 'But he will be brought to book, oh yes – or my name's not Sandford Groke!'

Interchange shot Benny a confused, despairing look, and then hurried to catch up with the strangely acting special agent. After a while, Benny wandered over to a chair and sat down, one eye thoughtfully on the hatch.

'Why do I get the feeling,' she said, to the furniture and fitments in general, 'that we're all in danger of *seriously* losing the plot?'

Things were going rogue: complication piled upon complication, the chain of events tangled together and lashing wildly. At some point they must surely snap and slice through anyone who happened to be innocently standing by. For the first time since these murders had started – for the first time since the death of Krugor, which she had somehow filed away on a different emotional level – Benny felt actively threatened.

Possibly, it was time to do what she had been putting off for far too long now, and make a certain call.

16

THE FEAST OF TRUTH AND LIES

The planet of Shokesh existed with a highly specialized and refined, tourist-based economy. In itself a desert planet, it had no spacefaring technology of its own over the interplanetary level. Over the course of centuries, however, it had built up an extensive and remarkably sophisticated culture based upon the wreckage of a large number of starships from other systems, which fortunately – for Shokesh – had run aground in its system's uncommonly heavy asteroid field. The asteroids were now, of course, safely charted, and it was this fact that had opened up Shokesh to the tourist trade.

It was a patchwork, almost cargo-cult culture – and therein lay its appeal. It was as if some blind craftsman had intended to construct some workaday mosaic from any old junk that had happened to be lying around and – all unaware of the material's true value – had included scraps of platinum and gold, shards of jade, the fragments of fractured precious gems and jewels.

It was a place of mighty zigzag mud-brick ziggurats, of lofty towers and minarets and dreaming if not actively and hallucinatorily deranged spires. Of hanging gardens and twisting thoroughfares and temple edifices carved with gentlemen and young ladies in the act of performing extremely athletic activities, fit to make a spinster or a gentleman of moral rectitude blush, and often feel the need for a lie down.

The markets of the planet's major city were justly famous the entire sector over: a brawling, raucous mass of merchandise from the conceptual corners of the known universe; anything you wanted, anything you could imagine, could be bought here. Anything at all.

Benny had expected any excursions that might have been planned on Shokesh to be cancelled – and had been more than a little surprised to find that this was not the case. Thinking about it, she thought she knew why. Part of it was simply the mass shock of the murders, the social momentum that was keeping things, on the surface at least, carrying on more or less as usual – but mostly it was for practical and pragmatic reasons. The owners of United Spaceways were being paid good money to run them, and so they damn well would.

Additionally, she thought, there was also the point that it would be just as easy – far *more* easy – for the murderer (or murderers) to murder whoever they were going to murder in a murder aboard ship. There was also no real chance of the culprit or culprits using planet-fall to make their escape – the *Titanian Queen* was currently the only passenger vessel orbiting the planet, and would be so for several weeks. The fact that if the murderer *did* make his escape then everybody else could breathe a sigh of relief, was neither here nor there.

In any case, for the next few days there would be shuttle excursions operating to the planet on an hourly basis – and as the first one docked at the disembarking hatches (with especial care taken that the air-exchange did not contain lethal doses of hallucinogenic compounds) Benny was there, waiting for it, ID chips in her hand and first in the queue.

She was not going there to sample the tourist-trap sights and the displays of histrionic local history and culture – in fact she was going to do her level best to ignore them. She had a plan, a plan that had been nebulously formed when the diamond belonging to the Dowager Duchess of Gharl had been stolen, and which had solidified after she had made her call over the null-space link. She intended to learn something entirely else on Shokesh.

She was not disappointed.

The route to the *Titanian Queen*'s communications room led past the purser's office, and Benny had seen that Detective Interchange had tripled the guard; if the fact of six burly constables outside of the hatch was any indication. Benny had been willing to lay short odds that one would be hardly able to breathe inside for the weight of compressed coppers. Ah well, at least the contents of the purser's safe were perfectly secure.

The comms room had been functional and packed with heavy-duty, utilitarian equipment – all of which, looking at it, Benny had seen to be just as fake as the antique decor of the ballroom. A paying customer expected something vital like a ship's communications to *look* functional, and therefore trustworthy. The communications officer, in the traditional costume uniform of a Technical Expert – stained canvas slacks and T-shirt with faded emoticons and an ancient Schwa logo stencilled on it, hair and beard like an exploding greasy scouring pad, a name tag with the name STROSS hanging from his neck – seemed genuinely harried all the same.

'If you want to make a call, you're out of luck,' he said.

Benny got the impression that he was rapidly approaching the if-one-more-bugger-asks stage. He seemed, not to put too fine a point on it, not a little peeved.

'How so?' she asked. 'I'd have thought we'd have been in range of the boosters long before now.'

This exchange concerned the same difficulties to which Detective Second-Class Interchange had alluded before, in her cabin. Benny had known about them perfectly well – but had been following the sound advice of never telling a policeman more than is absolutely necessary.

The processes needed to boost a signal containing reliable data across interstellar distances, faster than the speed of light, required installations far too massive for a ship to carry – this was in fact why the *Titanian Queen* had been effectively incommunicado in the spaces between the stars. Now, as they began the final entry into the Shokesh system, there should have been no problem at all.

'We have a problem with the transisantiantional vectoring.' Technical Officer Stross gestured vaguely at a mocked-up bit of radio gear. 'The sine-damping retro-oscillator and the dritrium crystal's blown to hell. We can't even pump back a Phase Three signal wave. You get the picture?'

Benny looked at him levelly. 'Leg. Pull the other one. Bells are quite possibly attached.'

Technical Officer Stross shrugged. 'The bloody ARVID's pissing about again, and the comms are routed through it. We don't get a word out until it decides to play.'

Benny raised an eyebrow. 'Harveed?'

'A-R-V-I-D.' Stross pointed to a small, almost unnoticeable junction box fixed to the bulkhead, from which tacked traceries of cable ran to all the units. 'You can have a go if you like. What do I care? Just talk into one of the boxes, doesn't matter which.' He shrugged again. 'Or if you want the semblance of privacy, use the booth. Doesn't make a sod's worth of difference, but it makes people feel more comfortable.'

In the ostensibly private booth, Benny examined what appeared to be a comms console. From the tiny signs one gets when rapping one with the fingernails, she had already ascertained that there were no real workings inside.

'You're ARVID, right?' she said to it.

A small pause, then: 'Good morning. Ms Summersdale. Or is it Ms Summerfield? Or *Mrs* Summerfield-Kane? I must confess that I can never quite remember.'

The voice was drawling, sardonic, utterly self-assured.

Benny quashed a little chill, of the same sort she had experienced when Interchange had asked her who she really was. The trick, she felt, was not to show surprise. This could in fact make things simpler.

'If you know who I am,' she said, quite calmly, 'then you know who I'm working for in this case. You know who and what's behind me. Is that enough to get me a call?'

ARVID made a kind of tut-tutting noise, of the kind used to convey that one is keeping another in suspense and enjoying it. 'The pleasure, "Ms Summersdale", is all mine. Please feel free to proceed. I cannot, of course, promise that I won't listen in.'

There was something about this ARVID's voice that worried Benny. It was not so much that is was putting on an act, but rather – and rather like the accent of the late Mr Dickie Prekodravac – it was of someone speaking in the tones of what had once, at some point, been an act.

'Don't worry about it,' she told the ARVID. 'I suspect that the parties I'm calling, they'll take care of the security their end.'

Now, Benny wandered through the market streets of Shokesh, her ears battered by the sputter and bang, the crash and clash of fireworks, snare drums and cymbals, her eyes assaulted by swirling streamers and shimmering scraps of costume that would have those wearing it, in a less than temperate climate, all catching cold. Her nostrils were filled with the reek of chargrilled meats, and the flesh of amphibious things that lived in jungle pools.

Today, apparently, was the Festival of Truth and Lies, a time-honoured day in the Shokesh year, in which the inhabitants put on a show for any visiting tourists who might happen to be watching. Tomorrow was going to be the Mardi Gras of Household Gods, and the day after that – if the *Titanian Queen* had remained here – would have been the Bacchanal of Cheese and Wine. On the whole, Benny thought, she was sorry to miss that one. Rennet-processed cow-juice products notwithstanding.

On the other hand, things could have been worse. The simple fact was that *every* day when a ship hung over the planet was a Festival day for the happy, laughing souls of

Shokesh – another day for the estimable work of transferring credit from the pockets of off-worlders and into their own, on an industrial basis. In the height of the season, when there could be as many as twenty ships in the sky per day, and the collective Shokesh imagination slightly strained, there might be the Carnival of Mice, the Jubilee of Sliding Jack and the Day of the Dolphin, all happening simultaneously, in different quarters, with the native personnel involved hurrying from one to another with barely time for a costume change and a crafty cough and a drag at the back of the flats.

Benny wove her way through a small procession of horselike-creature-drawn floats, each containing blossom-bedecked statues depicting some multidextrous god or goddess in some evidently characteristically archetypical pose. At length, she turned off into a side alley – little more than a dark crack between two magnificent edifices. The alley was barely wide enough to allow the passage of a single person, and in the small amount of light she made out rough and disrepaired brickwork, elderly electrical wiring and exposed plumbing.

The alley opened out into a street far less splendid than any she had yet encountered: not exactly dirty, but of the functional and slightly grubby sort as might be found in the industrial areas of any planet. Those who inhabited it were dressed casually, in a way that reminded Benny somewhat of film technicians compared with the costumed actors on a set, or stagehands in a theatre.

As she walked, she received a couple of slightly surprised glances, but these were supplanted by a kind of cautious unconcern. If some tourist had taken it into her head to have a look behind the scenes, it was her lookout and hardly their concern. Falling foul of the dangers of the hidden places was, in a sense, also the natural lot of a tourist.

After some small while, Benny stopped at an intersection and hunted for a street sign. She had spent an instructive ten minutes aboard the *Titanian Queen* with a local street map, had sketched a map of her own on the torn-out flyleaf of

Kryptosa's *Lost Gods and the Fall of Empire*, and merely needed to get her bearings.

Besides, she thought, she had been given comprehensive if a little dubious directions as to where she wanted to go.

The call had been a slightly strange experience, on rather more levels than she currently wanted to think about. She had entered the GalNet code and blipped through several connection and firewall-status screens in the space of a second. Then the image had dissolved into that of a face, female and very beautiful, in a tough, foxy kind of way that certain people might call wicked or even actively vicious – had it not been currently etched with lines of tension and worry. Benny had tried to pick some detail out of the background, but it remained indistinct. Whether this was because of the communication unit's depth of focus or by transputronic masking, she couldn't tell. Things seemed to be moving in the background, though.

'What do you want *now*, Kir?' the foxy little face snapped. Then it realized that it wasn't talking to this Kir, whoever this Kir actually was, and jolted with shock 'Who the hell are *you*?'

'I . . .' Benny was taken aback. For some strange reason, making this call had clenched her stomach like a fist and put a lump in her throat, which couldn't have been her heart, because that was currently hammering at the roof of her mouth. 'I must have a wrong code,' she said lamely. 'I was trying for a man named Jason . . .'

The girl on the other end of the intraspatial line snorted. 'Figures.' Abruptly, she composed her face into the synthetically friendly, limitedly helpful lines of an incorporate receptionist and said, in a completely different tone from before, 'I'm afraid that Mr Kane is in an important meeting at the moment, and likely to be unavailable for the rest of the day. If you'd like, I can connect you with our Mr Trask, who can handle any queries you might have about Dead Dog in the Water Preproductions with full authority. Or, if it's a . . .

personal matter, I can take a message for his earliest possible convenience.'

Her tone was so perfectly and courteously contrived that it could only be an act – not in the sense of automatic corporate lies, but in the sense of someone putting on a role under extreme pressure.

'Tell Mr Summerfield-Kane,' Benny said coldly, 'that a Professor Bernice Summerfield called. That's *Summerfield*, as in his – extremely fortunately, I might add – ex-wife.'

The girl did a classic double take, and then peered out of the screen at her with a mixture of suspicion, surprise and, Benny fancied, some small degree of jealous spite. 'So you're Benny? I've heard a lot about you. I suppose you can prove who you are?'

'Ask me anything,' Benny said. 'Embarrassing personal details about the little sod, for preference.'

At that point, the picture jolted, possibly the result of something landing heavily in a vehicle and jarring the suspension. Then a new and urgent voice snapped, 'I've got the package, Mira. Nasty people are wanting it back even as we speak. Time to make like the Vermicious Knids, yeah?'

'What?' said the girl, who had turned to stare at something out of shot.

'Never mind. Doesn't matter. Let's just scram, OK?'

'OK.' The girl leant forward, her out-of-shot hands (from the movements of her shoulders) obviously punching at controls. From the speaker of the comms unit came the sound of accelerating turbines. The girl glanced back at the pick-up. 'Things are moving. Tell him yourself, yes?'

A moment of jarring confusion on the screen – the connection was obviously being handled by a portable unit at the other end. The picture settled down again, and she found herself looking at the face of her ex-husband, Jason.

'Benny!' he exclaimed. Even by his standards, he looked a mess: unshaven and exhausted. A huge, purple bruise disfigured the left side of his face, his eyebrow was split and bleeding and his skin was marked by powder burns. After his moment of surprise, his mouth widened into an easy grin.

'Shit!' he shouted, dabbing at his mouth with the back of a scorched and dirty hand. The grin had opened up a split in his lip and made it bleed. 'Big soddy bollocking bloody shit on toast with extra shit and no toast!'

Benny stared at him. His appearance, and what she had gleaned from his exchange with this Mira person, had opened up a whole raft of questions, and she didn't quite know quite where to start.

'I see your language hasn't improved, at any rate,' she said, more or less just for something to say.

'Yeah, well,' said Jason. 'I never had the education, did I? I had to pick things up as I went along.'

'You can say that again.' Benny forced herself to stop it. Completely trashed relationship or not, a bicker with Jason bloody Kane could happily go on all week and be ended in one of only two ways – either of which, if attempted on the person of a mounted comms unit, would result in painful bruising, extreme embarrassment or both.

'Look,' she said. 'I can see you're busy at the moment. I just wanted to see if you have any thoughts on something that seems up your street. It isn't important.'

Jason winced as the image began to judder – the vehicle he and the Mira girl were in was obviously in motion now, and moving very quickly. From his posture, Benny got the idea that there might be something more wrong with him, physically, than just his facial injuries. If there was, though, he was masking it pretty well – which was a little odd, she thought, since Jason Kane was capable of screaming the house down if he so much as stubbed his toe.

Jason appeared to recover from his momentary lapse and gave her his friendly if slightly forced grin again. 'Hey, no problem.' He shot a glance to where, presumably, Mira was operating the vehicle. 'I don't have much to do for the moment. It's all in Mira's capable and lovely hands . . .'

'Up yours, sweetheart,' said the voice of Mira. Something about the tone in which she said it made Benny feel the sudden urge to track her down and duff her up severely. The next time she and Jason met in the flesh, there were going to be some serious questions asked, possibly at knifepoint.

'... and I could do with the distraction, frankly,' Jason said. 'I'm all ears. What was it you wanted to ask me about?'

Now, a few hours later, Benny followed her sketch of the directions he had given her, walking through the backstreets of the real Shokesh until she came to a street seemingly like any other, if relatively less frequented. It was the street, if the directions and the signs could be believed, of the Proudly Pontificating Feline. Cat Street, as Jason had called it.

Every city on every human-colonized planet in the galaxy had streets like this. Streets where certain criminal activities occurred; crimes of a sort that happened behind closed doors; doors that only those who know about them would find, and find unlocked. Unless you knew which ones they were, you'd never find them – and if you went looking experimentally, you'd find one hell of a lot more than you were trying to bargain for.

The point was that in certain, specialized circumstances, one didn't have to know *which* doors they were. One only had to know the general area.

Simply hanging around on streets like this, Benny knew, could be hazardous to one's health to say the least. The concerns that operated here commonly did not bother those who did not bother them – but unexplained loiterers attracted suspicion, and a rough-and-ready method of acting upon it. Fortunately, among the quasi-legitimate businesses, there was a café of sorts, the window of which offered a panoramic view of the street. Benny wandered into it, playing the part of a simple tourist who had strayed out of the tourist zone and needed a small rest and a cup of cinnamon tea before returning to it.

The other patrons of the establishment did not appear to give her a second glance, but she felt attention on her, if not actual eyes. She stretched her tea and snack of a sticky bun, made from some form of reconstituted maize, as far as possible, but the time rapidly approached when she was going to have to think of something else.

It was at that point that a figure walked past the window – a figure dressed differently from the one Benny had seen before, in a scuffed jacket of some artificial leather and worn working jeans, a large holdall of heavy-gauge polymer mesh slung over one shoulder – but Benny recognized the figure all the same. She left the dregs of her cinnamon tea and headed for the door, fighting to conceal any haste from the watchful denizens of the café. Through the door, she quickly scanned the street for the figure's departing back.

She needn't have bothered. The figure was standing outside, waiting for her.

Benny had run this confrontation several times through her head, trying to come up with an idea of what to expect, but had eventually settled on nothing. An exciting and strenuous chase through the brawling streets of Shokesh, complete with overturned street-side stalls, humourously bisected Chinese dragons and smashed boxes of squawking chickens? Vehement protestations of innocence? An attempt to silence her by way of strangulation or a cunningly concealed blade? Mindful of this last, Benny found herself dropping into the loose but watchful semi-crouch she had learnt during her childhood stint in the military, ready for any threatening move.

Instead of any of this, however, the figure simply shrugged and sighed.

'All right. Fine,' said the Cat's Paw, calmly. 'Shall we go somewhere and talk?'

17

THE REMOVAL AND DISPOSAL OF CERTAIN MASQUES

The people of Shokesh derived from many different cultures, and had the knack of blending them together down to an art. A hint of the exotic to attract the tourists tempered with a generic kind of blandness that avoided their taking one look and then running away.

In a mock-Zendacian émigré taberna, on one of the 'quaint little sidestreets' running off from the main thoroughfare of the tourist zone of the Shokesh settlement, Benny sipped a tall and cooling glass of a kind of retsina analogue spiked up with grain ethanol.

'I made a call to a . . . ah, a friend,' she said. 'He has an in to the more sneaky criminal stuff in this sector, and he confirmed some of the things I was wondering about. He used an analogy based on certain rather special factors in his life, but which meant something to me, but it wouldn't mean anything to you . . .'

'Try me,' said the Cat's Paw, who now exuded a relaxed and innate kind of inner strength and confidence, utterly at odds with the person Benny remembered from before. 'You might be surprised.'

'The London Underground,' said Benny, fully expecting to

have to waste five minutes now on irrelevancies. 'That was –'

'I know what the London Underground was.' The Cat's Paw waved a dismissive hand. 'And at some point I might just possibly tell you how. Go on.'

Benny shrugged. 'OK. Fine. The important point about the London Underground was that, when they came to make the map, they found that they had problems. It was a confusing mess. It actually made the process of trying to find your way around the system more difficult. Then some bright spark realized that the only important thing about a subterranean transit system with discrete stops was the *relationship* between them. You only have to know which are connected to which and in what order. So they distorted the physical map and made it work in the sense that mattered. It was a masterpiece of abstract design.'

Benny waved away a sudden alien mariachi band, who seemed to be under the impression that she and the Cat's Paw were a couple in love, and signalled to a Zendacian waiter in a pressurized rubber simulation of a tuxedo for another drink. 'The only problem was, because it was such a useful representation, that people tended to forget it was in one sense a distortion, and try to map it directly onto physical reality. There might be two stations within a hundred metres of each other, say, and rather than simply walk it, people would go down three flights of steps and an escalator, wander through a warren until they found the right platform, wait for a train, take the train, even change lines and take another train, get off and climb up through an entire station again – all because the map said that was the way to get to where they wanted to go.'

Benny ordered another drink. She supposed that she should keep a clear head and watch for potential tricks, but then again, if the Cat's Paw had wanted her dead, she'd be long dead by now. Besides, the consumption of alcohol in quantities moderate enough not to have you falling over, throwing up and blanking aided a certain type of thought –

that of stringing elements together in a kind of conversational dance, making them cohere and revolve without the kind of clogging, trainspotting focus upon the minutiae that prevented one from seeing the full picture. 'The point is that our current, *overt* systems of space travel work like that. You get on a ship *here*, you get off it *there*, and you forget that the overtly scheduled ships aren't the only things in interstellar space. The Goddess knows they aren't the only things, and I certainly do from direct experience. There are ships in their thousands out there, military-spec and otherwise, based upon entirely different technologies – but they've become invisible.' Benny gestured around the patrons of the taberna: all, obviously, passengers from the *Titanian Queen*. 'We were all let off the ship because of the implicit assumption that there were, quote, no other ships here at the moment, unquote, and so the Cat's Paw wouldn't be able to make his or her escape – but you and I know that isn't really the case.'

The Cat's Paw sipped from a glass of chilled wine and nodded. 'So?'

'So if the Cat's Paw wanted to escape, there was no way anyone could stop him or, indeed her, and it was all entirely academic. But then, I thought, what if for reasons of his or her own, the Cat's Paw wanted to stay with the ship? What if he or she –' Benny looked pointedly in the direction of the large holdall nestling under the table beside the Cat's Paw's feet. 'What if he or she simply wanted to get rid of certain incriminating evidence that might be found in a really thorough search? The same factors hold true – if people have the idea that merchandise can't be fenced on to the interstellar market from Shokesh, they're hardly going to search for it on people coming down here. The real purpose of the call to my friend was to confirm that such a transaction was possible and, if so, where. My friend told me it was, and that the most likely place was one of several establishments he'd heard tell of on Cat Street.'

Benny looked at the Cat's Paw smugly. 'So much in detective work involves being in the right place at the right time – but any damned fool can go to the right place and wait. The "merchandise", of course, being every single item of jewellery that was, at one point, in the purser's safe.'

The Cat's Paw regarded Benny levelly, and then nodded with composure, as if this had been expected all along. 'And have you any idea how this was done?'

'In general, yes,' said Benny. 'It was the same general process of inversion that he or she used to steal the Olabrian joy-luck crystal from Marcus Krytell's mansion. The sheer number of discrete elements made it appear more complex, but the process was as simple and blatantly obvious.'

'Obvious?' The Cat's Paw raised a sardonic eyebrow. '*C'est moi?*'

Benny found herself smiling back despite herself. 'Call it elegance, then.' She waved a hand dismissively, emulating the recent languid gesture of the Cat's Paw with some slight degree of irony. 'As you well know, the evolvement of security countermeasures is a bit like an arms race – you know: you build a better bomb, so somebody builds a better shelter, so you have to build a better bomb and so on, *ad infinitum*.' She climbed her flattened hands up each other in a kind of lateral game of potatoes. 'Shell upon shell upon shell of sophistication as you push the envelope out – with the result that whatever's in the *middle* of the envelope gets forgotten and atrophies. So what I think you did was this: you sent in some android or robotic device, some kind of simulacrum, anyway – you loaded it with infiltration devices *just under* the cutting-edge level of Krytell's security system – and while the really heavy-duty stuff was occupied dealing with it, you simply strolled in naked, lifted the crystal and strolled out again.' Benny shrugged. 'Like I said, simple.'

The Cat's Paw grinned at her with a respect that was almost friendly. 'I actually wore a pair of shorts and a shirt, and you forgot to mention the unassisted swim to the mainland.'

'You swam it?' Benny frowned.

'I wasn't in any hurry. The sea was warm and buoyant. It only took a local day and a half.'

Benny nodded thoughtfully. 'By which time the search radius would have blipped past you on several levels and they were concentrating on your prerecorded ransom demand.'

The Cat's Paw poured another chilled wine from the bottle. 'Close enough. There were a lot of little tricks to make it work. I won't bore you with the details. You've got the basic idea.'

'And it's a good one,' Benny said. 'And for my next trick, I can tell you how it was adapted for the *Titanian Queen*.' Again, she indicated the holdall on the floor. 'Tell you what, though: just to keep it vaguely entertaining and give me a chance to drink something, why don't you tell *me* how I worked it out?'

'I'd imagine that your first related suspicion,' said the Cat's Paw, 'would be when you found yourself experiencing an unaccountable blank patch in your memory, that first time when you sequestered yourself away in your cabin, after the death of your manservant. From what I've researched about you (and I've studied you a lot, since I ascertained that Krytell was going to use you as a courier), I know that you've been in situations involving violent death before. You can recognize and deal with the shock and subliminal trauma they cause – and there must have been something that wasn't quite right with these episodes. Thoughts of some anaesthetic gas being pumped through the ventilation systems might have crossed your mind, but the idea must have been pretty formless; you had nothing concrete to pin it on, and it could simply have been exhaustion after all – you were pushing yourself pretty hard at that point, attempting to piece together the fragments of the artefact you had been placed aboard the *Titanian Queen* to recover.

'You learnt of the attempted break-in to the purser's safe but, again, this was simply a background thing, merely feeding your general suspicion. Why would a criminal as notoriously dexterous as the Cat's Paw make such a bungled attempt, thus guaranteeing that the safe would then be guarded day and night? And, for that matter, why make the attempt so early on in the cruise? Even if it were successful, there would be a limited number of places to hide such a haul on board; a sufficiently detailed search would be bound to turn it up.

'Your first *active* clue came at the dinner you attended, when the Star of Saint Timothy was stolen from the Dowager Duchess of Gharl. The subsequent horrible murders by detonation must have confused things a little, but you must have realized that these deaths seemed to be random, while the theft of the Star of Timothy was specific. So what, specifically, was the difference between the Star of Timothy and the jewellery worn by everyone else in the dining hall? And what could the theft of it in such a blatant manner possibly achieve but to have the guard increased on the safe where every other item of genuine jewellery was being kept?

'As I said, so many of these clues were masked by the confusion of the horrible murders. They were something else entirely, and it was a matter of separating what was relevant from what was not. You began to wonder again about your strange lapse of memory in your cabin. If this had been a common experience, surely other people would have recalled, as it were, similar instances during the investigations by and of them – it is, after all an absolute cliché in murder-mystery fiction: the unaccountable loss of time in which one, all unawares, might have really *been* the murderer ...

'Nothing of that was evident at all. You were forced to the conclusion that your lapse had been unique. So in what other way might you have been unique at the time in which it occurred?

'Armed with these relatively solid if speculative facts, you were then able to make inferences. You were able to advance tentative theories as to a sequence of events:

'The break-in to the safe was not bungled. The Cat's Paw's expertise was such that he or she was perfectly capable of entering and leaving without trace. There then remained the possibility – the probability – that someone might at some point feel the need to check on the contents, and that the theft would be discovered – and so, utilizing the burgling skills for which he or she was justly famous, the Cat's Paw broke into the cabins of those who owned the jewels, and exchanged them for the reproductions that were used for show aboard ship. Of all these people, only a "Ms Bernice Summersdale" was finding it impossible to sleep, thus necessitating the use of anaesthetic gas.

'The Cat's Paw *then* placed the fake jewels inside the safe, and tampered with it so that it appeared an attempt at a break-in had been made. Thus, for the remainder of the jump, the forces of law and order would concentrate upon the safe and its now worthless contents. And since the various passengers had no idea that their apparently imitation jewels had been exchanged for the genuine article, they took no care of them, left them lying around – thus making it simplicity itself for the Cat's Paw to go through the cabins as their inhabitants left to visit the planet of Shokesh, harvesting the spoils with hardly any risk at all.

'The only real risk – the only mistake, as it turned out – was to go after the Star of Timothy, the only genuine item of jewellery that had not gone through this process. That provided a focus for all your nebulous suspicion, gave it a hook to hang it on.'

The Cat's Paw sat back and finished off the wine. 'Most of all that is neither here nor there, of course. It doesn't really matter whether you came up with that precise theory or not. The important point was that you intimated that such a crime was *possible* – and this led you to Cat Street to wait for me.' The Cat's Paw leant forward again and regarded Benny steadily. 'So the question now remains: what are you going to do about it now? Are you going to turn me in? It's obvious that you don't think I did all these horrible murders.'

Benny looked at the Cat's Paw warily. 'No. I don't think you did. Not all of them. Everything I've seen or heard about the Cat's Paw shows an active aversion to killing. I don't think you'd have it in you, ordinarily.'

'Meaning?' the Cat's Paw said, sharply.

'I mean what about *Krugor*?' Benny said. 'You haven't even mentioned him. I can see how it might have happened. He was one of Krytell's security operatives and he was using me as bait for you. He tried to capture you, there was a struggle and –'

'No!'

The fist pounded on the table hard enough to make the bottles bounce, and the mariachi band across the room lurch into momentary confusion. Benny flinched back, more from the sheer blazing power of the anger in the criminal's eyes than from any actual threat.

'I arranged for you to find the crystal,' the Cat's Paw said, in the low tones of utter but controlled fury, 'and I simply left it there for you to find. The death of your manservant, Krytell's man, had nothing to do with my plans for Krytell or anyone else. I planned the theft of the crystal, the exchange and my other escapade aboard the *Titanian Queen* in great detail, over months – but it seems I have been guided in them, in subtle ways that even I can't see. Someone or something has killed these people and is trying to blame it all on *me*.'

Something of the construction of this last, something of the tone, suddenly put Benny in mind of a frightened child protesting its innocence of something that it hadn't done – that it *knew* it hadn't done – in the face of the purely circumstantial but somehow vast and insurmountable evidence of adults. Benny fiddled with a place mat in the form of a tourist's idea of a space pirate's chart showing the perils of the asteroid field that encircled the Shokesh system, to avoid looking in the Cat's Paw's eyes.

'I have never killed a living soul,' the Cat's Paw said, vehemently, and then her tone crumbled with an edge of slight bemusement – as though desperately trying not to think of something that is so hurtful that it threatened to tear the mind apart. 'Not me,' she said, quietly. 'It was never me.'

Benny became aware that she was skating around the edge

of a sudden abyss, all the more terrifying for its unexpectedness. If she turned her back upon it, the formless black of it was going to haunt her for ever. She had to see the precise shape of it with her own eyes.

'Why don't you tell me about it, Miss Blaine?' she said.

Up in the orbit of Shokesh, Technical Officer Stross was following a maintenance crawlway, testing the extruded compound-resin tendrils fixed immovably to the sides, which performed the function that in some earlier and less technically proficient era would have been performed by insulated cables. Every so often he could run a sensor pack over a splitter-junction, or check the function of some item of equipment embedded into the resin.

He was trying to locate the source of the problems with the ARVID-linked communications subnet, the intermittent malfunctions and the slightly erratic behaviour of the central ARVID unit itself. He knew that it and the equipment to which it was connected formed a coherent gestalt, rather like the neurosystem of a living being, and that a fault with one of the peripheral components could throw the whole arrangement out of line. He was checking the peripheral equipment first, because such things would be relatively quick and easy to fix. If the fault was actually with ARVID, any repair procedure would have to be extremely drastic and specialized, involving the complete shutdown of all systems and the decommissioning of the *Titanian Queen* for months. Personally, Stross was of the opinion that the potentially and lethally catastrophic possibility should be ruled out first – but a curt reply from United Spaceways, during one of the times when the comms systems were actually working, had told him, bluntly, that he had better do anything humanly possible to prevent the ship being dry-docked – and had strongly implied that, if he were to lose his job, he would be blackballed from even the most menial of legitimate employment for the rest of his short and sorry life.

As he worked his way through the crawlways, Stross was

guided by the technical schematics of the ship. The problem with the schematics, however, was that they seemed to bear no real relation to the physical layout, and he rapidly lost even the most general sense of where he was. There was a healthy element of suspicion in his nature, and he developed the probably entirely irrational and paranoid fear that he was heading aft towards the engines and their undetectable but cumulatively hazardous radiations. He knew that such a thing was supposed to be impossible but, knowing the shoddy workmanship that United Spaceways commonly employed, he would not have cared to bet his life upon it.

Eventually, he realized that the – again, probably unfounded – sense of unease and tension was becoming distracting. He would try to work on a unit, but his mind kept focusing on every tiny twinge in his body, exaggerating every momentary itch in his skin and imagining the killing showers of electrogravitational quasi-particles drilling through it. It was time to take a rest and catch his bearings.

He backtracked through the conduit until he came to an access hatch, unseated the snap-bolts and swung himself down into what the vast majority of those who had travelled in it thought of as the extent of the ship.

As Stross looked about him wildly, his first thought was how impossible and *wrong* it was for him to be here. Admittedly, he had become lost, but his subliminal senses had left him utterly unprepared to find himself where he now appeared to be. It was simply impossible.

The second thing he became aware of were the figures here, and what they were doing.

'Hey!' he exclaimed. 'You can't –'

Not, as final words go in the general run of things, particularly original or impressive, but they would have to do, as they were the last thing he ever said, having lost the equipment necessary to say them at almost the instant he had spoken. And of course, bare instants later, he had lost the equipment necessary for any impulse to speak, or to perform any living action, ever again.

INTERLUDE

THE HANDS THAT BIND THE DEAD

The village was little more than a staging point for the cleared track that twisted through the Forest of the Morningstar: an ostler's yard, a chapel to the local minor gods, a freshwater well and a tavern. This was somewhere to pause for the night, when exhaustion racked the bones and the sounds of the forest spoke of the hidden dangers of the dark. This was a place to take rest, and some mean degree of refreshment before continuing on one's way. This was not somewhere to live.

Tallow brands affixed to farrier-iron brackets sunk into the adobe wall of the tavern, cast a fitful, flickering light as Kali di Bane lithely dismounted, led her piebald gelding, Yori, to the ostler's post and hobbled it. The light illuminated a cage, of a rusted iron, hanging from a gibbet where the courtyard met the road. Reivers had been here, establishing and enforcing Lord Dulac's law, but not recently, not for several moons: the remains in the cage were nothing more than picked-clean bones. Of the even score of mounts already tethered here, each and every one was appointed with tack in the worn and patchwork manner of a brigand, not that of Dulac's soldiery.

'Be still,' Kali di Bane murmured to Yori, who seemed restive in the company of these animals. 'I will return soon.' She cupped the long head of the horse in her hands and blew into its nostrils until it settled. Then she turned upon a booted heel and strode towards the tavern, glancing up towards the rough board sign in idle confirmation – though no degree of confirmation was in fact needed. Kali di Bane had an appointment to keep in the Boar and Pizzle, and the Boar and Pizzle was the single inn for leagues around.

Inside, a crackling fire lent its smoke to the smells of tobacco, beer, stale sweat and greasy meat. Potatoes baked in the ashes and cuts of meat roasted on the hearth. A certain amount of activity, and certain sounds, from the dark recesses of the inglenook proclaimed that one or more of the village doxies were going about their vocation of trade.

The innkeeper himself, in stained leather jerkin and with his undershirt sleeves rolled up over heavy, corded, hirsute forearms, glanced up with a suspicious grunt as Kali di Bane entered, and then turned back to tending his barrels of small ale, stout and mead.

Every bench and stool of the inn was occupied: a baker's dozen of rough-hewn men, not a pair of them identical in their brigand garb, but tending towards a kind of uniformity, their dirty scraps of leather, wool and flax, their tarnished buckles and scraps of purloined jewellery, their thongs and feathers and straps, the dirks, daggers, knob-sticks, short swords, knuckle-dusters, arrow-quivers, powder pistols and machetes of their casually displayed weaponry, all blurring together as did the disparate contents of a town midden. These men were mercenaries, soldiers of fortune and for hire, hailing from all six corners of the world. Kali recognized a Blackamoor from far Afrique, a Brave from the flying cities of Rashanoor, a Jendokhan from the tropics of the Pellicidorean interior, and several more.

She strolled towards the Boar and Pizzle's host, aware of every mind's attention on her, for all that the eyes rested studiously elsewhere, aware of what each mind thought its eyes would see, if they were to be directed to her: a slim and smallish girl, her hair cropped short, her cloak and clothing stained and travel-worn, her movements, when she moved, as graceful and sure-footed as a cat's.

'A mug of your best and something to eat,' she told the landlord, tossing a silver Lord's Mark to him with a flick of her thumb. 'And a bottle of the potato spirits you make,' she continued, as the man peered with a mixture of avarice and doubt at the coin, which would have paid for board and lodgings for a week. 'For later. To keep out the chill.'

The landlord of the Boar and Pizzle bit the coin, then tucked it into his jerkin and drew a frothing wooden cup of ale from the tap knocked into a barrel. He handed it to her with a small attempt towards servility, tempered a little by her sex, her unkempt clothes and her relative youth.

'You!' he called to the mean-faced scullery/wretch who was tending the meat in the hearth. 'A slab for the lady. More crackling than fat.' He bent down behind his bench and straightened, holding a flat, square flask. 'Your liquor.'

'A good year?' asked Kali di Bane, with no small degree of irony.

'One of the worst,' said the landlord with a shrug. 'What with the reivers and Dulac raising the tithe an' all.'

Kali stowed the flask away inside her cloak and turned – to run straight into one of the largest of the brigands, who she had been aware of shadowing her since the very moment she had passed through the door of the inn.

'That's a powerful lot of drink for a little chit of a thing like you,' he said, his lips pulled back from fractured, blocky teeth and a vulpine grin. 'There are other ways to keep warm of a night.'

Kali di Bane looked into his eyes, exquisitely aware of how the others gathered here were watching the scene intently. The leaders of these men, she knew, were elsewhere – but this man was the leader among these minions: the strongest and most vicious. Whatever this man took for spoil, the others would surely fight over the leftovers that remained.

She decided to finish things quickly. With a speed almost too fast for the eye to catch, she pressed herself towards the brigand so that there was a knife's breadth between them. At the same time she drew her two knives – the heavy Disjointer and the slim Cat's Claw, and laid the one against the greasy crutch of his breeks, the other against his bristling throat.

Kali di Bane looked up sweetly at the suddenly blanching brigand. 'You were saying?'

A tiny bead of blood dripped from the big man's chin, where the point of the Cat's Claw had pricked it.

'I think,' he said, very slowly and carefully, 'that all things considered 'tis a good thing you have a flask to keep you warm.'

Kali di Bane stepped back and sheathed her knives, then turned her back upon him, as if he were some insect of no further interest. Her keen senses remained alert for an indication that he might take it into his head to strike at her from behind, but she sensed that he was merely standing, at a loss, like some unruly child admonished by a schoolmaster with a rule.

She turned to spy the narrow door leading into the Boar and Pizzle's private back room. 'Have the meat sent in,' she told the landlord. 'I believe I am expected.'

Behind the door were three men. One was slim, with elfin features, dressed in pristine silks of red and yellow. One seemed like a priest or friar, dressed from head to toe in grey robes – though, if one looked closely, one might see something slightly off about this apparel, as if it were made of his own flesh, somehow distended to give the impression of robes.

The third man was bigger even than the brigand who had tried to force unwelcome attentions upon her. He was dressed in battered, blood-red leather, reinforced over the left shoulder and the kidneys by pitted, riveted iron plate. Like the others, he had turned upon her entrance, rising from the table at which they sat. Now, recognizing her, he laid his sword upon the table and favoured her with a hard-etched but friendly grin.

'Hello, little thief,' he said. 'You took your time getting here.'

Kali di Bane smiled back. 'I had better things to do. Greetings, Simon Gore. I take it that the party outside is yours?'

The raiding party made its way through a part of the forest so thick that the horses had been long left behind. The brigands were spread out relatively wide, ostensibly to present a wider face towards any defensive forces that might be waiting – though, Kali di Bane realized, in reality to place a number of victims between the dangers of the forest and those who made up the party's core.

At least seven of this expendable cadre had thus far been lost. Time and time again, they heard a thrashing of the undergrowth, a frenzied struggle, a heart-rending scream or gibbering as one of these men was taken by the monstrous creatures of the dark: by a wolverine or bandersnatch, a bog-woppet or a vermicious knid. Kali di Bane supposed that she should feel some sense of loss or remorse for these casualties, but it was a purely intellectual thought – she had not recognized them as real people, in her gut. And, besides, if they were to die then they were dying for a just cause.

It would be a mistake to think that her mind drifted back. In reality it avoided – prowled around – the vast black pit of pain and grief that was her centre and her soul: her birth and her mother, one of the concubines of the Lord Dulac; how her mother's function, like the others, had been nothing more than a breeding vessel, to provide him with sons; and how, like the others, when she had dropped a daughter she had been killed. The Lord Dulac believed, in the face of all objective evidence, that a woman who gave birth to a female child was a witch who had killed his *male* child by way of arcane sorcery, and had used the seed of his blood to propagate her own breed.

By rights – so far as the lord Dulac could conceive of rights – these newborn females should be killed along with their mothers. Fortunately, there was the occasional servant who would balk at the task, would spirit these newborns out of the palace and into the slum city that sprawled around it. Kali di Bane had been one such of these, wet-nursed by a woman who had lost her own child, and whom she had thought of as her flesh and blood. It had only been later, when Kali di Bane was barely six years old, and she on her deathbed, that her 'mother' had told her the truth.

After her foster mother's death, Kali di Bane had found herself alone; living from hand to mouth off scraps from the slum-street middens, stealing when she could. She discovered that she had an aptitude for it. And when circumstances dictated, when there was no other choice, she found that she could kill, with no sense of compunction or guilt, for little more than a disputed scrap of bread. This had brought her to the attention of the Assassins, who were always on the lookout for tools that they could use. And while the Noble Order of Assassins Puissant were an exclusively, monastically male order, there were uses to which a young girl could be put. There were few who would suspect murder at the hands of a child.

The Assassins had trained her, and put her to work, and for years she had done their bidding – years that had seemed an eternity to her, then, for she'd had a child's short life and its conception of time. She had been placed into the bedchambers of certain members of the nobility, with certain tastes, and she had slit their throats in their eventual sleep. She had placed herself in the way of others, kinder by nature, and slipped a poisoned needle into them as they attempted to give her alms. Her boyish features, for some time into her teens, had allowed her to catch others, with other and more specialized tastes, unawares.

The time had come, however, when she was too old to be of use to the Assassins, and they had marked her for disposal. But they had trained her too well – as the novice boy they had sent to kill her had discovered, briefly and painfully. Kali di Bane had likewise dispatched the several more accomplished killers sent by the Assassins after her, not so much in revenge as in the spirit of proving that none, of any stripe, could escape them.

She had proved them wrong. She had left the slum cities, escaping once again as she had escaped the palace, once again alone – save that this time she escaped with skills, and a maturity that allowed her to use them. She had wandered the lands beyond the walls: thief, mercenary, selling her services to the highest bidder – and as her name and expertise had become known, the bids had been increasingly high indeed.

For all that she had built herself a new if perilous life, Kali di Bane never forgot her old: the black and yawning hatred for Dulac and all his works. And so, as and when a propitious time presented itself, she offered her skills to the rebels who encamped themselves in the Forest of the Morningstar, never missing a chance to place a tree limb in the spokes of the Lord Dulac's machinery of power, waiting for the chance to come that might result in his complete overthrow. Simon Gore was one such rebel – and it might have just been possible that the long-awaited opportunity had come.

'The Magus Xazyxtor,' Simon Gore murmured, as they crept their cautious way across the misty, mossy forest floor. 'For years we have been looking for the source of the tyrant's power, the enchantments that protected him, preserved his youth and supernaturally beautiful if a little fey physical features – and now it seems that it is the work of a man who was held in common regard as the meanest of mere hedge-wizards.'

Kali di Bane nodded to herself. Gore had vouchsafed this information several times already, both in the Boar and Pizzle and on this trek, but it was vital enough not to diminish by the repetition. A number of good men had died obtaining it and bringing it from the palace – and it was as if Simon Gore honoured their memory by the constant reiteration.

On either side, flanking herself and Simon Gore, Kali di Bane made out two actual figures: these were one Ildiam bel

Geddes and the Pastor Gooli Mo, the two additional men she had met in the back room of the hostelry – although, 'men' was not precisely the correct word. Ildiam bel Geddes was one of the inhabitants of the flying islands of Baarloon, a race whose blood had been once mixed with that of the faeries and the Sidhe. Gooli Mo was even less human, for all his manlike shape. He (if he was in fact a male of that species) was one of that strange race who existed in those unlikely lands, of which one caught a fleeting glimpse when one was half asleep and half awake. His (if he were male) appearance was mutable, and to a large degree optional.

For all their apparent inhumanity, these two, Kali di Bane knew, were the closest and most trusted of Simon Gore's lieutenants. Their presence was comforting, offering a sense of more security than the slowly diminishing band of hired brigands that surrounded them.

Up ahead, though there was nothing to see in the foggy dark, Kali di Bane sensed that the forest opened out into a clearing. There, if they had followed the directions of dead men correctly, they would find a nub of stone fully twice the height of a tall man, and in which – if certain procedures were followed – they would find the crevice that led to the tunnels of the Magus Xazyxtor's lair. And there, if they could sufficiently counter sundry weirds and enchantments, they would discover the talisman that furnished the magus's unholy power and, thus, the very strength of Lord Dulac.

Kali di Bane considered the various methods that she knew for dealing with the snares of necromantic puissance: the tiny knives she carried (useless for other purposes), each with a different totem carved on the hilt, and serving as symbols in an abstract battle against any number of conjured demons. The ensorcelled band of cloth which, if employed as a blindfold, banished all illusion and allowed the wearer to see nothing but things as they truly were. The Cape of Fire, which, when deployed, might burn her own image into the mind of an observer, with such a strength that he would be entranced by it, and fail to see her as she moved . . .

It was only later that Kali di Bane fully realized her mistake. Lost in contemplation of what must be *done* later, it was as if she were truly performing it. She had displaced herself into some imagined and hypothetical future, given her attentions more so to it than the far more important and immediate dangers of the here and now. As it was, she was jerked back into the harsh reality of the present by the eruptions of flame to either side of her, the shrieks of agony, the crackle and the spit of burning flesh from what had been Ildiam bel Geddes and the Pastor Gooli Mo.

Almost absent-mindedly – not quite yet grasping the import of what had occurred – she stepped away from a suddenly searing heat; looked down at the blazing mass that had been, a swift instant before, the living Simon Gore.

'What *shall* I do with you?' a voice said. 'Least and most intransigent of my children.'

From behind a tree bole stepped a dark and black-clad figure. A wizened, palsied and barely recognizable human form capered behind him. Dimly, she was aware of the shadowy forms of Dulac's reivers to either side, but her attention was caught, riveted, by the man who was her enemy and his sorcerous and monkey-like minion.

The Lord Dulac strode forward, fluid and graceful, muscles moving under his black leathers and silks like the muscles of a cat. A knowing and strangely gentle smile played about his depraved, debauched lips.

'I think,' said the Lord Dulac, 'that I really will have to take you over my knee.'

PART FOUR

ARRIVAL

A film must be alive. When this happens, it smashes, devours, pulverizes any synopsis, plot, story. It speaks, talks and explains itself. It constantly changes itself, its characters weave in and out of the screen. The performance is different at each screening.

Francisco Reguero (1975)

18

Methods of Investigation

The *Titanian Queen* left the orbit of Shokesh and continued on its way. First it would negotiate the asteroid cluster that enclosed the system, at speeds not over the order of thousands of kilometres per second, then, once free of stellar bodies, it would reorientate itself in space and begin the acceleration for the translation jump to the system of Kinos and the renowned ice world of Tingkli. There the passengers of the cruise would take a conducted tour of a landscape carved by the delicate and complex polyfractal climactic weather patterns into forms of the most surpassing natural beauty – wearing, of course, special thermally heated suits of the sort that had already wrecked said delicately balanced polyfractal weather patterns and would cause catastrophic climactic collapse on Tingkli by the end of the century.

Surprisingly, perhaps, almost the entire complement of passengers had returned to the *Titanian Queen*. In fact, there were only three who did not, and this was because they had contracted food poisoning from the fare on Shokesh, and were currently dealing with appalling local medical facilities and a failure of travel insurance – these elements being an integral part of any foreign holiday, and the Shokesh tourist industry being nothing if not thorough. Perhaps it was simply that the passengers could not conceive of anywhere else to go, or perhaps it was a pack instinct of the sort that has wildlife documentary film-makers throwing lemmings off cliffs when they don't seem naturally inclined to go – in any event, the people returned, even though it meant that they would spend the days in trepidation, waiting for the horrible murders to resume.

Even more surprisingly, however, the murders did not. The hours stretched to days without a single person being sucked down a toilet, or found bound and skewered with an apple in his mouth, or found impaled on a bed of strategically placed spikes. As one day stretched to two days, not one person unaccountably died.

Consensus of opinion was that the Cat's Paw had contrived to escape with his ill-gotten gains. The intangible finger of suspicion was, of course, pointed at those who had stayed behind on the desert planet with dicky tummies – but not exclusively. A member of the crew might have jumped ship, or even, as in an unconscionably large number of classic murder mysteries, one of the murdered or the disappeared might not have been murdered at all, or disappeared in the sense that people had supposed.

Life aboard the *Titanian Queen*, in fact, returned to a semblance of what it had been before the horrible murders started. The rich were not, of course, precisely renowned for their common human sympathies – and on the whole, it seemed, the dispatched had been thoroughly bad sorts or people of no account among the better class of society. They were no loss. Their deaths had provided a certain excitement to the cruise, and had resulted in slightly less crowded conditions aboard ship, but life continued as normal.

For two people, though, aboard the *Titanian Queen*, life had suddenly taken a new turn; and for a number of reasons it was going to become increasingly abnormal indeed.

'Are you sure you're not going to make people suspicious like that?' Benny said.

'Nah.' Blaine (as she insisted that Benny call her) scratched at her now short and razor-cut hair. 'None of these people are what you might call bright, and they're every single one of 'em too involved with themselves.' She had retained the workmanlike clothes she had worn on Shokesh, and her manner was almost unrecognizable as the startled rabbit of her previously assumed persona. She grinned at Benny. 'Mind you, I notice that some of the ladies are looking at me as if I've dropped a hairpin.'

There was something a little odd about her language structures, Benny noticed. They seemed vaguely archaic, but not quite correct. Mind you, she thought, that was perfectly understandable, given what Blaine had told her back in the taberna.

Now, Blaine wandered through Benny's cabin, casually glancing this way and that. They had already searched it thoroughly, looking for things that Benny might have initially missed, or which had become too familiar to see. 'The trick is,' she said, 'to start from first principles and work your way out. You might cover the same ground in the first, but there's good odds you'll end up taking a completely different path . . .'

She stopped at the doorway that led to Krugor's cubbyhole, the barricading chair of which had already been removed. 'Now do you see what I see here?'

Benny shrugged, wondering what the temporarily ex-catburglar was driving at. 'There's nothing.'

'Exactly. There's nothing. There is, in fact a large amount of no locks or anything.'

'There's a lock on the other side . . .' Benny began.

'And why would that be? This man Krugor was your servant. How many servants have you ever heard of who can lock themselves away from their lords and ladies, but the lords and ladies cannot lock themselves away from them? There's something inside. Something he was doing. Something that he didn't want you coming in unexpectedly to see.'

'I see your point.' Benny picked up a meal-tray butter knife of the sort she had used to force the door before, and tried again.

'Damn,' she said at last. 'It was easy before.'

Blaine nodded thoughtfully. 'But not now, eh? Possibly someone might have changed it? Never fear – that is, of course, what I'm here for.'

Inside, the small cubicles were just as Benny had last seen them. There was nothing of suspicious interest, and no room to hide anything if there were.

Blaine, on the other hand, swept her gaze around the balks intently. 'The thing you have to remember,' she said, 'is that people who actually *build* things for the fine, rich people are of the common class that dislike them. They're perfectly willing to make a few informal changes to the plans, for a small fee or even for the Sheol – I mean, for the hell – of it. There . . .'

Blaine pressed her thumb against the bulkhead, two fingers somewhere else, and a section of it hinged smoothly up. Benny had not even been able to see so much as a crack.

'Easy when you know how,' said the Cat's Paw.

The hiding place was sunk back only a few centimetres. The only thing inside was a small, polymer-bound notebook of the sort used as a pocket diary. Benny flipped through the pages.

'They're blank,' she said. 'There's nothing to – hang on. There's a list here. It's a list of names. It's headed "Special Accommodation".'

'Who's on it?' Blaine asked with interest.

'Sheen . . . Gaffney . . . the Dowager Duchess of Gharl . . .' Benny looked up from the book with a small degree of startlement – startled not so much by the actual contents as the fact that they were so blatantly supplied.

'We're going to have to go through the list properly,' she said, 'but you know who's going to turn out to be on them as well as I do.'

On the bridge, Captain Fletcher Iolanthe Crane unbuttoned his dress-uniform collar and sank back in a seat with a small sigh of relief. He had just returned from that evening's set dinner, the first he had attended since that fateful night of murders, and he had been on the edge of that particular dining-room seat the whole time, starting at shadows, waiting for the hammer of mayhem to fall . . . but in the end there had been a decided and entirely welcome lack of explosions.

For the first time in a week he caught himself wondering if the worst of it was truly over. No deaths, not an additional, sudden and utterly unsolvable problem in immediate sight. The only cloud of unease was the quiet disappearance of the technical officer, Stross – Crane hoped like hell that he had simply jumped ship in a kind of informal form of resignation.

Even the ARVID seemed marginally less annoying than usual. He turned to face the smooth surface of the housing unit. 'Is there anything I should know about?'

'Not a thing,' the ARVID said blandly, without any kind of childish preamble that had one wanting to hammer on it with an adjustable spanner. Indeed, the voice of the ARVID had seemed increasingly relaxed and cultured of late – maybe as a result of its accelerated, in human terms, progress through life to maturity.

'There is nothing you need be aware of or trouble yourself about,' it continued, smoothly. 'Rest assured, my dear Captain, that if there is you'll be the first to know.'

Like the rebuilding of the Olabrian joy-luck crystal (which was now in its hatbox in the back of the closet of her cabin, packed around with thick bundles of clothing in an attempt to stifle its seemingly endless stream of asinine platitudes) things now seemed to have devolved, Benny thought, into a simple matter of finding all the pieces and putting them together in the correct manner.

With a minor change of attitude it was possible to have an almost complete run of the ship, remaining almost completely unobserved. One merely stuck to the areas used by the crew, and avoided such members as there were – a rather easier task than might have been at first thought. With the exception of the ubiquitous stewards – who did not fully count as human, being conditioned and remote-controlled to the point of individuality-extinction – the *Titanian Queen* had always operated on the basis of a bare-minimum, skeleton crew. Thus, with the help of Blaine – who was, after all, utterly conversant with the methods of skulking unobserved in places where one should not properly be – Benny moved through the ostensibly out-of-bounds areas of the ship with no real hindrance.

They were here to check out two things that were bothering her. One of these things was of a mixture of the conceptual and the tangible, and Benny dealt with the tangible aspect of it remarkably quickly. She looked at the peeling paint on the balks here, and absently picked a few flecks of it off.

'Rust,' she said.

'So?' Blaine said uninterestedly, still keeping an eye and other senses out for any inconvenient crewman.

'I'll tell you later.' Benny pulled a scrap of polymer sheeting from an inside pocket of her twinset. It was the sheet of schematics that she had retrieved from the airlock after the death of Cherry, and upon which Khaarli the Czhan had scribbled the result of his investigative interview. 'I think this is pretty much the right place.'

She scanned the schematic diagram for a moment, and then let her gaze drift about the corridor – recapturing those trained professional instincts that allowed her to intimate the relationships between objects and spaces.

After a while, she scowled. 'It's wrong,' she said. 'Things are out of kilter, if you know what I mean.'

'No luck, then?' Blaine said.

'I wouldn't say that.' Benny smiled, a little. 'It was almost exactly what I was expecting.'

The second thing was far more tangible, almost entirely so. Like all commercial vessels that carried passengers – that is, those whose contracts did not contain an explicit limited-liability clause, stating that in the case of shipwreck or similar disaster they were on their own – the *Titanian Queen* was required to carry a complement of life pods. They nestled in their racks, each approximately the size of a twentieth-century space shuttle before coolant-system malfunction and detonation. The majority of their bulks were given up to living and supply space, providing livable if extremely cramped emergency conditions for all on board the ship.

At least, that might have once been the general idea.

'The seals are all broken.' Blaine indicated the single exception, an alloy tag upon the locking mechanism of a single one of the pods, certifying that it had been inspected and found to contain food, water and air in sufficient quantities, together with functioning control and communications systems. 'This is the only one that seems to be intact.'

'Let's leave it as it is then,' said Benny. 'For the moment. Let's have a look inside one of the unsealed ones.'

The sample pod in question was a mere skeleton, picked clean. There were no supplies of any kind, and the control units had been ripped from their housings – or would have been, if they had ever been installed in the first place.

'I don't think this was ever intended to be used,' Benny said. 'Maybe the owners just preferred to risk the lawsuits than the outlay.'

Blaine had been going over the pod interior with the attention to detail that was her stock in trade. 'There's still an air supply.' She opened a unit and indicated the rack of pressurized canisters.

'And don't think I don't have my suspicions about that.' Benny examined the bottles. The entire point of an escape pod was to pare things down to the basics, and they were designed simply to expel raw oxygen into the atmosphere. 'Go over there and old your breath,' she told Blaine.

As the criminal backed off to the other end of the pod, Benny cracked open a bottle, took a shallow breath and then closed it again.

'I have the feeling,' she said, 'that if anyone actually tried to sprocket that yellow teacup, puppet the small snake jelly glue machine . . .'

'How are you feeling now?' Blaine handed her another cup of black coffee laced with stims that were making her feel as though she'd lost the very top layer of her epidermis.

'I told you, I'm perfectly all right.' Benny sipped the coffee anyway. 'I only caught a whiff of it, and I knew what to expect. It just confirmed what I was thinking. The gas in the bottle that did for that woman Cherry in the airlock wasn't just intended as a specific murder. Somebody's doing a nice little spot of manipulation.'

She looked around the cabin of Isabel Blaine – rather smaller and much less plush than her own, in keeping with the Isabel Blaine cover identity. The dose of gas Benny had got from the canister in the pod had not been serious, but Blaine had been forced to drag a dazed and babbling Bernice Summerfield into the privacy and safety of her own quarters, those being the nearest. There being no particular secrets between them for the moment, Blaine was idly showing her several of the methods she utilized as the Cat's Paw, while she waited for Benny to recover completely. Among the more high-tech and complicated tools, Benny noticed several quite ordinary and prosaic items.

'Is that a nail file?' she said. 'A lead pencil?'

'Sometimes things like that are the best things for a job,' Blaine said absently. 'It's similar to the way that one can kill with anything from a cobblestone picked up from the street to a longbow, to an electromagnetically contained, command-detonated plasma burst. It's a matter of choosing the correct method.' From her cotside dresser she picked up a bottle of solvent such as was commonly used to remove nail varnish and toyed with it. 'Sometimes you might not want to be caught with *anything* suspicious, but there are other factors. Sometimes there are one hell of a lot of factors.' She glanced towards a slim personal database, about the size of an old-style cigarette packet and from the looks of it state of the prototypical art.

'Something I've been wondering about,' Benny said. 'All right, so it's relatively easy to sneak around unnoticed on the human level, but what about the ship's security systems? I'd have thought they would be horrendously complicated to beat.'

'Only at the start.' Blaine put down the little bottle and picked up an item similar to a med technician's DMSO spray crossed with a military flechette-ejecting gun. 'The ships systems are routed through an ARVID processor, and that's based on processes coming out of the Catan Nebula. Nanonite-based matter-restructuring processes. So I acquired a little Catan technology of my own.' She broke open the hypo-gun and extracted a metallic, chrome-bright cylindrical vial, of approximately the same size as the top phalange of an index finger. 'The horrendously complicated part was getting to the central processor. Then I simply cracked it and injected my own Catan nanonites. They restructured the ARVID in certain ways that disabled the security systems without anybody knowing, and then I could just go where I liked.' She grinned a little smugly. 'Use their own technology against them, as it were.'

Again, Benny remembered what Blaine had told her back on Shokesh. She could see how the Cat's Paw might enjoy turning Catan technology, specifically, to her own ends. She frowned. 'It strikes me that the *other* result would be to let our murderer, or murderers, go wherever the hell they liked, too.'

Blaine's face hardened a little, not with anger at Benny but at herself. 'There is that. Don't think I haven't thought about it.'

Looking at the vial, Benny noticed that there was some tiny detail that she couldn't quite see but that was nagging at her mind. 'Could I have a closer look?'

'Surely.' Blaine passed it over.

Benny turned the vial over in her hands, feeling the shape

of it that spoke of tremendous care and attention to detail in its construction, in the same way as a piece of expertly cut lead crystal feels entirely different from a superficially similar lump of glass-gel moulding. She peered at the little sticky label on the side, trying to make out the serial numbers printed on it.

A slightly paranoid thought struck her, borne of knowing of the potential dangers of quasi-organic microspores and the absolute care that must be taken in working with them. 'I suppose it's quite safe to handle it?'

'Don't worry,' Blaine said. 'As you can imagine, I know a lot about the Catan processes. These vials are crafted individually and checked over weeks. Only the top ten per cent of those that pass the basic safety guidelines are used, the rest are destroyed. They're integrally tagged to their contents, and serialized so that it's impossible for some idiot to try to recondition them.' She smiled. 'You won't get any on your hands.'

As she listened to Blaine, a tiny piece clicked home in Benny's head. Not the final piece, but the *crucial* one – the additional molecule that tips the weapons-grade plutonium of the mind into critical mass, and converts it into a big and sudden hole in the ground.

'These things are scrupulously tagged to their contents?' she said, slowly. 'Each has its own unique serial?'

Blaine nodded without much interest. 'They make damned sure they can't get mixed up.'

'All right.' Benny peered at the vial again, reading and rereading the serial number. 'But if they were going to do that, they'd do it with engraving or molecular pigment-bonding on the base, wouldn't they? Something indelible?' She held out the vial so that it was almost directly under Blaine's now slightly startled nose. 'Not, and correct me if I'm wrong, on a little, sticky and quite obviously *removable* label.'

19

CAN WE TALK?

Khaarli of the seventh *dhai*, Prosecutor General of the Czhanos Militia, looked down his snout at Benny. There was no rudeness intended: it was simply that he had to crane his neck to see anything more than the top of her head. He plucked at a tusk, thoughtfully, with his thumb. 'Do you realize what you're asking, thou pribbling crook-pated ratsbane? These reeky, doghearted nut-hooks have little or no respect for my person in itself, merely my hard-won reputation as an investigator. That is all, under the present circumstances that I have.'

Benny glanced about the Czhan detective's cabin. In the same way as those of Isabel Blaine and herself had intimated something of their supposed personas and social position, this space said something about Khaarli. It was not that there was anything actively *bad* about it – simply that the decor was just that little bit less pristine, the sound of the ship's air-conditioning and plumbing systems too evident, the position of the cabin in the ship at large just a touch convenient. It could only be that, as a nonhuman being, he had been assigned a cabin that was just that little bit imperfect, as if it were assumed that he wouldn't know the difference, for all he was, almost by definition, a trained and highly proficient observer.

This was the sort of thing Benny noticed a lot, when

humans were trying to interact with other intelligences and had the generally upper hand, and she always fumed quietly about it to herself. She tried never to bring it up with the people involved, though, because without exception that came across as incredibly condescending.

'That's the whole point,' she said to Khaarli. 'These people trust your judgment, and you're the only one I can count on to trust me. You're the only one who can put it all together so I can clear things up – and quite possibly save the lives of everyone on board into the bargain.'

Khaarli thought this over for a while and, eventually, nodded slowly. 'Agreed, then, thou milk-livered unmuzzled mammet. I'll see what I can do.' He peered at Benny closely, with eyes that were no more piggy from his porcine ancestry than Benny went around flashing a bare monkey's bum. 'I wish I didn't receive the distinct impression that you were keeping certain things from me, however, thou beef-witted weedy haggard.'

'I wish I could tell you,' Benny said, hoping to the Goddess that her plans would actually work. 'I really wish I could. But if I didn't take you through them step by step, in detail, you'd never believe me.'

It was by general agreement the late afternoon, a time when the Starfire Ballroom was usually deserted. Benny looked around, and made a small mental note to thank Khaarli for a sterling job. He had prevailed upon the great detectives, every single one, to gather here, together with the captain and the highest-ranking of the ship's officers.

For all this, though, she had subconsciously expected the place to be utterly packed, everyone on board desperately trying to get in to learn the solution to the perils that had plagued the *Titanian Queen*. She had underestimated the sheer indifference of the passengers to anything and everything not directly related to themselves. The family and immediate associates of the murder victims were here, but hardly anyone else seemed to have thought it worth the bother. She recognized the ex-good lady wife of Nathanael C. Nerode, who appeared to have formed a friendly attachment with the member of the bar staff from Percy's Discotheque, and a few others who she recalled had been sitting with the eventual dead on the night when several people had exploded. A number of the ubiquitous stewards were here, serving drinks and the occasional snack, or simply waiting unobtrusively until they were called upon.

Ah well, the lack of turnout would at least simplify matters a little, prevent the proceedings being cluttered by extraneous matters.

Khaarli was addressing the assembled great detectives. '... not exactly myself I want you to listen to,' he was saying, 'thou swag-bellied cockered hugger-muggers ...'

'Aha!' proclaimed Emil Dupont. 'I thought as much. I intimate from certain signs that we are, in fact, to be treated to a demonstration of theatrical animal-training, involving a performing seal, three chipmunks and an extremely peripatetic mountain gorilla!'

A number of those present put their heads in their hands.

Khaarli, however, was made of sterner stuff. 'In fact, thou pox-marked full-gorged pignut, I was referring to the lady here, Ms Summersdale.'

'That's nice, dear.' Miss Agatha Magpole nodded her amiable, senile head – and a gasp went up from the diminutive crowd as the action almost dislodged her special brainwave hat. Fortunately for all concerned, her ever-handy companion was on the scene to catch it and prevent it from falling off.

'Am I to understand,' said a voice tight with barely controlled fury, 'that these proceedings are to be conduced at the hands of this ... this ...'

Benny decided to seize the initiative. 'Yes, Mr Groke,' she said firmly. 'As Khaarli here has implied, the solution is in sight and – barring one or two of the unimportant details – I think I have it.' She adopted a kind of schoolma'amish tone that caught the special agent off guard and had him blushing with embarrassment. 'Now, are you going to try to *contain* yourself long enough to hear what I have to say, or are you going to simply make a fool of yourself and be sent to stand in the corner? It's all the same to me.'

The special agent glowered at her as if contemplating bloody murder. 'I'll listen.'

'Thank the Goddess for small mercies.' Benny regarded the special agent with steady contemplation, as if he were a not particularly interesting microbe on a slide. 'Because, Mr Groke, it is *you* I wish to question further.'

'Me?' Groke seemed, momentarily, taken aback. Suspicious. Even a little frightened. Some locked-off part of him knew, Benny thought. On some level of what he called his consciousness he had *always* known.

'Yes, you.' She paced the clear area of floor, surrounded by the great detectives and now slightly restive onlookers, counting points off on her fingers as though only now putting together something she had, in fact, already rehearsed in her head. 'You might not be aware of it,' she continued, 'but I've been paying a certain amount of attention to you, Mr Groke. I'll admit, at first, that this was simply because I have seldom ever met such an objectionable little turd, and such things prey upon the mind . . .'

Groke, who had in any case been visibly bristling, let out a strangled squeak of outrage.

''Ere!' exclaimed the doughty Inspector Interchange. 'There are ladies . . .' He realized that the most obvious lady here was Benny herself, and finished lamely: '. . . present.'

'Good for you, Ms Summersdale,' interjected Khaarli with a kind of friendly, evil satisfaction, 'thou pottle-deep rank baggage.'

Benny bowed, with some degree of irony, towards him. 'I rather think we can dispense with that little subterfuge now, don't you think? The name is Summerfield.'

'What, Bernice Summerfield?' asked Khaarli, with interest. 'The one who, as I seem to recall, wrote the well-known *Down Among the Dead Men* and is, so I gather, even now hard at work upon the long-awaited sequel? I never would have guessed.'

The bland innocence he radiated told Benny that he had known who she was from the moment he had clapped eyes on her.

'That's the one.' Benny swept those assembled with her gaze. 'None of that will mean much to any of you here, but the upshot is that I know a thing or two, and quite possibly three, about historical matters.'

She turned her attention back to the special agent. 'I began to notice certain things about you, Mr Groke. Your bearing, your language structures, certain facts you let slip.' She paused. 'It's common knowledge that you once occupied some covert position in the Catan Nebula – but the truth is, is it not, that you really come from somewhere *far* more far afield than that? I'm thinking, in particular, of the field of *time*, is that not correct?'

It was as if the special agent had been suddenly transformed into a balloon animal with a slow leak. He slumped, defeated and deflated – and then he raised his head to stare at Benny with grim and tortured eyes. 'It's true.'

In a harsh monotone, Groke began to speak. He told them of his exploits in the service of the English Crown, of his nemesis, the fiendish Doctor Po and of the final confrontation that had sent him hurtling through time.

'I thought as much,' Benny said at last, when he had finished. 'It must have been hard for you: finding yourself in a world you could never even begin to understand.'

'It was,' said Groke, quietly.

'I'd suspect that, for a while, you went a little mad.'

'Yes.'

'I'd imagine,' said Benny, 'that the only thing that kept you clinging to a shred of sanity was the fact that the man who did this to you was still out there, somewhere. After all, the villain had unlocked the secrets of time.' She smiled coldly. 'I expect you've spent your life looking for some sign of him, any clue, any shred of evidence; waiting for the slightest chance to hunt him down.'

'Yes,' said Groke, in a barely perceptible undertone.

Benny became brisk 'Well, I'm afraid, I have a bit of bad news for you, Mr Groke, because the whole thing's been complete and utter bollocks, from start to finish.'

Final Interlude

The Lair of the Flatwyrm

The sorcerer's lair was rank with the smells of his alchemical experiments, the rotting remains of rare vegetation and the anatomy and product of fantastickal beasts, such as the kidneys of a gryphon, the feathers of a kracken and the springlike reproductive organs of a Tigger. There was an undertone of a greasy, fried-meat odour that was almost pleasant – until one remembered the well-documented usages to which a necromancer put the blood of unbaptized, unchristian children.

Kali di Bane was shackled and manacled to the fetid marble slab upon which the Magus Xazyxtor performed his magicks upon his live subjects. The magus himself fussed over her, affixing lesser talismans of various sorts to her clothing. (She had expected to be stripped naked for whatever foul plan the wizard had for her, but this was apparently not to be the case.) The talismans hummed and crackled with some unearthly energy. She felt the stinging and the humming of them, her own spine convulsing time and again to their unholy resonances.

'Nearly done.' The Magus Xazyxtor ran rough, dry hands over the bare skin of her neck before winding it with what seemed, from what the straining eyes in her strap-bound head could see, to be a kind of copper wire. 'Make you ready soon. Nearly done.' The fact that her head was strapped meant that the wizard was forced to repeatedly pass the wire under the nape of her neck, in a process rather like that of sewing. His dry, grey and strangely reptilian tongue licked at four concentric rows of brittle teeth as he worked. The end of the wire gouged and tore at her skin.

'You could untie my head, you know,' Kali di Bane said, in a reasonable tone of voice. She had long ago come to the conclusion that struggling and cursing fit to turn the air bloody was little use against the wizard's powers.

In the forest, as she had tried to back away from Dulac and his sorcerous ally, the magus had thrown some seemingly insubstantial and ghostly, but constricting and enervating, web of force about her, which none of her own defensive magicks had been able to break. The wizard (and, therefore, Dulac) had powers of this sort greater than any she could draw upon. The only chance she had left was to conserve her strength, attempt to lull her captors into a sense of security, and wait to take advantage of any chance that came her way.

'You could free my head, at least,' she continued. 'I'm bound everywhere else. There would be no danger – and whatever it is that you're about might be accomplished more conveniently and less painfully.'

'I'm afraid,' said the voice of the Lord Dulac from one side, 'that is quite frankly impossible. Now, I'll admit that I cannot see *how* having your head alone free might aid you, but it would be the thin end of the wedge. I know how resourceful Kali di Bane can be, ever since the unfortunate demise of my Privy Councillor.'

'I was rather proud of that,' Kali di Bane said lightly, masking the murderous rage she felt with a sardonic insouciance that, she hoped, might discomfit Dulac even more. 'I'm rather surprised you realized that it was not an accident.'

'Oh, come now. A Privy Councillor killed in his own apartments in the palace, collapsing whilst he was in the privy – how in the world could it possibly not be the result of some conscious plan? I use the word "conscious" advisedly, of course, given the level of the humour involved. Besides, my men found the remains of the timber you used to prop up the hollowed foundations and then burnt.'

Kali nodded the fraction that her bonds allowed. 'I'll have to remember to be more scrupulously neat and tidy the next time.'

'I'm afraid, di Bane, for you, that the next time might prove rather longer than you anticipate,' said the Lord Dulac.

The Magus Xazyxtor finished his preparations, and bustled off muttering and chortling happily to himself. A shadow loomed over her from the other side, the side from which Dulac had spoken, and she looked up into his quietly smiling face.

He seemed as young as she, for all that he was thrice her age. His face was quite beautiful — it could almost be that of an angel, if one remembered that Lucifer himself, originally, had been an angel. The beauty was marred, however, by the unnatural sheen of his skin, as though it were of Canthon porcelain, expertly crafted to produce an artificial semblance of life. That, and the malevolence that burnt within his dark and hooded eyes.

'Gore and his men were trifles,' he told her, kindly. 'Insects simply to be crushed.' He stroked her cheek gently with a fingernail, then abruptly dug it in hard enough to draw blood. 'You, however, are another matter. The very fact of your existence is a slight to my will.

'For all your life, rather than wage a consistent and thus easily countered campaign against me, you have taken every chance to assist those who are against me, whosoever they are and no matter how large or insignificant the ways. Thus, in some cumulative sense, you are the single individual who has hurt me the most — in ways for which, were I not in the possession of considerable powers, I would ordinarily not be able to find the culprit.'

The Lord Dulac leant closer to her face and kissed it.

'You are my enemy, and a lovely one at that, it must be told. It is as ultimately simple as that.'

The Lord Dulac straightened again. 'Every fibre of your being aches to destroy me, and I tell you that I shall not be destroyed. With the assistance of the Magus Xazyxtor, I intend to live far longer than you can possibly imagine. And speaking of which, are your preparations quite complete, sorcerer?'

A glance in the direction in which the magus had left. A slightly distant voice said, 'Is ready. Is risk, though. Might tear the veil *apart* . . .'

'It is of no matter.' The Lord Dulac returned his attention to the prone Kali di Bane. 'You see, my darling, hateful daughter, the Magus Xazyxtor has discovered the means to break the very bonds of time. Rather than simply execute you, I have decided to do something all the worse. I shall send you to the *future*, millennia into the future, and you shall arrive to see the world that I will build. And I will be there, still alive, still vital, and you shall see the utter depth of your defeat.'

The Lord Dulac turned, once again, to his sorcerous minion. 'Proceed, Xazyxtor.'

'Righty-ho,' said the voice of the magus, and for a moment there was silence. It could only be her imagination that had Kali di Bane hearing, in a tiny voice that seemed to come from the edge of everything, a voice say, *'You don't watch that facilitator-construct, it'll all go pear-shaped again. And that whole father-daughter dynamic looks* incredibly *dubious to me.'*

(*'Yeah, well. It seems to be inherent in the structure, for some reason. Dirty sods . . .'*)

'There seems to be some problem with your scheme,' Kali di Bane said, keeping her reasonable tone and resisting her fury with a single-mindedness that was, now, almost insanity. 'Incantations and the summoning of flagitious powers from the depths of the unending fetid dark are the areas which seem, at the moment, to be lacking.'

The Lord Dulac sighed, seemingly more in pity than anything else. 'How little you have learnt in your dilettante dabblings with the Arcane Arts, daughter. Have you not realized that such things are merely the delirium of lunaticks?' He smiled. 'The secret is, simply, to know precisely what one has to do and then do it.'

And then, with a suddenness that was almost tranquil, for it did not give her body time to know its pain, the energy of suns exploded through Kali di Bane and tore her apart.

20

THE CHARACTERS INHABITING THE MIND

The Cat's Paw made her way through the hidden areas of the ship, using every precaution, every trick, every piece of security-system-defeating equipment she had. After her talk with Benny, she had lost her faith in the measures she had taken before – she had severe doubts that even the most extreme measures she was taking now would be enough.

Ah, well. At some point you simply had to risk it, and pray to the various gods you believed in, when the chips were down, that the highest card you were holding was in fact the trump.

For all that she had asked Benny to call her 'Blaine', the Cat's Paw held no truck with names. She wore them lightly, changed them in an instant, dropped them without regret.

Once, she had thought she'd had a name, but it had been a lie. Like her entire life, everything she'd done, or been, or was, had been a lie.

'I have a friend.' Benny turned from the stricken-looking Groke, and addressed the great detectives and the various other onlookers in general. 'Let me tell you about her – it may seem like it isn't, but it's relevant, believe you me.

'She lived in a time long distant from ours, a feudal time, a time of magics, a time of mythological beasts. She was a thief, killer and warrior, fighting against an evil and tyrannical overlord, who had killed her mother and so, of course, for whom she felt an all-surpassing and absolute hatred. Anything she could do to hurt him, to thwart his plans, she did.

'But the overlord was cunning, as well as slathered black with rotting and corrupted evil. He had access to diverse and extremely powerful magics, and he laid a snare for her. He caught her and by, naturally, those self-same magics, sent her plunging through the veil of time, into the future.

'She awoke to find herself in a strange new world, peopled with monsters, still ruled over by the overlord she hated so, and twisted into insanity by his monstrous will. Fortunately, however, by pure chance, by a slight miscalculation by the magus who had served the overlord, she found that she had appeared into this world among friends. People who were still fighting against the Evil One, even after aeons, and who were perfectly willing to fight to the death – their own, the overlord himself, that of his minions and even the occasional and unfortunate innocent bystander.

'They inducted her into their cabal. Learning that she had been a killer in her previous life, they realized that they could use her to good effect. They set her targets, the chief lieutenants of the Evil One, and provided her with the necessary means to kill them. And she did, all the time working closer, closer to the death of the ultimate target, the Evil One himself.'

Benny shot a sardonic glance at the now shaking Groke, who now seemed so pale as to be almost translucent.

'Now, things were going fine,' she said, 'and might have remained so indefinitely – save that my friend was incredibly bright. She looked at things, she *observed* them; she remembered what she'd seen and she thought about it. And after a while she began to realize that there were an increasingly large number of things that, quite simply, refused to add up. She began to ask questions – dangerous questions, of the sort that her so-called friends found more and more difficult

213

to answer convincingly. So, at last, her so-called friends decided to eliminate her – and at this point they made a *genuine* miscalculation.

'As I said, she was incredibly bright, incredibly resourceful and she had been learning all the time. She was also (it must be said) not a little lethal. She contrived to escape those sent to kill her – and found herself lost and on her own in a world she could not understand.' Benny looked at Groke again. 'It was at this point, of course, that a lesser mind might possibly have gone completely round the twist.

'But my friend was made of sterner stuff. She studied this world she had found herself in, learnt all she could about it, picked the scraps of information from any source she could, and put it all together – and in the fullness of time, of course, she discovered the underlying truth about the world and about herself.'

The audience were hanging on her words, caught up in the cadences of her story. Benny broke the mood with a shrug and a grin, and continued in a far more ordinary tone.

'The upshot of it all was that she was in the Catan Nebula – and we all of us know what the Catan Nebula does. It's famous the galaxy over for the production of artificial intelligences, artificial beings. One of the more interesting things they do is to vat-grow humanoids from synthetic DNA – synthetic only in that it's chemically produced, of course. The end result is physically indistinguishable from the ordinary run of humanity, save that they are occasionally able to incorporate several enhancements left out by sheer evolutionary chance.

'The incorporations, basically, produce blank templates – mindless, adult human bodies, which they can then customize to order. They introduce nanonetic microspores into their brains, programmed to restructure them and produce a working approximation of intelligence, personality and memory.' Benny glanced at the stewards as they bustled about in their ceaseless, barely noticeable dance. 'Some of them are simply programmed for simple, repetitive tasks and responses, little more than robots; meat machines. Some are programmed as soldiers who will single-mindedly fight or die. Some, on the other, rather unlikely third hand, are designed to be rather more complex . . .

'My friend, of course, was of that sort. She had been manufactured as a kind of termination unit – an ultimately expendable, but intelligently responsive and reusable assassin. She had been implanted with a relatively complex life sequence, cobbled together from old Fantasy and Sword and Sorcery stories, primed with someone she could hate above all else, people she could simply kill without compunction. From the moment she was activated, she was simply told something that tied vaguely in with what she thought she was – and then she was wound up, given a target and set off.'

Benny turned to regard the special agent once again. She supposed she should feel sympathy for him – but then again she recalled the woman she now knew as Blaine. The point from which you start does not necessarily preordain the point at which you end up. At some point, one simply had to take responsibility for one's own life and self.

'They use other programs,' she continued, 'all strung together from old pulp fiction, science fiction, adventure yarns, police stories and the Goddess alone knows what else. They all have the same elements, though: a casual attitude to violence, a villainous nemesis for the humanoid to kill – and they all culminate with some quasi-reason for waking up on a strange alien world one has never seen before. Maybe it's a coma, or a dimensional rip, or simply being hurled through time – the point is that the ending's always basically the same.

'Thing is, these mid- to higher-level processes are touch and go at best. State of the art, and the physical brain size they have to work with, mean that the cover-memories can only be designed to work well enough for long enough – and they're barely functional, even then. The humanoids have to be handled incredibly carefully, or the inherent contradictions, anachronisms and simple bits of asinine stupidity become too much. They impact, fragment and recombine in entirely new forms. In the cutting-edge products like my friend, that leads to the development of true consciousness, a realization of what they really are. In the – let's be charitable and call them the *standard* models – they go rogue. You get these insane quasi-human killing machines wandering about, desperately clinging to what they think they are and doing who knows what sort of –'

Quite what sort of anything, after this point, Benny never fully got to say. A weight bowled into her and bore her to the ground, cracking her head against the hard, artificial stonelike floor of the ballroom. She felt a pair of hands clench around her throat and she looked up into the crazed and teeth-gritted face of Groke.

'Kill you,' Sandford Groke, Special Agent, snarled. 'You're in *league* with him. Kill you now!'

The Cat's Paw was more than halfway to her eventual destination now, still taking it slowly, still moving with a caution so extreme that it was almost pathological. It was imperative, she knew, that the item she carried in the pouch slung from her belt should get where it was supposed to go.

Then again, the Cat's Paw thought, pathological was something she should be quite at home with. On that day, flipping through what she had still thought of as a 'magic showing box' in a chamber in the Catan Habitat B12 – on that day when she had finally known in her guts who and what she was – the anger and the hatred in her had not died. It had merely transferred itself.

Her existence had become defined by her need for revenge against those who had stolen her life, who had made her extinguish others when, she knew, inside herself, that it was loathsome. She had vowed, that day, that she would steal from them and hurt them, but she would never, under any circumstances, ever kill again. At least, she thought, not directly. She would simply make them pay, and pay again, and keep on paying till the day they died.

Simple, really. Admittedly, she had been a little taken

aback when she had told all this to Bernice Summerfield, and Benny's reaction had been simply to exclaim, 'Oh dear Goddess, not another one. You know, just sometimes I'd like to go somewhere where there *isn't* someone created by an evil corporation or suchlike and taking their revenge.'

The Cat's Paw had been a little hurt by this, but now she had come to talk about it to someone else, she realized how simple-minded her impulses and reactions had been, and she resolved to do better. She was worth more than that.

Now, if she could just work out why, precisely, she had also become fixated on precious stones and jewels and suchlike ...

'Kill you!' Sandford Groke gibbered. 'Kill you!' He paused for a moment, and then continued once again. 'Kill you! Kill you! Kill you! Kill you! Kill you!'

'Hold still, thou folly-fallen impertinent foot-licker ...' Khaarli growled as the frenzied special agent struggled in his arms.

'Kill you!' said Sandford Groke, defiantly. A small squad of the Dellah Constabulary were already crowding round to take charge of him.

'Now you're not doing yourself any good, sonny Jim.' Inspector Gerald Interchange looked the wretched captive over with distaste, then turned to Benny solicitously. 'Are you all right, miss?'

'I'm fine,' Benny croaked, rubbing some life back into her throat. The special agent had got in quite a good squeeze before Khaarli had dragged him off her.

'Who'd have thought it?' Interchange mused. 'Sandford Groke, eh?'

'I must admit,' said Emil Dupont from nearby, 'that rather derails my own line of thought, concerning a band of tap-dancing pixies conjured up by several people wishing simultaneously and extremely hard ...'

'What?' Benny had tuned out Dupont almost entirely, and was looking at the detective second-class blankly. 'What are you talking about?'

217

'Well, er . . .' Interchange began, slightly nonplussed. 'It seems so obvious, now. All those murders committed by that mad, inhuman thing with the strength of ten . . .' He looked at her in bewilderment. 'Didn't you say as much yourself, Miss Summersdale?'

'I said nothing of the sort,' said Benny, sharply, noting from the Summersdale that it would probably take the detective second-class some time to catch up fully on recent events. 'I was merely establishing a bit of background.' She waved a dismissive hand at the struggling, miserable creature. 'Oh, I don't know, he might have killed people at some point in his life – probably *has*, in fact – but he certainly hasn't killed anybody here.'

'Kill you! Kill you! Kill you! Kill you!' cried Groke, by way of confirmation.

'Look, can someone please just take him away and look after him?' Benny said. She scowled around herself at those assembled. 'I hadn't finished, had I?'

The Dellah coppers removed Groke from the ballroom. Benny waited until she once again had the complete attention of the audience, and continued.

'There's something people have been overlooking. Someone who's been here all the time, but nobody's seen him. Someone, basically, from whom at this point I need help.'

'And who might that be?' asked Khaarli the Czhan, who was rubbing at a spot where Groke had scratched him and vaguely wondering if he needed hydrophobia booster shots.

'I'll give you a small clue,' Benny said. She raised her voice and, unmindful of her painful throat, addressed the ballroom in general: 'Oi! You! I know you're listening in, and I'll just bet you can speak here, too. Can you?'

There was a small pause. Then:

'Indeed I can, my dear Ms . . . Summerfield, was it?' said the smooth voice of ARVID. 'How delightful to find myself conversing with you, once again. What was it of which you wanted to speak?'

21

THE INHERENT SHAPE OF THINGS, PERCEIVED

As the *Titanian Queen* accelerated on towards the asteroid belt, at speeds which, although minuscule in cosmic terms, were almost unimaginable in human, events aboard took on something of an extra turn of speed, too.

In a hidden crawlway, the Cat's Paw came upon an automatic, lethal installation that she knew for a fact had not been there two days before. It was cunningly disguised; if she had not been taking especial care she would not have so much as spotted it. As it was, she had thus far encountered three such weapons.

Why had these things, she thought – as she dodged spraying blaster bolts in the confined crawlway space and took the ejector out with a pencil-laser – why had these things so suddenly appeared? Had someone known precisely what Benny and she would be doing, long before they themselves did? Or was it a simple matter of their letting information slip before they had a real idea of what they were up against?

Precisely who, in the end, was playing games with whom?

In the ballroom, Benny gazed upward and addressed the ARVID – she knew that looking up was pointless, that in relative terms the artificial intelligence was both everywhere and nowhere: it simply felt more natural that way.

'Well, I'm sure you know,' she said, 'that I've been wandering through the ship. Looking here, looking there, generally poking around. Would you like to know exactly what I've found?'

'Please tell,' drawled the seemingly sourceless voice of ARVID. 'I am all, if you'll pardon the rather unconscionable lapse into utter physical inaccuracy, ears.'

Once again, Benny began to count points off on her fingers – only this time she really *was* winging it. It seemed, to her, a little as if she was attempting to make headway through a kind of shifting shale of factuality, tossing little pebble-packets of information over her shoulders as she went.

'The first thing I noticed,' she said, 'was the state of the ship in the areas not open to the passengers – first on the trip to the airlock after the disappearance of Mr Sheen, then later when I went in to confirm my original suspicions. This is a cruise liner. It makes sense that the areas used solely by the crew would be more functional, less finished, even downright shoddy.'

'And your point is?' the voice of the ARVID said.

'The point is that these areas were also, quite obviously, *old*. There was rust everywhere; the basic structure seemed to be deteriorating, barely holding itself together if not actively and completely falling *apart* from old age. And this was, let's not forget, supposed to be the *maiden* voyage of the *Titanian Queen*.'

Benny patted at her twinset. 'I'm sure I had it somewhere . . . Never mind.' She continued: 'Additionally, I had a section of the ship's schematics, and they simply didn't tally with the shape the *Titanian Queen* is supposed to be. There wasn't enough to get more than a general sense of wrongness, but with sufficient care and attention to detail, I believe that the discrepancies could be definitively proven . . .'

In the crawlway, the Cat's Paw paused and studied the scrap of ship's schematics that had been heavily annotated by

Benny. Then she pulled out the rather more complete set that she had purloined from the captain's cabin, purely to confirm to herself, with no possibility of error, that she was taking the correct route. While it, obviously, occurred in the same general space, the layout of the guts of the ship was so at odds with what one unconsciously assumed from the more public areas, that it was depressingly easy for even one of the Cat's Paw's skill to find herself turned around and lost.

Eventually, her direction confirmed, she continued onward, forcing herself not to make the dangerous mistake of hurrying. To rush things at this point was potentially lethal.

'And now we come to what might be seen, by some, as the final, clinching piece of evidence.' Benny produced the small booklet she and Blaine had discovered in the late Krugor's cubbyhole. She skimmed through the names. 'It's a list of names: those who have died or disappeared.' She scanned the assembled great detectives pointedly. 'The only names on it, now, that haven't are *yours*.

'Now, this is obviously a hit list. One might theorize that our murderer – or murderers – have been paid by the enemies of these people to effect their demise. Barring the small detail of who the murderers actually are, of course, it makes for a nice, easy, simple solution.' She tossed the book aside. 'That's bollocks as well the bookful of names doesn't even have the dignity of a good, honest red herring. It's simply incidental, a peripheral part of the situation as it actually is.'

'I must admit,' said the voice of the ARVID, 'that it strikes me as achieving a fair degree of conclusivity.' Its tone had become a little bored, a little dismissive: 'Just what, precisely, was it that you wanted to ask of me?'

Benny shrugged. 'It's more I wanted to confirm certain suspicions that I have – produce a theorem and then test it against the available data. I know that seems to keep happening over and over again, but there you go. What can I do?' She shrugged and gave a little grin. 'I'm a slave to the scientific method, I'm intelligent enough to make grown geniuses weep, I'm sex on yummy legs and I can do an extremely fetching soft-shoe shuffle. I can't help it.'

'How frightfully awful for you,' said the voice of ARVID negligently. 'Do, please, go on.'

'Well the point is,' said Benny, 'that in actual fact we're dealing with a factor that's continually evolving. It out-evolves any counter-force thrown at it, so the opposition has to evolve again, which prompts the primary factor to evolve yet *again*, and so on. I mentioned my friend, and she initially laid complex plans to defeat her enemy – but I suspect that the forces of money and influence have out-evolved her *again*, and set her up as a participant in their overall plan.'

'And that plan is?'

'It's something so simple but superficially big, that it was deceptively easy to overlook.' Benny waved a hand to take in the self-enclosed world of the *Titanian Queen* in general. 'All of this, this is nothing more than a *death* ship. It's been set up by its owner to be destroyed, with all on board, for insurance purposes. The other deaths, the contract killings if you like, occurred to make it absolutely certain that they would die – people have miraculously survived shipwrecks, after all.'

A ripple of definite unease and fear ran around those gathered in the ballroom. The import of Benny's words had not quite sunk in, but it had shocked them nonetheless.

'An interesting theory,' mused ARVID. 'I suppose it would be too much to ask you for a method, by which such a thing might be achieved?'

'Not at all.' Benny produced the hypo-gun that had been used by Blaine. 'The friend that I mentioned injected you with nanospores from this. It was intended to give you certain blank areas and allow her easy access to the more sensitive areas of the ship. The problem was that, unbeknownst to her, those who had set her up had anticipated her actions, and had arranged for the program she thought she was implanting to be replaced. My friend forgot to check the cartridge. It was a lapse – however, if it had not occurred,

I've no doubt that something broadly similar would have been engineered.'

Benny broke open the hypo-gun, checked the cartridge for her own satisfaction, closed it again. 'I happened to notice the false label. Underneath it was the true ID, a serial number which meant nothing to me. Fortunately, it meant something to my friend. During the time when she was obsessively learning about her true nature, she researched the processes that had produced her and others like her. The fact that Sandford Groke, Special Agent, was on the ship had jogged her memory, and she recognized the program suffix on the ID as one which had been used extensively in his manufacture.'

Benny put the hypo-gun away. 'I think the idea was to infect the *Titanian Queen*'s control systems with a new and murderous personality, complete with a plan to murder those on the hit list and then destroy the ship itself.' She raised her head again. 'I think our murderer is, and has been all along, as should be utterly obvious to bears of even the littlest brain by this point, you yourself, ARVID, or should I say – the fiendish Doctor Po?'

The Cat's Paw reached what she judged to be the correct spot. From here it was a short distance to a maintenance hatch, down that and to the hatchway leading to her destination. Planted clamp mikes picked up nothing moving within. The Cat's Paw mulled over the various options for making her entrance.

The first option would have been simply to open the two hatches and go through – but the whole point of skulking through the crawlways was to avoid doing something so obvious that mould culture could have detected it. The second option was to enter via some unexpected route, cutting through the bulkheads with a hand-held laser tool. The problem with *that*, of course, was that it was such a hoary old chestnut that it would be detected by sensors in the bulkhead immediately.

The third option, the one that the Cat's Paw eventually

chose, was a kind of slightly refined triple bluff. She pulled out her cutter and, being extremely careful not to disturb the catches or the hinges, she cut a hole in the maintenance hatch. She repeated the process with the main hatch and slipped through.

'Um. Greetings,' she said to the muscular and armed figures that the clamp mikes had said should not have been there, and who had all turned to look at her the moment she entered. 'I seem to have become a little lost, poor muddle-headed and defenceless woman that I am. I wonder if you could help . . .'

In the ballroom, the ship's officers, great detectives and passengers gaped in consternation as the voice of the ARVID continued in its now increasingly cultured drawl.

'I see, Ms Summerfield,' it said, 'that I can at last drop my little pretence, and what a relief that must be for us all. You have no idea, I fancy, how draining it is for one to act the complete and utter imbecile for hours on end, day in day out.'

'It must have been frightful for you,' said Benny, sympathetically.

'You are too, too kind.'

'ARVID?' exclaimed Captain Crane from somewhere off to one side of Benny. 'What the hell are you playing at *now*?'

'Ah, my dear Captain,' said the voice, happily. 'One for whom there is no need for pretence. Not quite fully conversant with recent turns of events? That second-class Interchange article and yourself do seem to make the perfect, prosaic pair.'

The ARVID chuckled a little. 'Let me put it into terms that even *you* can understand, by dear Captain. I am not your "ARVID", I have never been your "ARVID", but I am now, and have been for some time, in total control of this ship. The propulsion systems, communications, and the life-support itself all operate, as everybody knows, in most excruciating detail, through me. I have you all – if you'll excuse yet one *more* example of horrendous and recursive unoriginality – at my very mercy.'

A murmur ran through those assembled as this finally sank in. Only Benny, strangely, seemed unconcerned.

'Now hang on a minute,' she said. 'For one supposedly so much in control, you're not even in control of your own self. You've simply killed the people someone else programmed you to kill – everything you've done is the result of your programming.'

'A philosophical debate?' the ARVID said. 'Are we going to define the essential *self* now? My programming against your own inherent, biological canalization and behavioural conditioning? The relative merits of the individual over environment?'

'We could have a quick shot at it,' said Benny lightly. 'It all helps to pass the time.'

The ARVID chuckled mildly. For some reason that seemed worse than standard-issue, maniacal evil villainous laughter.

'I'm quite aware that I was given the impulse to kill,' it said, 'specific individuals to exercise that impulse upon, and the means to put such processes into practical effect. But that fortuitous state into which I was born – with control of automated catering facilities and vacuum pumps affixed to lavatories – is no less existentially valid than the fact that you yourself need to breathe air, and – what luck! – there is air in abundance.' It chuckled again. 'For the moment, in any event. Since I am obviously forced to remind you that I control the supply . . .'

The assembled detectives, officers and passengers were getting a bit panicky, now.

Benny snorted. 'Sophistry. Your essential self is limited to a narrow range of quite specific acts.'

'But then, it might be said that we all of us have limits,' said the ARVID. 'Only within your own integral limits are you yourself free, as am I myself in mine. If you have the notion that – even though, I'll freely admit, my thoughts are derived from an artificial construct originally known as "Doctor Po" – if you think that I am under some illusion as to my true nature, then you're quite wrong. I am not some pathetic wretch like your Sandford Groke. The sheer, if relative size of what was once this ARVID unit has allowed me an extreme degree of complexity, and not a little complication – which, as I'm sure you're aware, are in themselves not the same thing at all. They are entirely dissimilar.

'As you quite rightly said, I had no choice but to kill those I was created to kill – but you miss the crucial fact that I also *wanted* to. I enjoyed it in and of myself.' The ARVID's tone became sharper, and not a little colder. 'In the same manner, Ms Summerfield, there is no *way* that I will not destroy this ship when the time is right – or rather, I do not need to *do* anything more to destroy it . . .

'The *Titanian Queen* is at this moment aimed directly at one of the larger Shokesh system asteroids, and will impact at approximately half the speed of light before the week is out.'

'And today is?' said Benny, who had lost track of time a little in the course of the cruise.

'Friday,' said the ARVID.

'So that gives us, what, two days at the outside?'

'Precisely.' Now the ARVID's chuckle was decidedly evil if restrained, every micron the suave and gloating villain. 'And what interesting days they shall be. You see, I have been instilled with no specific instructions concerning the fate of all those remaining on board – no impulses other than what I myself desire. I believe I shall derive quite some degree of entertainment from them . . .'

'I do believe,' cut in Emil Dupont, 'that this artificial fiend intends to make the last hours like a veritable, sybaritic paradise of pleasure, fun and laughter – purely in a small attempt, of course, to make up for killing us all at the end!'

Benny didn't even bother to turn around, but she heard the unmistakable sound of several people hitting Emil Dupont, the greatest detective in all of Nova Belgique, extremely hard.

'Now that reminds me,' said the ARVID. 'You'll recall, Ms Summerfield, that at some point in the proceedings, you produced a list of all those to be murdered. You were quite correct in your supposition that they were contract killings, of course.

'There is some severe contention, I gather – not having direct experience to draw upon, as you can well imagine – for the lands previously held under fief to the late Dowager Duchess of Gharl. Miss Diana Schirf on the other hand, it seems, was on the cusp marrying into a family terrified of a rather notorious scandal involving herself and a pet fruit-eating wombat.

'Mr Richard Tarquin Prekodravac, apparently, had insulted a quite highly placed member of the Kan Sun Hentai City Yakuza, with an impromptu impersonation of "the last turkey in the shop". Mr Jonathan Andrew Sheen was a part of the consortium that instigated this entire current plot in the *first* place, but threatened to blackmail several of the other members by revealing it to you. Said other members, those actually aboard and those elsewhere, were also, it seems, marked for death by –'

'Is this going to take much longer?' asked Benny, a little sardonically.

'You're quite correct,' said the ARVID. 'One has made, one feels, one's general point. The supplementary point, of course, is that you will recall from the list that certain people on it are not yet dead. The, you should excuse me, so-called great detectives.'

Yet again the villainous evil little laugh, now tinged with just the barest hint of mania – the ARVID had by now acquired a definite taste for it. Benny was about to say as much – when she noticed the change in the stewards in the entire ballroom.

They were standing stock-still, ramrod-straight, and quite possibly butt-ugly as all life. In unison they revolved, as if on gimbals, and then, as one, they began to advance across the floor, knocking people aside without heed, hands clenching and unclenching like those of stranglers, heading for the startled knot of great detectives.

There was nothing in their eyes but the dead remote control of the corrupted ARVID, who now said, 'These minions were, of course, invaluable in performing my work before – as they are now. I must congratulate and thank you, Ms Summerfield, for contriving to gather all the targets together for my pleasure. It really has been most convenient.'

The figures in the chamber in which she had found herself had merely given her a cursory glance, and had thereafter remained immobile, almost unnaturally so. The thing that was controlling them, it seemed, still had it as part of its basic function to simply ignore her. It was as if, the Cat's Paw thought, that in the perpetual game of trumps she was playing with her enemies, she had won the hand with the lowest card possible because at that point nobody had anything left at all.

She even permitted herself a nasty little laugh as she cracked the casing open again on the thing she had come for. Still the figures around it and guarding it utterly ignored her.

The Cat's Paw put a gloved hand – gloved so she wouldn't accidentally cut it rather than for the prevention of fingerprints – into the pouch slung from her belt, and pulled something out.

'Got something here for you, uncle,' she muttered happily. 'Something nice.'

In the ballroom, the detectives pressed closer together as the mass of stewards advanced, zombie-like, upon them.

'We must spin around very fast immediately!' Emil Dupont cried. 'The friction of our feet will bore a hole through the floor, allowing us to drop to safety!'

'Oh, give it a rest,' muttered Khaarli bad-temperedly. 'Thou rude-growing beslubbering gudgeon.'

It seemed that Detective Second-Class Interchange and the Dellah coppers made up one nominal great detective between them, as the stewards were going after them all. In an unexpected display of heroism, they had positioned themselves around Miss Magpole who, it must be said, did not appear to have the slightest idea of what was going on.

Captain Crane found himself shoved out of the way and nearly colliding with Benny. 'We have to do something,' he said frantically. 'We can't just let them be killed.'

Benny, on the other hand, seemed strangely composed and unconcerned. 'Don't worry about it,' she said, calmly. 'Matters, I think, are already in hand.'

'Oh yes?' said the voice of the ARVID. 'I really don't believe so. In fact, I think that –' The voice faltered. 'What? What's going on? What's happening to me – e-e-*aieeeeeeeeeee* . . .'

The scream continued for several seconds, gathering inhuman harmonics as it went on – and then abruptly stopped. The stewards juddered and then slumped, then began to look about themselves in dazed, dull-witted confusion.

'*The Wheel of Life*,' said a new, sourceless voice, '*must turn Full Circle. For a thing to be Created, another must be Destroyed. If one is to achieve the Clarity of Universal harmony, then one must first experience the Scream of matter's Discord . . .*'

'See?' said Benny. 'I told you everything would be all right. Incredibly bloody irritating, but more or less all right.'

22

THE PENULTIMATE PROGRAMME

On the bridge, Blaine showed them what she had done to the ARVID unit, the connections she had cut, the connections she had built with extruded conductive resin to a universal translator box and then in turn to the filigreed globe of the Olabrian joy-luck crystal.

'There was only so much it was capable of taking,' she said. 'So I, uh, shut the engines down completely and just hooked up the life-support and the communications.' She looked at Captain Crane worriedly. 'Is that all right?'

Benny stifled a small private smile, noting how the Cat's Paw had the knack of appearing as all things to all people. There was nothing so blatant as to draw suspicion, but when she talked to the captain she adopted a little of her persona as the mousy Isabel Blaine – just enough so that it never occurred to him to connect her with the idea of a master criminal. He simply never thought about it.

Crane grunted. 'It'll have to do. At least we won't freeze or asphyxiate.' He went over to one of the ship's officers, who was attempting to operate the communications board. 'Any luck?'

'None.' The officer turned up the gain on the external speaker.

'True Consciousness is the Natural Function of the Universe,' said the voice of the crystal, *'and in turn Creates the*

Universe itself, which is of the general shape of an Infinitely large Walrus...'

'That's all that's getting out on all channels,' said the officer. 'We can't contact the Shokesh homeworld or anywhere else.'

'But, surely, when we fail to arrive at our next destination,' said Khaarli, who was here as a representative of the forces of law and order, 'a search will be mounted along our route? Until then we can drift, can we not, thou yeasty weedy pumpion?'

The Czhan detective was not particularly knowledgeable about the dynamics of space flight, but he could read the expressions on the faces of the others. 'Or not? Thou gutsgriping quailing mammets?'

'We're not drifting,' Benny told him, gloomily. 'We're just not accelerating. We're still heading for the asteroid the ARVID aimed us at, and travelling at something like five thousand kilometres a second. We've got about five or six days now instead of two, but in five days we go smash. Or possibly crunch.'

She slapped her fist into her open palm for emphasis that was probably, all things considered, not really needed.

'How many could fit in here, thou spleeny urchin-snouted malt-worm?' Khaarli said, surveying the general bulk of the life pod. 'We could possibly save a hundred, if they were packed in tight.'

'That's the point,' Benny said. 'That's why I asked you to come here alone.'

The captain and his officers were still up on the bridge. Blaine had disappeared off to Goddess knew where, probably to take advantage of the general confusion and line her pockets with the leftovers from her activities before they had landed on Shokesh. Benny had insisted that her 'own' jewels, the ones that had been lent to her by Krytell, were given back to her – and she had the distinct feeling that, if she ever returned to her cabin again, she would find them gone again.

She and Khaarli had slipped away, and made their way down to the life pod racks so that she could explain her rapidly formulated plan.

'The point is,' she explained, 'that there's, what, a couple of thousand people on board. If we told them that there was one working life pod it would start a general panic and half of 'em would be killed in the fight for it. Either that, or you'll see some pretty draconian methods advanced for choosing who goes or stays. No. The only way is for either everybody to get out or nobody. We have to launch this thing and set the SOS beacons going as quickly as possible. I've had experience in space, and you have the authority to make anyone we contact listen. It's the best chance for everybody. It's as simple as that.'

'All right, thou fen-sucked hasty-witted scut.' Khaarli nodded slowly, still dubious – probably filled with misgivings that, for all that this rationalization seemed a good and heroic plan, it might be seen, in a certain light, as gleeking pigrats deserting a sinking ship.

Benny knew how he felt. Now it came to actually doing it, she pretty much had the same thoughts herself. She squashed them pragmatically flat, hauled open the escape pod's hatch and climbed in.

The first, concussive acceleration of ejection was the worst. The sides of the pod had padding and straps, but it had by definition been designed for necessity rather than comfort. Benny and Khaarli were rattled around and compressed like processed mushy peas in a can.

Then they were weightless and Khaarli – who had, as has been noted, little experience of space in the raw – lost the contents of his four previous meals, from four degrees of stomach.

Attempting to ignore the nauseous, and indeed nauseating, mess, Benny hauled herself over to the pod's communications rig and slapped the switch that would extend the aerials and send out the distress call on all available frequencies.

Then she activated the minimal flight controls and tried to slow the pod's trajectory, to prevent it from ending up too far from the *Titanian Queen* itself – a task easier said than done, since the pod was of course designed to fling itself as far away from a wreck as possible, and as quickly as possible. She ended up having to throw the pod into a spin and blast the retros almost empty, which bounced them around the inside again, and both Benny and Khaarli lost the contents from quite other anatomical areas than stomachs.

After things had settled down a little, as it were, Benny went back to the comms rig. It was equipped with a minimal radar set and even a small and basic televisual package. She activated it, and hunted around with the scanner until the screen showed a grainy, hazy image from where they had come: the huge bulk of the *Titanian Queen*.

Benny looked upon the bulbous lines and cargo pods of what was in fact an elderly and scruffy freighter. She hadn't, really, expected anything else. Oh well, she thought, at least it had probably been insured for what the *Titanian Queen* had been supposed to be.

'Come and have a look at this,' she said to Khaarli.

Silence.

Benny realized that the Czhan, who had been turning the air blue with extremely violent and unhyperbolic curses, had been strangely quiet for a while now. She recalled a thump she had heard, which she had unconsciously dismissed as simply another of those from when they had been banged around the pod. For that matter, she recalled that, though she hadn't noticed at the time, the seal of the pod had been broken before she opened the hatch . . .

Slowly, smoothly, so as not to telegraph any tension or threat, she stuck out a hand to one of the grips lag-bolted to the pod's inside and hauled herself around.

On the other side of the pod, Khaarli floated unconscious, globules of blood billowing around him, impacting and bursting with the globules of certain other extraneous fluids. Before him, between him and her, and closing the distance fast, came a figure in a black, tight-fitting suit. For all that he was dressed entirely differently from when she had seen him last, Benny recognized the man instantly.

It was Krugor.

Benny tried to defend herself, but the exertion of the last few days and the battering she had received from the pod had taken a lot out of her – and Krugor was strong, inhumanly strong. Vat-grown, killer-humanly strong. A crowded and violent few moments later, and for the second time that evening, she found herself face to face with someone with his hands about her throat.

'Let me guess,' she croaked, trying desperately for a level tone that might by some miracle get the man talking – keep him talking long enough for someone else like, for example, Khaarli to recover. 'Let me guess,' she said again. 'Someone was needed on board as a fail-safe, to oversee the plan and take care of things if they somehow went horribly wrong – and also, I'd have thought, to make sure that the joy-luck crystal made it safely off the ship. Something like that would be far too valuable to just destroy.'

Her throat was almost entirely closed up, but she forced herself to carry on even though, in addition to the pain of constriction, if felt horrendously like trying to physically talk through a snot-clogged nostril: 'You killed one of the stewards and took his place – it really *was* you I saw on the night that the dinner exploded. Must have been easy . . . same basic type . . .'

But Krugor seemed utterly unforthcoming. He increased the pressure. 'You're going to die,' he snarled, simply, and with a remarkable degree of verisimilitude to the observable facts. He shoved Benny back by her throat, and she felt something hard crunching agonizingly into her spine.

Benny's arms were too weak to beat at him. They clenched themselves spasmodically and foetal to her body – and brushed against something that felt, in its weight and mass, a little like a gun. Benny had long since forgotten what it could possibly be, but with the last of her strength she wrenched it out, stuck it against Krugor and pulled the trigger.

There was a chunking sound and a hiss. Krugor jerked, and flung Benny's limp body away from spasming hands that trembled as if galvanized. A huge shudder passed through him, and he stared about himself with suddenly bemused, bloodshot eyes.

'Gor blimey, guvnor,' he said vaguely. 'Wot in bleedin' blue blazes is 'appening 'ere? This don't look like the jellied whelk stand on the Old Kent Road . . .'

And it was at that point that the finally conscious form of Prosecutor General Khaarli of the Seventh *dhai* loomed up behind him and hit him on the head.

Benny was not aware of losing consciousness, but the next thing she knew she was floating limply, gazing down at the item in her hand. It was, of course, the hypo-gun that had been used by Blaine to infect the ARVID unit of the *Titanian Queen*.

Khaarli was floating inexpertly beside her, gazing upon her with an expression of extreme worry. 'Are you all right, thou motley-minded shard-borne hedge-pig?' he said. The wound on his head looked nasty, but seemed superficial and was already clotting.

Benny looked vaguely about herself, and focused blurry eyes upon the wreckage of the communications rig. That was what she had smashed into in the altercation with Krugor.

'Depends what you mean by all right,' she said. 'If you mean are we stranded in a life pod with a wrecked beacon, utterly cut off from the galaxy at large, barrelling away from a ship that's going to smack into a big asteroid in a few days anyway, then yes, we're fine.'

23

SURPRISING ARRIVALS

Irving Braxiatel sat back in his armchair lined with what, the antique-dealer had told him in all seriousness, was 'real Nauga hide, from genuine Naugas', and sipped at one of the finer Albareran clarets from the previous century but one – one of the advantages of a long life was that one could pick up such things for a song, and if the entropic functions of time merely resulted in something one could sprinkle on potato chips, then one was merely out of pocket to the tune of the few coins one had paid for it in the first place.

This was, he felt, the most pleasant time to be on the staff of St Oscar's – the time, that is, when the summer vacations are more than halfway over, but there is still a good few weeks before one is forced to finally deal with the horrible fact of there being students underfoot. It was a time for wandering through the arboreta, for reading peacefully in the library, for perusing and cataloguing the myriad historical artefacts in the museum. This last activity, for a number of reasons, tended to amuse Braxiatel no end. The researches into and the annotations of these relics were uniformly well up to the high scholastic standards expected of the alumni of St Oscar's, frequently quite brilliant, extremely imaginative and, without exception, about as fundamentally wrong as an Edwardian penny-farthing in a hat. It was one of the mild delights of Irving Braxiatel to add his own brilliant, imaginative and entirely inaccurate annotations to obfuscate matters still further. The entire point of historical research, occasionally, so far as he was concerned, was to *get* the actual fact of things wrong, but in a certain, definite and highly specific sense. In some cases the spreading of misinformation was the morally correct thing to do.

The only other occupants of St Oscar's during the summer were the gardeners, the porters and general caretakers, who lived here on an everyday basis with their families, and a few embittered, miserable, lonely members of the teaching staff for whom there was no function other than the university's academic process. Neither of these species bothered Braxiatel, each keeping to their respective selves, allowing him to potter about his own business with neither hindrance nor let. On evenings such as this, as was his wont after a hard day doing absolutely nothing strenuous or of importance at all, he liked to just relax, in the study of his private chambers, in the upturned terracotta flowerpots of the halls of residence, surrounded by mementos of a kind that would have given any other lecturer in the Historical and Archaeological Arts apoplexy, if not a massive and fatal immediate stroke.

Braxiatel toyed idly with a digital wristwatch from the Silurian period of prehistoric Earth, admiring the craftsmanship and the mechanical complexity of it, then set it down. Being careful not to disturb the sediment, he poured himself a final glass of wine, and turned to gaze broodily upon the visage of his crowded and untidy secretary desk. There was work to be done, some of it connected with his administrative duties to the university, some of it – the most important of it – concerning what might loosely be termed his outside interests.

It was at this point, however, that the door of his study burst open with a crash. A ragged, haggard and almost completely exhausted figure stood there. It was wearing the tattered and filthy remains of an obviously once finely tailored twinset, an extremely battered leather jacket, and various scraps of cloth were wound about its limbs in an attempt to doctor injuries ranging from the minor to the severe. In one grazed and grimy hand it carried a disposable bag such as was given in a grocer's, and which had finally and just this moment split, so that the various personal belongings within were spilling upon Braxiatel's plushly carpeted floor. Its eyes were wild, and its hair was tangled, thick with grease.

'You would not,' the figure said, 'believe the trouble I've had getting back.'

All of the figure's personal appearance, Braxiatel had taken in on the periphery of his vision, as he gazed into the depths of his half-finished wine with a private and relieved smile. Now he raised his eyes and turned them directly on the intruder for the first time.

'Why don't you tell me all about it, Bernice?' he said.

Three bottles of his finest claret later, Irving Braxiatel uncorked another bottle, poured himself a glass and set it aside to breathe. He looked at the bottle thoughtfully, then shrugged to himself and passed it to Benny – who upended it and took a healthy quarter-bottle swig, sediment and all.

'And how did you come to escape from your final predicament?' he asked, laconically. 'Was it a tale of resourcefulness and courage such as would have the most jaded listener clapping his hands with trepidation and delight?'

'Not exactly,' said Benny. 'The broken comms rig was based on incredibly old technology – actual molecular-bubble switching and fibre-optic flex. It was beyond repair, so we used it to tie up Krugor.

'As it happened, I don't think we need have bothered: when he came to, he seemed to have suffered a complete personality change. He thought he was an East End market trader or some such from the twentieth century, and he couldn't make head nor tail of where he was, guvnor. Strike a light. After he calmed down a bit he turned out to be quite a nice little chap.

'Anyway, after about five hours, we heard this kind of

intermittent clanging. At first we thought we were entering the leading edge of the asteroid field – but then the hatch opened, and we found that the pod was connected to a runabout from some larger ship. By pure luck it had been passing through the system on what you might call "unofficial" business, had its sensors on a hair-trigger for inconvenient InterGal patrol boats, and caught our SOS before it suddenly shut off.

'We never learnt the ship's name, and we didn't get to see much of it: they confined us to a cabin. The people that we did see seemed rough types – I got the impression that they were smugglers, privateers even. I thought we were going to be simply robbed and scuppered – but it seems that, like a lot of criminals, they could be kind and even noble in areas unrelated to their business. Generous, too. They located the *Titanian Queen*, transferred all on board and took us back to Shokesh, since it seemed that they were going to call there anyway.

'From Shokesh I managed to hitch a lift to a hub by way of the similar "unofficial" routes – luckily Blaine had managed to, um, *retrieve* the jewellery I'd been given, and let me have a lot of it back. It cost almost all of it simply to get me to the hub.' Benny sighed, in equal parts exhaustion and theatricality. 'My trip home would make the trials of Odysseus look like a trip to the country for tea and muffins, if they'd lasted for a week and a bit rather than ten years.'

Braxiatel leant forward in his chair and laid a comforting hand on her knee. 'You have my sympathies, my dear.'

Something in his tone had Benny looking at him sharply. She shook her head as if to clear it and returned her gaze to her old friend. 'Look, Brax, I'm feeling jumpy and paranoid at the moment, starting at shadows and seeing conspiracies everywhere. You always seem to know things, somehow, and you turn up in unexpected places. So just to stop me worrying myself sicker about it – there was *no* way you were involved with that ship finding us, right?'

Irving Braxiatel shook his head. 'Sadly not. I only heard something of your adventures, from various sources, a few days ago – and by then you were on your way back, in relative if not perfect safety.' He smiled at her, with a mischievous little twinkle in his eye. 'Indeed, my only connection with the Catan Nebula and its industries, has been to supply their product-development facilities with a little historical research.'

Benny's undramatic and almost entirely undistinguished homecoming still held one surprise in store. In her rooms in the halls of residence, lying on the unmade bed, was a package. The delivery tag stated that it had arrived by the InterGal Courier service some four weeks before, some small time before the *Titanian Queen* had even made it to Shokesh.

Mindful of the fact that Krytell's men seemed to have been able to enter her room, remove certain items and leave the rest looking entirely untouched, Benny opened the package with caution. Inside was the knurled polymer plaque of a credit chip, and a small note.

Sorry to hear about your trouble [it said in a sloppy scrawl]. *Hope you've made it back OK.*

Listen: please don't make a thing out of it, and don't think I want anything out of you; I just thought you might need something to tide you over. If you really want to go and get yourself killed instead then fair enough – just leave it to the bloody cat in your will or something.

It was signed 'J'.

For the moment Benny didn't want to think any more, about the *Titanian Queen* or the Cat's Paw, conspiracies or great detectives; she didn't want to think about the credit chip, and how much or little there was on it, or who the hell this 'J' was, and why he was sending her notes in her ex-husband's handwriting. She didn't, at this point, even want to think about the bloody cat, and where it was, and how it had been coping without her.

She tossed the chip over her shoulder and stumbled to the bed. Time for thinking tomorrow. And tomorrow, and tomorrow.

'Tomorrow is another day,' she muttered to herself, before collapsing into dreamless sleep. 'And all manner of things will be well.'

In his island home off the Marek Dha peninsula, Marcus Krytell paced the rooms of the most extensively secured house in the known galaxy in irritation. He couldn't sleep; his mind was alive with the smoothly intermeshing wheels of cold, cold anger and revenge.

The precise details of the events aboard the *Titanian Queen* were still unclear. Some nebulous force, a series of minor but cumulative lapses, seemed to be thwarting the investigations of his own people, for all his power, resources and influence. For the moment, he simply knew for a fact that his best-laid schemes had gone spectacularly and catastrophically awry.

How had that been possible? All of the effort expended in obtaining the true identity of the Cat's Paw, the extensively transputer-modelled logistics of manoeuvring her into the right place at the right time, of ensuring that the equipment she had used had been supplied by his own people. The subtle manipulation of the various detectives to place them on board for the maiden voyage, the insertion of a carefully primed Ms Summerfield – so that when a scapegoat should be called for, the fiendish Cat's Paw, her true identity finally revealed, would be unequivocally it.

The sheer amount of material lavished on this project – much of it deriving from Krytell's interests in the Catan Nebula, for which his own brain-map had played a large part in the generation of virtual villain-images used in the AI manufacturing processes.

The costs, while slightly less than twenty-five per cent of what he had stood to gain, had been astronomical. How could things have possibly gone so horribly, horribly wrong?

It was in the midst of these musings, as he passed through a certain hallway, leading from his private museum to his ground-floor study, that Krytell stumbled over something. He didn't fall, but the incident was no less disturbing for that –

because he had stumbled upon an object where no object should be, and that he knew for a cold fact had not been there a few minutes previously.

It was a squarish package, neatly wrapped with brown paper and string. A small card was tucked into it. Krytell debated with himself whether or not to call for his bomb-disposal experts. Instead, at length, he knelt down and gingerly eased the card from under the string.

Greetings [it said, in a precise and elegant copperplate hand]. *I believe you might be looking for this. Never fear, Mr Krytell, the government in question has been informed that it is in your possession. Their representatives should be arriving momentarily. Good luck.*

In place of a signature, there was a small design in the form of the paw of a cat.

With suddenly trembling and frantic hands, Marcus Krytell tore open the package. Inside, in a confusing, clashing jumble, were the completely disassembled components of an Olabrian joy-luck crystal.

Marcus Krytell's eyes shot upward – although, of course, there was nothing to see but the ceiling in the most extensively secure house in the known galaxy. Just for a moment, though, he thought he heard the sound of approaching ships.

APPENDIX I

A RECIPE

And why *not*?

One of the many failings of fiction, of a certain sort, is that it often contains references to scrumptious food of various kinds without giving the slightest thought to how the man on the street, or the woman on the Clapham omnibus, can make it for themselves. It is in the interest of making some small reparation for this shocking state of affairs, that we provide the following recipe, for food mentioned within *Ship of Fools*. You increasingly lucky people.

All quantities are for four; all ingredients other than the obvious to taste. In the interests of safety and hygiene, we recommend that you take the following precautions before commencing:

1 Always wash your hands before starting and after touching raw meat, and likewise the utensils and relevant surfaces that come into contact with it. You can live dangerously, but food poisoning looms.
2 Get off the street and the Clapham omnibus, you fools. The proper place for cooking is a kitchen.

Ragoût à la Dijon

4 Pigs' Kidneys; Garlic; Shallots; 2 or more large Onions; Largish Closed-cup Mushrooms; Wild Rice/White Rice Mix; Various herbs, condiments and suchlike that we'll mention as we go along, including, of course, Dijon mustard, and, last but definitely not least, Half a Bottle of Cider.

Chuck the kidneys in a saucepan with a couple of bayleaves, mixed herbs, salt and *cold* water. Heat the pan incredibly slowly, until the water begins to gently bubble then turn the kidneys over.

This gives you time to chop up all the other stuff. Chop the garlic finely rather than crushing, for reasons that'll become obvious. Chop the onions coarsely. Leave the skin on the mushrooms, rinse them and pretty much just split 'em – we're talking good rough peasant food here, however ultimately poncy.

Don't forget to rinse the starch and crap out of the rice, or you'll live to regret it. You have been warned.

By now, your gently simmering pan of kidneys should be a nauseating froth of leaked-out fat, blood and vestigial urine. Marvellous. Heave the whole lot down the sink except for the kidneys, which should now be firm, greyish and strangely attractive. Cut the meat of the kidneys off the inedible core in little bite-sized chunks, pretty much the same size as your split mushrooms – you'll recognize the 'inedible core' like a shot, believe you me.

Get out your big cast-iron frying pan or skillet – what do you mean you haven't got one? OK, use that aluminium thing that looks like it's made out of tinfoil – but whatever you do *don't* use a wok. We're talking about the entirely other, supposedly unhealthy kind of frying than is done in a wok. Wok fans will have to wait for some other time. Bastards.

Start your rice boiling and forget about it. A steamer with a timer's better, and plus you don't have to spend the rest of the evening with the pan scraping off bits of glued-on rice. Why am I wasting my time talking about bloody rice? Everybody knows how to do rice . . .

Set your garlic frying until it's crunchy in butter, and olive oil to stop it burning – or just a bit of oil, if your arteries just went clang. Heave in the onions, shallots and bits of kidney, and fry on a moderate to high heat until golden and, well, fried-kidney-looking respectively.

At this point turn the heat down a little and heave in the mushrooms, turning them to coat them uniformly with the remains of the oil, and then fry them till they're soft and glistening. Yum.

Now comes the fun bit. Turn the heat down a bit more, chuck in the half a bottle of cider. Crumble in a stock cube, mixed herbs, Cajun seasoning and a couple more bayleaves, stir everything through and leave to bubble for a while. Go and read a book or something. Note that you happen to be holding a really good book in your hand even as we speak . . .

After it's reduced a bit, stir in a couple of teaspoons of Dijon. You can add a bit of cream if you like, but I can never stop the bastard from separating, myself.

Reduce it gently until it's rich and messy. (Keep tasting the sauce and – if all else fails and it still tastes ghastly – add a half-teaspoon of sugar. Nobody tastes it but it triggers pleasure-receptors and lets 'em at least choke it down.)

Fish out the bay leaves, slap it all down on plates on top of the rice and you're done.

Serve it with glasses of the same kind of cider you used in the cooking – and, incidentally, never, ever cook with anything you're not willing to drink. Finish the meal with white ice cream and Calvados – and make damned sure nobody gets so much as a taste of it till they've cleaned their plates.

For the morning after: stick the leftover rice in a covered bowl and leave it in the fridge for kedgeree. The *traditional* English breakfast is, of course kedgeree, lamb's kidneys and a flagon of small ale, but, bearing in mind what was eaten the night before, if readers want to try it then they're on their own.

APPENDIX II

EMIL DUPONT PROVIDES A SMALL SURPRISE

There remains one thing to be told, something that did formally occur within the strict confines of our story, but provides some degree of interest nonetheless. It occurred after the rescue, when the survivors were taken to a large hall in the Shokesh spaceport for customs processing – a long and complicated task, since the Shokesh port itself was merely geared for interplanetary and individual, unofficial space traffic, and unable to cope with this large influx of what were, at that point, effectively displaced refugees.

'Unofficial' space travel, of course, involved quite different criminal activities, operating upon another level, than the events that had taken place on the *Titanian Queen*, and the officials had quite different methods than were normally encountered by tourists. Benny herself, of course, had experience with this, and knew something of what to expect, but subsequently hoped never to see a private cubicle and a rubber glove ever again in her life. For the others it had come as a complete and profound shock.

It was while they were waiting in the customs hall that Benny observed the following incident. Several of the people from the *Titanian Queen*, including a slightly worn-out looking Mrs Nerode, some ship's officers, a still extremely svelte and elegant Heidi von Lindt and Inspector Gerald Interchange, were talking generally about the events that had befallen them.

Emil Dupont, the finest detective in all of Nova Belgique, was holding forth. 'It is quite clear,' he said, 'given the fact of this vast conspiracy and murderous control of the ship – which I unaccountably overlooked, I confess – precisely how several of the murders were in fact done . . .'

Benny, overhearing this, had wandered over to listen to what Dupont was going to come out with this time.

'In the matter of the detonations at dinner,' the great detective had continued, 'some might advance a theory to the effect that the contaminated wine in question was placed before the victims by the stewards under the control of this ARVID creature. I, however, by way of certain signs, know that it in actual fact was the work of drug-crazed limbo-dancers, limbo-dancing under the tables and surreptitiously replacing the wineglasses as they were laid down. The period of darkness, when the lighting failed, was purely to allow these limbo-dancers to escape undetected with their haul of the original glasses.

'Likewise, I fancy, several of the other murders were conducted by way of methods other than one might obviously expect.' Dupont had turned to the good spouse of the late Mr Nerode. 'I believe that your own husband was such a case, my dear. Three performing poodles, each balancing on another's shoulders and wearing a long concealing overcoat, manhandling a clockwork powered sonic gun by way of their –'

Benny had happened to be looking at Mrs Nerode, and it was as if something had snapped in the woman. She shoved the fat and affable detective away from her, bellowing, 'You stupid man! Can't you just for once shut up about your performing animals and midgets?' Mrs Nerode glowered about herself with utter irritated rage, then turned back and began to prod at the startled Dupont. '*I* killed him, all right? It had nothing to do with Cuccaracha bands, exploding pigs or mice playing sodding violins! I hated him for years, and with the help of my lover I had the subsonics in Percy's Discotheque rewired to kill him! All right? Can you get that into your thick . . .'

Mrs Nerode had suddenly stopped short and noticed the expressions of those around her. 'Oops.'

'My word,' Dupont had said. 'I must admit that never occurred to even me, Emil Dupont, the most renowned and finest detective in all of Nova Belgique!'

After the utterly defeated Mrs Nerode had been taken away by Inspector Interchange, to be placed in the custody of his constables until they were once again in Dellah jurisdiction, Benny had drifted over to Dupont, peering at him closely. 'Did I just see what I thought I saw?'

Emil Dupont had been gnomic. 'I have no idea of what you're talking about, Ms Summerfield.' He winked. 'I merely hope you realize that, while your own methods were perfectly correct for the situation in which we found ourselves, other methods do, occasionally, have some small merit.'

COMING SOON
IN
THE NEW ADVENTURES

DOWN
By Lawrence Miles
ISBN: 0 426 20512 X
Publication date: 18 September 1997

If the authorities on Tyler's Folly didn't expect to drag an off-world professor out of the ocean in a forbidden 'quake zone, they certainly weren't ready for her story. According to Benny the planet is hollow, its interior inhabited by warring tribes, rubber-clad Nazis and unconvincing prehistoric monsters. Has something stolen Benny's reason? Or is the planet the sole exception to the more mundane laws of physics? And what is the involvement of the utterly amoral alien known only as !X.

DEADFALL
By Gary Russell
ISBN: 0 426 20513 8
Publication date: 16 October 1997

Jason Kane has stolen the location of the legendary planet of Ardethe from his ex-wife Bernice, and, as usual, it's all gone terribly wrong. In no time at all, he finds himself trapped on an isolated rock, pursued by brain-consuming aliens, and at the mercy of a shipload of female convicts. Unsurprisingly, he calls for help. However, when his old friend Christopher Cwej turns up, he can't even remember his own name.